Trajectories

Trajectories

Stories of Space Exploration

Edited by Dave Creek

Hydra
Publications

Hydra Publications
Goshen, KY 40026

www.hydrapublications.com

DEDICATION

To Mary Jewell, my favorite centenarian.

TABLE OF CONTENTS

Introduction by Dave Creek 1

The Breath of Mars by Marianne J. Dyson 3

High Jack by Bud Sparhawk 34

A Matter of Timing by Maya Kaathryn Bohnhoff 53

Seeds by Mary A. Turzillo 80

Formal Charges by Jay Werkheiser 93

Trajectories of the Heart by Arlan Andrews 109

The Adventures of Star Blazer by John F. Allen 132

In Its Shadow by Martin L. Shoemaker 143

The Ghost Conductor of the Interstellar Express by Brad R. Torgersen 165

INTRODUCTION
By Dave Creek

Do you realize how tough it is to write an introduction to yet another anthology of SF stories about space exploration? How the heck do I keep from using the phrase "final frontier" or referencing Kirk, Spock and the rest of the STAR TREK gang?

How do I talk about the dangers we might find out there without bringing up the Xenomorph from ALIEN or Fred Saberhagen's Berserkers?

Then we have the more benign aliens such as the unknown intelligences from Arthur C. Clarke's ODYSSEY books or Steven Spielberg's E.T. You gotta mention them!

Other stories take the wide-screen approach, such as Isaac Asimov's FOUNDATION series, C.J. Cherryh's stories of the Alliance-Union universe, or Ursula K. LeGuin's Hainish Cycle.

The fact is, the tropes of such stories are familiar to almost everyone, including starships, aliens, strange new worlds - oops!

See how hard it is to keep such phrases from cropping up?

Don't worry, though. Familiar though they may be, the conventions of classic space-oriented SF are far from played out. Older readers eagerly snapped up the latest chronicles of their favorite heroes contained within books or short stories by Leigh Brackett, Edmond Hamilton, E.E. "Doc" Smith, Poul Anderson, Andre Norton, and manyothers.

Today, readers both old and young thrill to the adventures chronicled in tales from Alastair Reynolds, Ian McDonald, John Scalzi, Steven Baxter, and many more.

Trajectories

All the writers in this volume had a single assignment — tell us a story in any genre, with any mood, as long as it takes place in space or on an alien planet. Harsh planetary dystopias could fit in with light-hearted space opera. Think anything from "The Cold Equations" to "Captain Future."

And they delivered! Marianne J. Dyson brings us a suspenseful tale from the surface of Mars; Bud Sparhawk shows us blue-collar workers finding danger while just trying to make a living; John F. Allen explains how a TV production assistant can go from fighting racial prejudice in the 1950s to defending against an alien invasion in the far future.

Brad R. Torgersen wraps it all up in a story that features one of my favorite titles ever, "The Ghost Conductor Of The Interstellar Express."

In all, we have nine authors who love traveling to distant stars and new planetary landscapes; even better, they're willing to take us along for theride.

Enjoy!

THE BREATH OF MARS
by Marianne J. Dyson

Take a deep breath, in fact! Marianne J. Dyson starts us off with a suspenseful tale of a Mars explorer who scrambles to rescue the crew of a crashed ship, which includes his best friend — only to find himself in danger as well.

Marianne Dyson is a physicist and writer who was one of NASA's first women flight controllers, the subject of her memoir, *A Passion For Space: Adventures of a Pioneering Female NASA Flight Controller* (Springer 2015). Her children's books have won the Golden Kite Award (for *Space Station Science* from Scholastic/Windward) and the American Institute of Physics Science Writing Award (for *Home on the Moon* from National Geographic). Her most recent children's book is *Welcome to Mars: Making a Home on the Red Planet*, coauthored with Buzz Aldrin for National Geographic (2015). A frequent contributor to Ad Astra, the magazine of the National Space Society, she serves on their Board of Advisors and also reviews books for them. She welcomes speaking invitations, with experience on BookTV, C-SPAN, Great Day Houston, NPR, and as a National Geographic Explorer. Contact her via www.mdyson.com.

■■■■■■

Thomas checked the Mars topographical computer map clipped to his knee as he guided the one-man ultralight up from the canyon floor. The angry-looking red dust that clung to his spacesuit matched his mood.

If he could just check one more spot, he was sure he'd find the fossil he needed to prove his theory, that the Martian mold his German friend Karl Orth had discovered evolved as part of a complex ecosystem. Thomas believed the fossilized evidence of that ecosystem lay buried under the sands of the Nirgal Vallis canyon floor because that was where the mold spores had originated. During his two-year-long search, he had found only frozen water deposits, valuable discoveries in themselves, but not the fossil record he wanted so badly. Now, with the dust season upon them, he would have to leave Mars with his search unfinished and no hope of renewed funding to complete the job.

As Thomas maneuvered, the bundle of drill poles across the front of the ultralight shook like they were laughing at him. They reminded him of his last girlfriend, sharply mocking him for throwing his life away looking for dead rocks on a dead planet. *Some people will never understand. Mars is the god of war, the endless war of Life against the elements. I intend to beat him.*

Checking that his altitude was high enough for a clear transmission, he touch-selected the Columbus base frequency on his radio.

"Columbus Control, this is Ultra One Niner Foxtrot calling on two seven six."

A squeal in his helmet receiver indicated other traffic on the frequency. A frantic sounding voice replied, "Ultra One Nine clear the air ways, am handling an emergency reentry!"

"Oh shit," Thomas mumbled as he punched "Listen Only" mode. "Crackle, Repeat, this is Shuttlecraft Motel Alpha Roger Sierra Two. Burn completed. Coming in steep over Nirgal Vallis to Columbus. Estimate power cells will last only a few more minutes. Nelson out."

Power cell failure! Damn. Thomas searched the sky for the ship. Commander John Nelson was among the best space jockeys alive, but without power to control the vehicle, there was little hope of an intact landing.

Thomas's stomach burned. Nelson had taught him to fly the ultralight, and he'd let him handle the controls on some hopper flights, too. And his best friend, Karl Orth, was probably in the copilot's seat learning to fly a shuttle right now because Nelson never wasted an opportunity to teach someone something that might save their life one day.

Just last week Karl had teased him for being jealous that he was getting to join Nelson on the rendezvous flight with the incoming Earth-Mars transport. Karl's sister Lorena was on that transport. Karl had a secret to share with her, an experiment that, if successful, could change the whole economic climate of Mars. Thomas knew about it, but wasn't allowed to say a thing because Karl wanted to tell her in person. But now . . . *Oh no! Lorena is on that shuttle, too!*

Just above the haze layer, Thomas spotted a bright streak and quickly thumbed on his radio. "Columbus Control, Ultra One Nine Fox has Nelson in sight. Tell him to pull up! He's not going to clear the canyon!"

"Ultra calling Columbus, we have lost contact with Shuttlecraft Mars Two. Can you provide location information?"

The Breath of Mars

Thomas hardly heard the controller's words as he watched the shuttle disappear behind a bend in the labyrinth of canyons. He whispered a prayer for Nelson, Karl, and Lorena.

"Columbus Control, this is Ultra One-Nine Fox," he said into his helmet mike. "The shuttle has gone down out of view. I'm going to overfly the area and check for survivors." *My friends, be alive. Please, be alive.*

"Roger, One Nine Fox. Godspeed."

*****

Sunbeams slowly marched up the length of the drill tools as Thomas yawed away from the base and into the wide red mouth of the canyon. He would guide himself down its throat and search its twisting tributaries until he found the shuttle.

He pushed the ultra-light to its greatest speed, which was still painstakingly slow. He didn't want to waste precious time or fuel raising his altitude though, so he continued bumping along just above the canyon rim. The afternoon thermals made level flight difficult, and Thomas could almost hear Commander Nelson chewing him out for feeding so much sand to the engine.

But the low-level haze was nothing compared to the yellow and orange cloud of sand and dust steaming up from one of the tributary canyons. *Impact debris and outgassing. Got to be the crashsite.*

As he turned toward the west, Thomas recognized the area as the section nicknamed Razor Ridge Fossae after the gigantic thin rows of parallel ridges which jutted up from the canyon floor, shaped by some ancient flood. The edges had been sandblasted over the eons to reveal a bone-white interior.

The cloud originated between the canyon wall itself and one of the ridges. From the shape and thickness of the cloud, it looked like the shuttle had miraculously come in parallel with the ridges and skidded along the thick bottom sand. *Nice flying, guys.* Thomas allowed himself a small burst of hope that his friends had survived. Unfortunately, the cloud made it impossible to determine the condition of the shuttle. Most likely, it was partially or completely submerged in the deep loose sand characteristic of this area. He'd have to wear snow shoes to walk across it.

"Columbus, this is Ultra One Nine Fox. I have located the shuttle in the western side of Razor Ridge Fossae about twelve kilometers from its Nirgal junction. The canyon floor is not accessible by rover. Send a rescue flight to the rim. I'll park this thing there and wait for them. Tell them to bring sand shoes and ropes." While they were on their way, he would scout out the best route down.

"Negative, One Nine Fox. No flyers are available. A rescue rover is on its way to you now. Over."

Thomas swore under his breath. "It will take a rover at least six hours to reach here! It will be dark!" Even an experienced explorer like him wouldn't attempt a descent into Razor Fossae at night. The dry ice fog would make footing treacherous and visibility nil. That meant the rescue team wouldn't reach the shuttle until several hours after sunrise tomorrow!

"Shuttlecraft Mars Two, this is Ultra One Nine Fox, can you read?" Static.

Thomas repeated the call several times, with no response. If there were survivors, they were unconscious, which meant they needed help, and they needed it now, not tomorrow morning. If the hull were intact, he could climb aboard and treat the injured using his emergency kit. If the hull were breached, well, he wouldn't think about that too much.

He tried to contact the shuttlecraft one more time. Still no answer. There was only one thing to do. "Columbus Control, the shuttlecraft does not answer radio calls. I'm going to land and offer assistance."

There was a pause. Were they worried about him landing on the sand? It might foul the gear so badly he'd have to abandon it there until after the storm season. He'd be gone by then, so it would be their problem to retrieve it. Still, there wasn't much choice, and they probably knew it. "Understand, One Nine Fox. But be advised we do not have you on radar."

Thomas swallowed dryly. The Phobos Positional Relay must have gone below the horizon. As he descended, he would lose voice contact as well. Usually, he enjoyed the solitude compared to the cramped noisy atmosphere of the base. Today, however, he would have preferred the company of voices. "Roger, Columbus. Over and out." *I'm coming, Karl.*

* * * * *

The ultralight's engine strained and shook as Thomas reduced power and descended. His heart raced. The shuttle's furious reentry had stripped away millions of years of accumulated sand which started a chain reaction. Rocks broke loose from the canyon wall tumbled down and uncovered others. It was a treasure trove for him. If only he could get the funding to stay!

The Breath of Mars

The ultralight's filters choked with sand and coughed uncertainly. Still, Thomas urged the craft lower.

As he threaded his way down into the cloud formed by the shuttle's descent, a boulder careened off a ledge and struck the thin mylar wing of the ultralight, silently crushing it. The craft pitched violently and tumbled.

The canyon walls sped past in a blur of fantastic colors: orange, red, brown, pink. Thomas struggled to regain control, spinning round and round like a kid's kite with its string reeling out of reach. The wings folded up and scraped alien graffiti into the sandy rock pinnacles.

On impact, a sharp pain shot through Thomas's ankle as the bundle of drill tools, impacting a rock, slid and slammed violently into his left leg. A cloud of warm life-giving air puffed out of his suit like the last breath of a dying Mars. Red snowflakes of blood froze around the opening in the minus forty-degree air.

*****

The insignia on the spacesuit read, "Shuttlecraft Mars 2/Passenger." Inside it, Dr. Lorena Orth fought her way back to consciousness. She opened her eyes to blackness.

"Dummkopf!" She had neglected to turn her helmet light on! She raised an arm and pushed a button on her helmet. When the red light flickered on, she was only partially relieved to discover she was not blind but that the ship was dark. *Why are not the lights on?* She struggled to sit up, her first attempt unsuccessful because she forgot to unbuckle the chest strap.

She swung her booted feet to the floor and tried to stand. A wave of dizziness and nausea overcame her. She hated throwing up. She especially hated throwing up inside a pressure suit. But, after days of being space sick in orbit, she didn't have anything in her stomach. *It is no wonder I fainted during entry.* She'd endured it all because her brother Karl insisted she must come in person to share some discovery with her. The spots in front of her eyes slowly cleared, and it occurred to her that there was gravity. They must have landed. "Karl?" *Why doesn't my brother answer?*

"Commander Nelson? Karl?" she repeated. Neither answered.

Apparently the ship intercom was not functioning. *Something is wrong.*

She held her wrist up close to her face to find the button for the wrist lamp and turned it on. *At least that works.* Antiseptic white light bathed the cargo boxes surrounding her. There was a fine white powder on them.

Snow! They had lost pressure! Some of the water vapor and CO2 in the air had condensed to frost.

Quickly she checked the front of her space suit, the only thing between her and death in the thin Martian atmosphere. Her suit was at 10 psi, the same as Martian standard, though still not high enough to prevent her from suffering "altitude" sickness since leaving the transport. The air gauge informed her she had a little over five hours of air remaining in her primary supply. She took a deep breath. *I must remain calm.*

Still dizzy, she pushed open the partition that blocked her view of the cockpit. She emerged between the backs of the two cockpit seats. Pale sunlight gleamed through a ragged gash in the port side of the hull. Ancient sand trickled through the opening, slowly measuring the limited minutes of human lives.

"Commander Nelson!" She gasped as her wrist-mounted flashlight illuminated a gruesome scene. The commander's helmet had been crushed when the ceiling caved in above him. As an intern, Lorena had dealt with death in the emergency room, but it was never easy. She'd spent the last week with this man. She swallowed the bile from her stomach and concentrated on her brother. His suit appeared intact, but his head lolled forward on his chest.

"Karl? Karl! Please answer!" she cried.

The dial on his suit front read 8.0 psi. She panicked thinking he had a suit leak, and then remembered that Martian crew suits were at a lower pressure than those used for passengers. The lower pressure allowed better flexibility in the fingers, but unless the crew breathed pure oxygen ahead of time, they ran the risk of the bends. According to his suit gauge, he had 5 hours and 30 minutes of air remaining in his primary supply compared to her five. Five hours in a space suit seemed both a terribly long and terribly short time. *Surely someone will come for us quickly!*

Her wrist light was totally reflected from Karl's mirrored face plate, so she activated his interior helmet lamp. In its red glow, she studied his face for a twitch, any sign of life. Her face plate bumped into his as she leaned closer. His eyelids quivered. "Karl!"

Lorena released his seat straps. Remembering the intercom didn't work, she switched to the emergency radio band, and found the control to switch Karl's, too. "Karl, can you hear me?"

She slid him sideways so that his helmet rested on the seat, hoping to increase the blood flow to his head and bring him around. She gently tapped on her brother's helmet and called his name again. His eyes blinked and opened.

"Lo . . re . . na!" He gasped for breath. "Where does it hurt, Karl?"

"My chest. Ribs," he panted.

The violent impact had thrown him against the hard shell of his suit torso, and probably broken some ribs. He may have a collapsed lung or other internal injuries, making it hard to breathe. "Do not try to move or talk, Karl. I will get help." She checked his heart rate on the suit monitor and was relieved to see it was only 95. A bit high, but not dangerous. She must get help before possible internal bleeding sent him into shock.

"My discovery . . . ." he whispered.

"Please, do not stress yourself, Karl. You can tell me your secret later. I must try the radio."

"Forgive me," he wheezed, and closed his eyes.

The words temporarily paralyzed Lorena. How long she had waited to hear them! Is that why he made her come? Did he want to apologize for allowing their father to test a new drug on himself? For the pain he'd caused Mother, for ruining the family financially? If they had consulted with her, she might have warned them of the danger, made them take precautions that might have saved Father's life. But they were researchers. They didn't need her advice, her permission. She was merely a family doctor — what did she know about research? Now her brother, the one she'd loved and hated, admired and blamed, was very possibly dying, inside a space suit where she was helpless to save him. *My brother, do not die now. There is too much yet undone between us.*

She leaned over the copilot's seat to reach the communications unit above the center console. Her helmet scraped against the ceiling of switches, dials, gauges, and meters. She often chided her patients for being afraid of technology, yet here she shared their intimidation and frustration at the rows of unfamiliar cockpit switches with their incomprehensible abbreviations. But she would find the radio controls. She must!

Finally, she found one highlighted with red tape and labeled, EMER CCU. It could stand for emergency communications control unit. She stuck her finger under the switch guard's upside-down U shape and pushed it ON. The small light did not come on. Maybe she had not made a good connection? She yanked her finger loose and pushed the lever using a pen that was velcroed to a nearby checklist. "Why does it not work!" she said, frustrated tears coming to her eyes and being sucked away through the suit fan system. But even as she said the words, she knew the answer. Though she and her brother could talk on their suit radios, the ship's radio had no power. Was there an emergency beacon? If so, she didn't know how to activate it. She should have asked more questions before boarding this shuttle.

Feeling like a trapped animal, she looked for a way to escape. She crawled over the console to the narrow aisle leading to the side hatch. She threw her full weight where it said, "PRESS HERE FOR EMERGENCY EXIT." All she succeeded in doing was rubbing her slim figure around inside the spacesuit like a heel in an over-sized shoe.

After this exertion, she took a few sips of water through her suit straw to clear the bitter taste from her mouth and calm her rising sense of panic. It didn't help. She turned to the airlock which was over her head, wondering if she could crank the handle open. She wasn't quite tall enough to get a good grip from the floor, and it was extremely awkward to turn the crank with one hand on the ladder. She tried it anyway, and was rewarded with a slight movement before she ran out of strength. All those hours of being sick in orbit had drained her. "Where could I go anyway?" she mumbled, hating the truth of it. She was stuck on this horrible planet, trapped in a spaceship that would become her tomb. *Forgive you, Karl? What have you done?*

She slumped to the floor by the ladder, sweat steaming inside her visor. Her gloved hand hit her face plate as she absent-mindedly tried to wipe the tears stinging her eyes. She squeezed them shut and began rhythmic breathing to stop the nervous shaking and shivering racking her body. *Rescuers were surely on their way and would be there momentarily. Karl would be fine.*

The calm only lasted until she opened her eyes to the vision of Commander Nelson's dead body. Her reflection, seen in his cracked, mirrored visor, was a horrible distortion of white skin with pink hair and bluish lips. She switched off her helmet light to end the nightmare. She sat in silence as pink Martian sand continued to slowly pour through the hole in the outer hull.

* * * * *

Thomas fought against the pain, the loss of pressure, and the numbing cold. He must stay conscious! Pieces of his ultra-light lay scattered all around him. Where was the emergency medical kit with the suit patches? It had been under the seat, with his extra O2 bottle. It must be buried in the deep sand. He slid an arm down his side and felt for it. Spots formed in his vision. He would never find it in time.

Frantically, he searched for something, anything to use for a patch or tourniquet. The suit had automatically shut the valves feeding his lower leg when the pressure flow reversed, but against the pull of near vacuum, air continued to escape. He had to plug the hole enough for him to reach the shuttle. There were plenty of patch kits there. His geologist's sample pouch was still attached to his belt. He'd emptied the contents into his storage bag before heading home for the day. He could use it for a tourniquet under his knee. But first he must "deflate" the suit.

Using the front pack of the suit, he deactivated the fan, turned off the O2 supply, and waited for the suit to collapse around the tear in his leg. His lungs protested the sudden drop in pressure. He squeezed his eyes tightly shut and counted the seconds he was without fresh air. *One*. Through his eyelids, he saw the helmet light flashing red to warn Thomas's nonexistent companions that his oxygen level was in the danger zone. He wished he could turn it off. *Two*. He forced his aching eyes open and applied pressure to remove any bubbles near the hole. The opening was caked with frozen sand and blood which he decided would be best left in place. It might help seal the hole. He secured the pouch over the mess as best he could, pulling the Velcro straps as tightly as he could manage. *Three*. He might lose his foot to frostbite, but at least he'd be alive to complain about it. His lungs were about to explode.

Praying the plug and patch would hold, he turned the O2 supply and suit fan back on. *Four*. He gulped oxygen greedily. The sand and blood bulged outward meaning the leak was not completely contained, but the flow rate was certainly reduced. The red helmet light thankfully quit flashing.

Now to reach the shuttle. From the nearby sand, he retrieved one of the drill tools that had gouged him. He shoved it into the sand in front of him. It hit something solid about one meter below the surface. Using the tool like a vaulting pole, Thomas propelled himself onto a wing section of the ultra. He gritted his teeth against the renewed pain in his ankle. The movement had probably broken his frozen scab loose and started him bleeding again. He gingerly put some weight on his foot. The pain didn't get any worse. *Good. At least no bones arebroken.*

He gathered pieces of the frame that were within easy reach. He took the two best pieces and knelt on one while laying the other in front of him. He then crawled onto that one and picked up the one behind him. He repeated this process, lay down, crawl, pick up, lay down, crawl, pick up, slowly, making progress toward the canyon wall. He would follow the wall until he came to the shuttle. He told himself it couldn't be far.

What seemed an eternity of pain later, the drill tool indicated a manageable depth of only a few inches of sand above solid ground. He leaned on the tool for support and pulled himself to a standing position. His leg ached with frostbite, his head throbbed, and his throat felt like he'd just had his tonsils removed without anesthesia. Three seconds of near vacuum certainly had not improved his health.

His helmet light began flashing red again. Thomas checked the patch had not come loose when he stood. It looked the same. That meant there was another problem. He had used a lot of oxygen to feed the leak, but his secondary system should have come online, unless . . . . "My automatic switch-over must be jammed!" Thomas dropped to his knees and then onto his back, rolling against a rock to activate the manual switch the way Nelson had trained him. He remembered thinking he'd never need this procedure, but Nelson had insisted it was best to be prepared. It worked.

He lay there breathing deeply until his vision returned to normal.

Thanks Commander. Then he sat up, set the pressure controller to hold at 6.0 psi instead of the normal 8.0 psi. "That should give me more time." He'd been breathing pure O2 all day, so there was little danger of the bends, though the lower pressure didn't help his headache any. *Karl, at times like these, I could sure use that new drug of yours.*

He set the event timer on his chest pack so he could later determine the leak rate. His secondary supply held enough for three hours, plenty of time to reach the shuttle.

Pulling himself up onto a boulder, he scanned along the base of the cliff. Was that white area the shuttle or a patch of dry ice? He'd find out soon enough. He slid off the boulder and limped toward the white area in the distance.

His boot struck a rock under the sand causing him to stumble and fall headlong. Using the drill tool for a crutch, he got back up and resumed limping to the crash site.

The Breath of Mars

Twenty-eight minutes later, he confirmed that the white spot was indeed the shuttle, or rather the shuttle and a patch of white that he feared was vented cabin atmosphere turned to snow.

Thomas used the pieces of the ultra light again to crawl over the deep sand to the shuttle's wing. Panting with effort, he uncovered the recessed toe holds used to climb to the ship's upper hatch. The side hatch did not have an airlock, and he hoped to need one. Pulling himself up with his arms, Thomas reached the airlock hatch. He scooped sand away from the handle and punched the pressure equalization valve. It flashed green instantly. His heart sank. The hull must have been breached after all. He forced the manual crank to turn. His head throbbed. There were spots in front of his eyes again.

He heaved one more time and slumped over the handle to rest. Bang! Bang! He felt rather than heard the sound through the hull. "I'm coming!" he shouted on the radio, hope restored. He took a deep breath and pushed. The handle turned. He pushed again. He threw aside the hatch and stuck his helmet into the dark hole of the airlock. The banging was someone opening the inner hatch. He twisted and slid in, feet first, supporting his weight on his good foot. He grabbed the inner hatch handle and felt it give.

From a wrist light, he saw a suited figure clinging to the hatch ladder. As the helmet light flickered on, Thomas instantly recognized the face from vids in Karl's lab.

"Dr. Orth!" Thomas exclaimed. "I'm Karl's friend, Thomas. Thomas Miller."

She tapped the side of her helmet with her hand to indicate she could not hear him. She must be on the emergency transmit frequency. He quickly reset his radio. "Can you hear me now?" he asked.

"Ja," she replied.

"I'm Thomas Miller. You okay?"

"Ja, Dr. Miller, but the others are not," she replied. "Please inform the rescue unit we need immediate medical evacuation."

Thomas was momentarily confused by her request, and then realized Lorena would not know the situation. "I'm not with the rescue unit," Thomas explained as she stepped off the ladder to let him enter. "I was returning to base in my ultralight when I saw the crash."

He hopped down the ladder on his good foot, nearly falling when he reached the bottom.

"You are injured?"

"My ultra-light was hit by debris," Thomas said, suddenly feeling the full weight of his ordeal. With no cabin pressure, there was no way to treat his leg wound. Thinking about it seemed to be a signal for it to begin throbbing anew. With Lorena holding his arm, he gently lowered himself to the floor. *I feel like I'm going to throw up.* As he settled against the bulkhead, his eyes adapted to the dim interior. "Where are . . . . No!" he shouted, as he took in the gruesome scene through the open cockpit door. "No!"

As he took in the horror of what had happened, he heard a familiar voice. "Thom . . as?"

"Karl! Yes, it's me, Thomas." He dragged himself through the doorway to his friend, stretched across the copilot seat and center console. "How are you?"

"She doesn't . . know," he wheezed.

Lorena moved closer. "I think perhaps one of his ribs has pierced a lung. He really should not talk."

Oh god. He didn't tell her he has been testing the new drug on himself. If he dies . . . . "What do you want me to do, Karl?"

"Take . . data," he said.

"Karl?" Thomas quickly punched up Karl's suit monitor display and noted he had 5 hours and 14 minutes of primary supply remaining. *Take data, he'd said. He wants to know if the drug works, if his oxygen usage is down. But you are injured, my friend! How does that change things?*

"I think he has fainted," Lorena said. "How long until arrives the rescue unit?"

Thomas took a deep breath to clear his head. He checked his timer. "Columbus Control sent a rescue rover about thirty minutes ago. They should reach the rim in about five and a half hours, but I doubt they will attempt to climb down until morning."

"Morning! I only have five hours more air!"

"No, actually, you have nine counting your secondary supply," Thomas said. "But that is still cutting it pretty close." He didn't mention that he would never last that long, not with a suit leak. "That is why we will climb to the rim and meet them," he concluded. "They will pick us up in a pressurized rescue rover."

The Breath of Mars

"But you are injured, and my brother should not be moved," Lorena said.

"I'll be fine once I get a proper patch on my suit, and we can rig a stretcher for Karl. Don't worry," Thomas said with confidence he didn't feel.

"Germans always worry, but they do not let it keep them from work," Lorena said. "Let me see your ankle, please."

Thomas sat with his back to Karl's seat and stretched his legs out in front of him.

"Are you in much pain?" she asked as she held her wrist light above his ankle to examine it.

"Not much," he lied. "I don't think any bones are broken."

"How did this happen?" She poked around the edges of the sample pouch. Pink flakes and sand came loose at her touch.

"A drilling tool took a sample of me," he said. "I couldn't find the medical kit with the patches, so I used my sample bag as a tourniquet."

She shook her head. "It is impossible to determine the extent of tissue damage from the exposure to low pressure without removing the tourniquet. I think this I should not do. Instead I recommend applying patches over the top of your work. Do you agree?"

"You are the doctor," he said.

He heard her sigh. "It seems that being a doctor is of not much use on Mars."

"I don't know why you say that. Karl said it was because you are a doctor that he needed you here." *To confirm his new drug works. But what if it doesn't?*

She rose and pulled the medical kit from the pouch behind the copilot's seat. "He did, did he? That is new," she said. "He had no use for doctors when he let our father kill himself." She pulled a large patch from the kit and slapped it onto Thomas's leg. He winced with the pain.

"I thought your father died of a stroke."

Lorena smoothed the edges of the patch and proceeded to wrap his entire lower leg mummy-style with tape. "It was actually an intracerebral hemorrahage: a blood vessel burst in his brain. It was likely a direct result of using the drug he made from my brother's Martian mold."

"I don't understand," Thomas said. "The drug was supposed to help people adapt more quickly to our lower pressure environment. Why would having some extra red blood cells and a more efficient metabolism cause a brain hemorrhage?"

She carefully replaced the scissors and tape in the kit. "During his test, he fell and hit his head. He reported a slight headache, but no one thought it was any problem. Then he just didn't wake up the next morning. My brother later determined that the drug had acted like a blood thinner, and caused excessive bleeding in the brain that would not otherwise have happened. He should not have been testing this drug on himself!"

"I'm sorry," Thomas whispered. *That must be why Karl did so many brain scans of his lab mice and himself.*

"I am sorry, too," Lorena said. "But that is now behind us." Before he could reply, she patted his leg with her gloved hand.

"Good as new as you say. What next?"

"Why don't you see what we can use for a stretcher while I get some extra O2 bottles?"

"He must have his arms pinned to his sides. A window shade might work, Ja?"

"Yes. Get one," Thomas agreed. He didn't want her to watch what he was going to do next. He wished he didn't have to either.

Thomas shivered as he pulled John from his seat. The movement dislodged small pockets of trapped air from within John's suit and sent bits of frozen blood and flesh spouting onto the cabin floor. Thomas's stomach reeled at the sight. He rolled the body onto its front so the backpack was in view. The secondary O2 bottle was intact and unused. "Someday we'll build a suit that's as invulnerable as one of these," he whispered to John.

Lorena appeared in the hatchway with a small bag and a rolled foam bundle and knelt down beside him. The sight of the body did not seem to disturb her. He supposed doctors must get used to that sort of thing.

"Even if we are not hungry," she said, "I think we should eat before we go rather than carry it with us. We will need the strength."

"Good idea," Thomas said. That was something he hadn't considered. He was beginning to see why Karl had wanted her here for his test.

She retrieved something from the small bag and squeezed it into his food container. He could then access it via a straw inside his helmet once it had warmed to suit temperature. "What is that stuff?" he asked.

She looked at the label. "Turkey Tetrazzini."

"My favorite. How'd you know?" He wanted to see her smile like on

Karl's video letters, but instead he saw her lips pursed in concentration.

She was obviously having trouble opening another pouch for herself. "Can I help?"

"Ja, danke. My nimble surgeon's hands are not so nimble in these over-large gloves."

"The crew suits like mine are a lot easier on the hands. When we get to base, we'll have to order you one."

"There is no need. I will be here a few weeks only," she said.

"You're going to turn around and go right back to Earth?" After spending the near fortune it cost to come to Mars, most people stayed a standard two-year term.

"I only came because Karl insisted I be here in person for the announcement of his new discovery." She looked up at him. "Has he told you about it?"

"A little," Thomas said, squeezing the tetrazzini into her food transfer unit for her. "But I am not a bioengineer. Most of what he's told me went right over my head." *Like the bit about the rats. I should have asked more questions.*

"I see," she said. "Karl mentioned that you will be returning to Earth now also?"

Thomas sucked a mouthful of tetrazzini, barely thawed. It felt good sliding down his raw throat. "Unfortunately, yes. My money's run out."

"If you found another sponsor, would you want to stay?"

"Absolutely," Thomas said, though he had to admit, a trip back with her might be appealing. "I'd clean toilets if someone would pay my room and board. I love it here."

Lorena sat the food bag aside and unfolded the window shade across the floor. "Perhaps Karl's new discovery will attract a sponsor for you?"

Thomas nearly gagged on his tetrazzini. Was that why Karl had been so anxious to do the test now? His guilt level started flashing red. *Of course, you idiot!* "I hadn't really thought about it," he said. Working for Karl would be perfect. He could gather mold samples and continue his fossil-hunting on the side.

"Well, we will find out, assuming we survive this day."

"Right," Thomas answered simply. He pulled himself stiffly erect, using the seat back for support. He ignored the intense pins and needles sensation from his foot as the blood flow returned. "I assume you've tried the radio?"

"Ja. No power."

"I was afraid of that. But the 'black box' will transmit our location." He picked up the O2 canister he'd disconnected from John's suit and fastened it to his belt. With that bottle and what remained in his suit, he figured he'd have enough to last the five hours until the rescue team met them on the rim. There was no way he'd make it until morning, though.

Thomas peeled a checklist from the ceiling and turned to the tab labeled PHOBOS AOS/LOS. Columbus control hadn't had him on radar, which meant Phobos was out of sight when he crashed, but once it came back up and he got out in the open, they should pick him up. He frowned as he scanned the table. "I was hoping Phobos was in sight now so they'd have a fix on the shuttle and also our suit transponders from orbit, but no such luck. It won't be in sight again for three and a half hours." He shut the book. "Once we're above the canyon rim, the rover should be able to pick us up on their radio, though."

"I understand."

Thomas noted the readings on Karl's chest pack had not changed since he checked earlier. *So far, so good, my friend.* "We're going to have to stand Karl up to get him up the ladder," Thomas said.

"No! He must remain horizontal," Lorena said. "The greatest danger is that a rib will pierce his heart. Do you understand?"

Thomas blanched at the thought that he might have killed his best friend had Lorena not been there to advise him. "Okay, then. We'll have to clear the side hatch."

To Thomas's surprise, without any water to compact it, the sand flowed away from the door fairly easily once he cranked it open.

The two of them secured Karl to the stiff window shade Lorena had found, and used bungie cords to hold his arms to his sides. Thomas automatically took Karl's head and swung it toward the hatch.

"Stop," Lorena said. "He should have his legs higher. You are taller than I am, so I will take the head."

"Okay," Thomas said. Another thing he wouldn't have considered. Not only was she thinking clearly, but Thomas marveled at how calm and accepting she was of their desperate situation. Just the kind of person you'd want for your family doctor. *Mars could use more people like her.*

Thomas swung him around the other way and began backing out the hatch. The movement roused Karl. "Lo . . re . . na," he gasped. "Are we

. . at base?"

"Nein. Karl. Your friend Thomas and I are taking you to the rover. We will be safe soon."

"You can . . trust Thomas. I . . love you."

"I know," she whispered.

Thomas tried not to think about what Karl said while he slid out the hatch. *She can trust me? Trust me not to say her brother is risking his life testing a drug, so I can stay on Mars? Testing the same drug that killed their father?*

Once he was out, he lay flat on the wing and pulled Karl out after him. It wasn't as hard as he thought it would be. The tetrazzini really had helped.

He scanned the sky as Lorena climbed out to join him. The impact dust had mostly settled, but the horizon was changing from pink to an ominous yellow characteristic of dust storms. He estimated the dust layer to be about four miles up and thickening. They would have no time to waste.

"Columbus is to the south. We'll have to climb out over that way." He waved an arm in the direction of some sheer cliffs. "We can use that pinnacle over there for a guidepost. If I can't make it, you keep heading that direction. One of us has to get over the rim to make radio contact."

"I understand," Lorena said.

They slipped and slid slowly toward the base of the canyon wall. "Good thing we're not farther downstream," Thomas said. "The canyon's only about half as deep as Grand Canyon here."

Lorena moaned, and Thomas decided maybe he should keep these cheerful thoughts to himself.

The air inside Thomas's suit was growing steadily colder. *Perfectly insulated suits do not need a heater,* instructor Harold had replied to Thomas's question. *In the unlikely event one of these suits is punctured, the victim will likely die before help can reach him. At least freezing to death is supposed to be a pleasant way to go.* The numbness in his left foot was creeping like gangrene up his leg. Despite Lorena's patching, he was already having trouble bending the suit at the knee joint. "There's our guidepost again," he said as they approached an ominous looking overhang. "Do you have any climbing experience?"

"Nein," she replied. "I left always the exploring to Karl."

"Oh," Thomas replied, wondering what Lorena would think if she knew the kind of biological exploring Karl had been involved in?

"With the stretcher, we won't be doing anything fancy, anyway," Thomas added quickly.

They plodded along in silence, the grade becoming much steeper despite his chosen route around the sheerest rock faces.

"See that yellow haze in the southwest? You can click once on the radio for yes."

She clicked.

"That storm could blanket the whole planet in a matter of days. We have to get out of the canyon before it hits and blocks our call for help." After another long moment of silence, Thomas thought about what he had just said and mentally slapped himself on the forehead. "I'm sorry, Dr. Orth. You have enough things to worry about without me adding the weather to the list."

"Do not apologize," Lorena panted. "I would much rather know these things than not. I have never forgiven my father for not sharing his concerns." She paused to get her breath. "He did not want me to worry."

Karl, should I share your secrets with her? Is there something she would know to do for you now that might save your life?

They continued climbing. Newly fallen rocks blocked the path. Under other circumstances, Thomas would have been screaming to stay and examine these newly uncovered pieces of Mars' history, but between the pain of his leg and his worry over his air supply, he hardly had time to note their types as he stepped over them.

The constant flexing of his left knee was becoming increasingly difficult. Thomas needed to talk to keep his mind off the pain. "I'm sure that more complex life once existed on Mars," Thomas said, as he made his way around a particularly promising boulder. "Did Karl ever tell you how Mars has been keeping me from finding out its secrets?"

"Nein," Lorena puffed from her end of the stretcher.

"I had this great plan," Thomas continued, gritting his teeth as he landed on his foot after crawling over a rock. "I would search as many canyons as possible using a light-weight ultra." The two of them balanced Karl's stretcher like a teeter-totter over a big rock. Thomas waited while Lorena scrambled over the rock, and they resumed the climb. "I told the selection committee I could cover as much territory in a Martian year as the Russians cover in two. But Mars had a plan of its own. First a dust storm that lasted seven months, then troubles with the ultra, then nothing but dirt and an occasional new batch of mold." Thomas paused to choose a path around another large boulder. "At least the mold was useful for Karl." *If it doesn't kill him.*

* * * * *

"Dr. Miller, can we stop for a short rest, please?" Lorena gasped on the suit radio. He wanted to say no, but she had already propped her end of the stretcher on a rock and collapsed to the ground. Thomas stumbled over to her, trying to sit without bending his bad leg. He didn't want to put more pressure on the patch than necessary.

He closed his eyes and relaxed. He probably needed this rest more than Lorena did, but he would never have initiated it. He had a feeling she knew this. *Karl, you were right to bring her here, but why didn't you tell her the whole story? Why didn't you tell me?*

"We had better go now before your leg becomes more inflexible," Lorena said.

Thomas opened his eyes. He'd been falling asleep! "Yes, yes, of course," he mumbled.

But Thomas wasn't the only who was a little stiff. As she put her arms in front of her to stand, Lorena looked like a kid on roller skates for the first time. She straightened, but, unused to the force of her muscles in the low gravity, she overcompensated. When Thomas realized she was going over backwards, he reached to help her, but only succeeded in grabbing her boot. She tumbled onto her back dislodging eons of accumulated dust from the surface of the rocks. "Oh!" she cried.

"Sorry," he said. "You okay?"

She propped herself up with one arm. "I think so. My body is most confused going from false g to none to one third all in one week."

"I know what you mean. Last time I took a flying lesson with Commander Nelson, I . . . Never mind."

"Try not to think of your lost commander now."

"I know, delay grief until there's time and all that. But I was hoping to get a hopper certification flight when he got back. One of those things we'd both been too busy to do until the last minute, and now . . . ." He took a deep breath and stood.

"Now it is too late for that," Lorena said, then added softly, "But not for other things."

Trajectories

Like saving Karl? "Let me help you up," Thomas said quickly.

They resumed marching along, the stretcher swaying between them. Thomas scanned the canyon rim with his flip-down ocular. They had reached the base of a series of ledges. Climbing the first few had been relatively easy. Thomas would have enjoyed it if he could have blocked the pain in his ankle and stopped worrying about Karl.

Thomas continued to watch Karl's oxygen readings. His usage was low, but that might be because Karl was not moving around.

Thomas stopped, looking up a long shaft cut out between two sheer faces when the rock he was standing on had slipped down like an elevator. There was no easy way up from here. While he contemplated what to do, his helmet light started flashing a warning. As he suspected, his O2 bottle was empty. While Lorena was preoccupied checking her brother, Thomas sat there ignoring the ringing in his ears for a full minute, running over the manual procedure for changing out O2 bottles in his head. Then, unclipping Commander Nelson's scavenged bottle from his belt, Thomas closed the valve to prepare it for manual hookup. He tried to attach it behind his back, but there was something wrong with the connection. "Doctor, I need your help," he said. He held out the bottle to her indicating the small adapter. "I can't get this spare bottle to attach. Will you do it for me?"

She reached for the bottle as if she expected it to explode. "Do you not have an automatic secondary supply?" she asked.

"I've already used it," he said. He imagined her eyes growing wide. She must not have realized the extent of his suit leak.

"If I cannot attach this, you will die?"

"Try not to think about that," he said. "I'll talk you through it."

"Ja," she replied and shuffled around to his back.

"Look for the yellow banded plug marked MAN O2," Thomas said.

"I see it."

"Is it clear of sand?"

"Ja, but it is bent."

He suspected that was why he wasn't able to do it himself. "Poke the plug with a rock or something." He wished he had his old scout knife with him, but regulations prohibited him carrying anything sharp on him while wearing a spacesuit . . . .

"I have an unused clip on my belt," Lorena said. "It is the right size to fit, I think."

"Sounds good," Thomas said. "Go ahead and try screwing the adapter onto the plug as soon as you can. If it doesn't seal properly, the air leak will pop it off. It's kind of like attaching a pump to a bicycle tire. If it pops off, keep trying."

"Trying to poke this thing with gloves on is like trying to thread a needle in mittens!"

Lorena's frustration seemed miles away. "Just keep trying," he said.

"I am."

He was feeling a bit light-headed already from the CO2 build up in the suit. It wasn't a bad feeling. *I wonder which is more pleasant, CO2 poisoning or freezing to death?* Lorena's first attempt at attachment failed. He felt a little whoosh of air, and sucked it in, like Mars holding on to its last thin breath.

Thomas tried to concentrate on something. The stars. They were barely visible through the thickening dust. His hard-learned star navigation wouldn't help tonight. He felt another whoosh. His peripheral vision was going black. Mars had lost its air and died, and now he would, too. "Doctor," he gasped, "Hurry." Then he passed out.

* * * * *

"Herr Miller! Please wake up!" Lorena was shouting, as Thomas felt the cold air reviving him.

Slightly dazed, Thomas blinked his eyes and saw Lorena bending over him, studying his face. A lock of her blonde hair stuck to her pale forehead. *She is so beautiful.* He thought it ironic that she was hot and sweaty inside her suit, and he was freezing in his. He could almost feel frost forming on his unshaved whiskers. "I'm okay," he managed weakly. His head felt like a truckload of anvils had landed on it.

"Your suit pressure is only 4.3!"

"That's what they used in the old Shuttle suits," he said. But he was worried that meant the leak rate had increased beyond the capacity for the supply to make it up. No wonder he was so cold. "We'd better get a move on," he said, sitting up. "By the way, please call me Thomas," he added. Karl had told him that for Germans it was a measure of friendship to be on a first name basis with someone.

"And you may call me Lorena," she said. Just as she finished talking, Karl cried out, startling both of them.

"Lo . . re . . na," he gasped. "Must . . tell . . you . . . "

"No, Karl, save your strength," Lorena pleaded. "We will be at base soon."

"No . . if I don't . . make it, please . . ." His arms struggled against the bungie cords.

"Karl, do not move!" She punched up his display, checking his heart rate. Lorena turned a wild look at Thomas, tears streaming down her cheeks. "His heart rate is 190!" She laid her helmet against Karl's.

Thomas thought of what she'd said about her father dying after hitting his head. "We'd better hurry, then," Thomas said, pulling himself up on one knee.

"No," she said. "There is too much danger. He is in shock. If we should bump or drop him, the extra trauma could be fatal." She waved her gloved hand at Thomas. "Go on and radio our position. I will stay with him."

Thomas did some quick calculations. They were probably not more than an hour's climb from the rim. The rescue team was still several hours away, but their oxygen supply should last until then, assuming he made it to the rim and told them where to look. But he still didn't want to leave them.

"Look, Lorena, I know you don't want to leave him, but his best chance of survival is for us to get to the rim as soon as possible."

"You can climb faster without me, and I must monitor his condition," she said. "His breathing is shallow and his heart rate high. I may need to manipulate him to clear his breathing."

There was no arguing with her logic, especially considering the sheer walls above them. He would have to wedge himself between them, what climbers called chimneying, like a kid climbing a doorjamb. He'd never tried it in a pressure suit, but somehow he must make it. "Okay, you've convinced me." He stood up unsteadily, leaning on a rock for support. The extended time of no activity had cost him in mobility. He could barely bend his knee at all now. He viewed the walls above.

"Keep your suit radio on despite the static. I may need to call you," Thomas said.

"Take a sip of water, Thomas. You must not get dehydrated," she replied.

He smiled, glad for the reminder. She seemed to really care what happened to him, and that made what he was about to do easier to face. "Yeah, doctor, I'll do that." He shuffled over to the 'elevator' shaft, and pressed his back to one side and his feet to the other. Slowly, he began painfully walking up the shaft.

* * * * *

Over an hour later, Thomas scrambled onto another ledge. He had made good time. The sand impacting his helmet sounded like a distant hive of bees, meaning he was likely getting close to the rim. The sand had just enough force to stick to his suit and prevent his helmet light from penetrating more than a few meters in front of him. There was also a lot of CO_2 snow condensing onto the rocky surface, making it extremely slippery.

A large boulder blocked Thomas's path and he almost hit it head on in his haste. He lunged around it only to find another, and another. "Come on!" he panted. He must get help fast, before his air ran out. "Which way Mars?" He scooted along a narrow ledge, looking for a way up and over the rock pile.

Thomas followed the curves of stone using his wrist light. It suddenly went dark like the sky above him. "I can't believe this! How am I supposed to climb out of this canyon without a light!" With only his dim head lamp, he couldn't see where to put his boots. He placed his numb foot on a slippery section, and it gave way abruptly, his bad leg collapsing into a crevice. He tried pulling it free, but the movement only seemed to loosen more sand to bury his leg deeper. Mars had finally stopped him.

"Lorena, can you hear me?" There was no answer. The rocks must be blocking his signal. "Columbus, this is Thomas Miller. Please respond." Miraculously, he heard voices mixed with the static.

"Thomas Miller, Thomas Miller, this is Columbus. Please give us your position. Over."

Thomas knew they were repeating first sentences because his signal was weak. Even though it would drain his batteries, he upped his transmit power to FULL. "Columbus, Columbus, I am on the southeast rim of Razor Fossae. Repeat, southeast rim of Razor Fossae. I have a suit leak. Estimate one hour of air remaining. Karl and Lorena Orth survived the crash and are on the ledges below me. Over."

"Thomas Miller, Thomas Miller, this is Doctor Engle. Rescue vehicle enroute to you. Expected arrival three hours, repeat three hours. Recommend you return to the Orth's and utilize Karl's secondary supply. He should not need it. Over."

Doctor Engle must have known Karl was taking the drug! *And if the drug worked, Karl would not need his secondary supply! Lorena, if Karl had briefed you on the drug, you would have known what Dr. Engle knows, and had me take that supply, wouldn't you?* But it was too late now. He hoped she'd never know, and thus blame herself for his death as she blamed Karl for her father's. "Columbus, Columbus. Copy that rescue vehicle will not arrive for three hours. Negative on your recommendation to use Karl's secondary supply. I am trapped in a crevice and unable to reach Karl."

The airways were silent for a moment as if in prayer for Thomas. At least he had the comfort of knowing he had saved Lorena, and possibly Karl. The rescue team should be able to find them easily once they had a fix on Thomas's suit transponder.

The Columbus flight controller awkwardly thanked him for his report and asked if there were any messages he wanted her to relay to friends or family. He thought of his old friends back on Earth. He didn't have much in common with them anymore. *Searching for dead rocks on a dead planet. Why did I do it? Because I want to prove that Life can win against the god of war?*

Apparently, he had lost his battle, but he hoped others would win the war eventually. He wondered if his parents would come to Mars for his funeral? Would they want his body shipped back to Earth? Did he?

He suddenly had a terrible fear of his body being yanked from this place where his soul would depart for the next world. If he couldn't find life here, then he wanted to at least mark his struggle with a grave. "Columbus, I just have one request. Please let my parents know that I'd like to be buried here, in this canyon," he said.

He couldn't think of anything else to say. Eventually, Columbus informed him that Phobos was going over the horizon in fifteen minutes. He was alone now. Trapped in the crevice, his body warmth was not enough to counter the cold that crept with icy fingers up his leg to his hip. He imagined his fingers wrapped over Lorena's, watching Phobos rise in the West. *Phobos, fear; and Deimos, panic. Great companions for a soldier dying in battle.*

His eyes became heavy with the urge to sleep. *So cold. Concentration was slipping.* "Great Rock, nice to meet you," he mumbled. "I'm a geologist you know. Wanna be my tombstone?"

Part of his mind knew the low O2 pressure was affecting him, making him silly when he needed to think. He was startled momentarily when his radio squealed loudly in his ear as if more than one user was transmitting at the same time. It reminded him to turn the power back down to NORM. "Karl," he whispered. "Don't die."

Peaceful and warm at last, Thomas closed his eyes. The darkness that engulfed him was blacker than the depths of space.

*****

The darkness was complete except for Karl's red-lighted face. Lorena had left her suitcomm on as Thomas had instructed, only to hear a broken, one- sided conversation. She couldn't be sure if Thomas were delirious or actually talking with Columbus Base. But either way, he was in trouble. Only one hour of air left and the rescue team three hours away!

She checked Karl's O2 reading. How could he still have three hours of his primary supply left? Hers had switched to secondary a short time ago, meaning she had used six hours of air since it activated in orbit. Even with his lower suit pressure and inactivity, he should use more oxygen than that! Unless . . .

"Karl, can you hear me? Karl!"

"Lo . . re . . na," he whispered.

"Did you take father's drug?"

"Ja," he gasped.

Lorena closed her eyes and clenched her fists in anger. "How could you?" she said. But Karl was not listening. He never listened. "Is this why you brought me here? To watch you kill yourself like Father!"

"Thom . . as," he gasped.

"Thomas? What about Thomas? You want to be buried with him in this canyon?!" *Was there nothing but death on this planet?*

"*Nein*," he wheezed, coughing weakly. "Save him."

She turned away, not wanting to look at her brother. How did he expect her to save Thomas? Lorena pictured Thomas's face as she had seen it when she fell. She thought he could almost pass for German with his sandy hair and blue eyes. *The kind of young man Mother would approve.* He was going to die unless he got air soon.

But wait! The drug not only increased the number of red blood cells to make more efficient use of existing oxygen, it altered the body's metabolism, so a person actually needed less oxygen. She turned back to face her brother. His eyes were closed. He was so silent, she had to check his suit display to make sure his heart was still beating. Then she checked his O2 supply again. It had not changed! He may be going to die of his injuries today or a brain hemorrhage tomorrow, but in the meantime, the drug seemed to be doing what it was supposed to do — lower oxygen requirements. That meant he would not need his secondary supply.

"Oh, Thomas! If I had known!" she cried. "Is that what you were trying to tell me, Karl? To take your secondary O2 to Thomas?" She would have to move her brother, risk his life to save his friend's.

Dare she roll him over to get the bottle? He might die! But his friend would die for certain if she didn't. Still, she hesitated. "What do you want me to do, Karl?" She heard his words, *Save Thomas* repeated in her mind. And once again, *Forgive me*.

"I do," she whispered.

Deep inside she knew he was not to blame for their father's death. Father was the most stubborn man she'd ever known. He did things his way or not at all. Karl's weakness had been only that he was unwilling or unable to challenge him, especially when Father's gambles had paid off so many times. So when Father's sponsor had demanded immediate results to continue funding, it was not surprising that Karl had gone along with Father's plan to test the drug on himself. They would provide the struggling Martian industries a solution to their worker productivity problem and also make it possible for people with low blood pressure, like Lorena and her mother, to visit Mars without being sick. Lorena thought those dreams had died with her father, but it appeared her brother had inherited some of their father's stubbornness. He had obviously invited her here to confirm his results, but the accident had instead challenged her to trust his life to the drug like he had trusted their father's life to it. Her brother had not been able to save their father, only continue the work. She prayed that Fate would be kinder to her.

She carefully removed the bungie cords holding Karl's arms to the window shade stretcher. Taking a deep breath, she rolled him onto his right side and located the secondary supply bottle. It attached the same way as the one she had done for Thomas. She quickly removed it and clipped it to her belt. She pushed Karl back so that his lighted face was upward again and struggled to slide him as far out from under the ledge as possible. That should make it easier for the rescue team to locate his suit transponder. She propped his head up on a rock, to aid his breathing, and his feet on another, to ease his shock. There wasn't any more she could do.

"Karl, I am leaving. I will send the rescue team as soon as possible." He didn't respond. She realized he may be listening though, and her words may be the last he would hear. "Karl, I . . . I am sorry for the way things have been between us. I love you."

* * * * *

Thomas heard voices. They sounded foreign, and they sounded far away. He commanded his eyes to open, but they wouldn't obey him. His thoughts were a jumble as he tried to concentrate on the words.

"I think he comes around." A female voice.

"Ja." A male voice.

"Herr Miller, this is Doctor Engle." The male voice again. "You are in the Columbus Hospital. Can you hear me? If so, open your eyes."

Thomas forced his eyes open. The room whirled around. *I must be drugged.* He tried to speak. There were tubes in his nostrils, his lips were crusted shut. He couldn't feel his left foot.

"This is good, no?" the blurred image of the doctor said. "Do not try to speak, Herr Miller," he continued. "Your lungs are still recovering."

Thomas closed his watering eyes, trying to figure out how he'd gotten here.

"I'm sure you have lots of questions," the doctor continued. "First of all, your surgery went quite well."

His surgery? How much of his leg had he lost? He attempted to sit up and look, but found he was strapped down. There were tubes leading into both arms. Thomas writhed in frustration, moaning. The movement awakened a considerable pain down his left side.

The doctor adjusted the tubes in his nose. "Blink three times at me if you are experiencing pain."

Thomas blinked.

The doctor nodded. "I will adjust your medication so you can rest. If you need anything just press the call button by your left hand." He placed Thomas's hand on the button. "Blink three times if you understand."

Thomas blinked. The doctor adjusted his IV and then left.

Thomas lay still, the sedative overtaking him.

* * * * *

The next time Thomas opened his eyes he was alone. The room was darkened. His mouth felt like he'd swallowed a bucket of sand. He pressed the call button.

A few moments later, the door opened. "Water," he heard himself whisper. "Water!" That was better.

A young Asian woman that he suspected had been recruited from the greenhouse to serve as his nurse brought him a pouch of water with a straw sticking out. "Doctor Engle said for you to only take sips so you don't choke."

He did as she advised. The water was cold going down his sore throat.

He tried wiggling his toes and moaned in pain. "My foot?" he asked. "How bad?" Had they amputated it?

"Doctor Engle removed three of your toes and grafted some skin from your thigh," the young woman said. "You should be almost as good as new in a few months."

"A few months?" He nearly choked on some water, and then found his voice. "But I'm supposed to leave for Earth at the end of the month!"

The woman frowned. "I'm sorry, Dr. Miller, but I was told I'd be needed to help you with rehab for at least three months."

Thomas lifted the blanket to stare at his bandaged foot. He'd wanted to stay on Mars, but how would he pay for another two years on top of his medical expenses? Then he shook his head. He was lucky to be alive. He recalled the view from inside the crashed shuttle. It could have been worse. Much worse. He looked up at the nurse. "Did Karl and his sister, the Orths, make it?" he asked.

She hesitated. "Let me get Commander Cary," she said, bustling out of the room.

The news must not be good if she is summoning the head of the Mars Exploration Team. To lose both his flight instructor and best friend and a woman he'd hoped to get to know better all at once . . . *Oh Karl. I'm so sorry. You risked it all for me. This just isn't fair.* He thought of the rocks newly exposed by the shuttle crash. *Even if I have to dig outhouses to pay for it, I'll find that fossil evidence and dedicate my life to proving that life once did, and still can survive here!*

Commander Cary arrived a few minutes later. Dark circles under his eyes betrayed his lack of sleep. Thomas braced himself for the bad news.

"Dr. Miller, it is good to see you awake again. I trust the foot is not giving you too much pain."

"It's not bad," Thomas said. "Can you tell me what happened? How did I get here, and what happened to Karl and his sister?"

Commander Cary ran his hand over his five-o'clock shadow, then through his short hair. "From what Dr. Engle told me, Lorena Orth saved you. She took Karl's secondary oxygen and brought it to you. Good thing you left your helmet light on, so she could find you. The rover picked you up a few hours later."

Thomas was relieved to hear that Lorena had survived. *Thank God. But Karl must have died or Lorena would never have left him.* "So Karl didn't make it?" Thomas asked.

"Oh, yes, he did," the commander said, "though he was pretty banged up. Apparently that drug he was taking kept him from needing much oxygen. When his sister figured that out, she brought his secondary supply to you. So that drug saved both of your lives."

"He didn't have a stroke or anything?" Thomas asked.

Commander Cary shook his head. "No, I don't think so. Dr. Engle says he is recovering even faster than normal, possibly because of the drug." He looked off into the distance and then back at Thomas. "Can you imagine what it will be like to have the ability to do week-long explorations without having to carry tons of oxygen along? Why, think of all the canyons you can explore!" He gestured widely with his hands.

Thomas nodded slowly, seeing the exposed rocks of Razor Ridge in his mind's eye. "Yeah, about that . . . I've been told I won't be able to return to Earth on the next transport because of my foot, and um, well, you know my funding runs out soon."

Commander Cary patted Thomas's arm. "Don't worry, we've got plenty of work needs doing around here." He grinned. "In fact, Nelson had already talked with me about making you a transport pilot."

"He did?" Thomas struggled to sit up straighter.

"Yes. He and I were looking for ways to keep you here on Mars," he said.

Thomas felt a lump forming in his throat realizing that Karl, and now Nelson, had been working on his behalf without him having a clue.

The commander continued. "So, as soon as the doc says you're able, I can take you for hopper certification and then start shuttlecraft training if you're interested."

Trajectories

He'd always dreamed of flying a shuttlecraft into space and back! Thomas wiped the tears that somehow had started rolling down his cheeks. "Thank you, Commander," he choked out. "I'd be honored."

"Good, good. It's settled then," the commander said. "I'll inform Mars Central. By the way, I'm recommending the canyon be named 'Nelson's Fossae' after John." He looked at his large hands then continued, "I recovered his body myself yesterday. We'll have the funeral as soon as you and Karl are up to it."

Thomas knew he and Commander Cary would share that same gruesome memory forever etched in their minds. Unable to speak, he just nodded his head.

They were interrupted by a knock at the door. "Time's up for this visit," the commander said, rising to leave. "I'll be back tomorrow to collect a full report after I get some sleep." Thomas realized that for the commander to have recovered Nelson's body, he must have driven to the canyon, led a team down and back out, and then driven back. No wonder he looked so tired.

The drape between Thomas and the next bed was still swinging when he heard the door again. Someone quietly entered the darkened room. At first Thomas thought it was the nurse again, until she poked her head around the drape. "Lorena!"

She smiled a broad smile. "Ja, it is me," she said, moving quickly to perch on the bed next to him.

As she pushed an errant blonde curl from her blue eyes, Thomas thought she was probably the only person to ever look ravishing in a hospital gown. "I understand that thanks to you, both me and Karl are going to be okay."

Her expression was difficult to read. Happiness mixed with anger? She sighed. "When I overheard you talking to the base, I realized that Karl's O2 readings might be low because of Father's drug."

She looked down at her hands briefly. Thomas had a feeling when Karl was recovered, he would have some tough questions to answer from her. Thomas wrapped his cold fingers around her soft, warm hand. "He loves you more than anyone in the world, you know."

"I know. From talking with Dr. Engle, I begin to understand what he did to Father's drug. He not only took care of the stroke problem, he took the drug a step further. His system used about half as much oxygen as normal. It really is a wonder drug. It will have many applications." She stopped talking a moment and her eyes became unfocused. "I think this means he will not trouble have getting a sponsor now." She looked into Thomas's blue eyes, like a palm reader looking for a clue. "Karl has asked me to stay and help him."

"Are you considering it?" *Did he dare hope?*

Her eyes studied the sheets for a moment. "Ja. He is not so reckless as I had thought. Dr. Engle was intimately involved in the experiment and with the animal testing also. He showed me the test plans, and I agree there would have been a minimal risk to Karl. But the accident has proved the drug's safety under much worse conditions. In fact, once I am rested, I have agreed to volunteer as a test subject. With Karl's drug to stop the adaptation sickness, Mars will not be so terrible." When she looked up, she flashed a slightly embarrassed smile at Thomas. His heart fluttered.

"Oh, I brought you a little present." She pulled a pouch from her gown's only pocket.

He read the label on the plastic bag she handed him. "Turkey tetrazzini!" Thomas laughed until tears came to his eyes. He imagined the two of them out on a mold-fossil-hunting expedition, feeding each other packets of the white glue under the light of the two moons. After what they had survived together, nothing could stop them. *Mars, it's time for you to surrender!*

HIGH JACK
by Bud Sparhawk

Not every space traveler is an intrepid, square-jawed explorer concerned with the Big Issues of life on other worlds and humanity's tiny role amongst in an infinite spray of stars in an infinite universe. Instead, some of those who leave the Earth will be blue-collar types just trying to use their common sense to make a living while finding someone to love or cherish, just like Phil in Bud Sparhawk's story, "High Jack."

Bud Sparhawk has published several novels and over a hundred short stories in major SF magazines and anthologies. He has been a three-time finalist for the Nebula award. A complete bibliography can be found at: http://budsparhawk.com or on Wikipedia. He resides in Annapolis, Maryland with his wife of fifty-five years and writes a weekly blog on the pain of writing at http:// budsparhawk.blogspot.com.

■■■■■■

"Brace yourself, Phil," the pilot warned.

I looked over the shuttle jock's shoulder at the bright speck we were chasing. From here our destination looked no different than the hundreds of other specks dotting black space. I kept my eye focused on the one particular speck that was our destination and tried to ignore the vast mass of Mars hanging overhead, ruddy and menacing.

The speck grew rapidly to the rough potato shape of Phobos. Closer, the moon revealed details across its pocked face, including the sparkle of light that marked Stickney Station.

"We aren't going to land in the dark, are we?" I asked nervously. Overhead and slightly behind our position, Mars's Elysium Planitia was darkening so I knew it wouldn't be long before Phobos also went dark, shielded by Mars from Mother Sol.

"We'll be down to Stickney before dark, Phil," the pilot answered nonchalantly. "Why are you worried? I thought all you 'jacks were pretty fearless."

I took another nervous look at Mars, ominously huge at this distance. "Yeah, when we're in free space. This close to the planet . . . ."

High Jack

I let the phrase hang. "Scary."

* * * * *

The pilot feathered down so smoothly that I hadn't realized we'd arrived until the pilot got out of his seat. I expected to feel at least some effect from the moon's miniscule gravity, but I'd been in the business long enough that making adjustments for low or lack of gravity was second nature.

I hand-walked the safety line to the new installation and immediately began inspecting the footplates of the new rig. The welds looked smooth and bright with Pham Ra's signature, a little rippled bead, at the end of each run. He was one of the best welders in Mars orbit, and one of my former teammates.

Next, I checked the runs on the crossarms, smacking them with the impulse hammer to make sure they weren't weak cold-welds that might break under stress.

The other bonded sections made up ninety percent of the structure. Adhesives were easier to work with, lighter, and needed little expertise to apply. They were preferred where a weld's brute strength wasn't needed. Besides, transporting a container of glue was cheaper than moving heavy welding gear.

By the time I finished my inspection Phobos was nearly eclipsed, so I could appreciate the spectacular view of Marineris slipping into night while Olympus Mons passed directly below.

Julie was down there now, I knew. Probably drinking a cold one with the other rats and bragging about the strikes she'd made. Mars prospectors were like fishermen whose tales grew with each telling.

I'd met her a few weeks before, when she was between prospecting trips. Since then we'd gone out a few times, had a few laughs, and generally found that we enjoyed each other's company.

I didn't know if this brief relationship was going anywhere. At our ages and occupations any sort of long-term relationship was doubtful; orbital construction workers and prospectors weren't an insurance company's favorite people. Just the same, having someone waiting for me was enough, out here in the cold emptiness of the frontier.

"Coming back," I called to the pilot and took one last look at the darkening face of Mars.

* * * * *

Trajectories

JBI's recruiting manager was a pinch-faced corporate weasel that I disliked on sight. His handshake felt soft against my calluses. They came from constantly palming the control ball in a construction rig, something I'd done for nearly thirty years, before taking my current position.

"I already have a decent job," I replied, sensing what he wanted. "Inspector."

The weasel smiled, showing a perfect set of teeth. "I know, a very critical position and one in which JBI is deeply appreciative, witness your somewhat substantial salary."

"It's enough to get by."

He raised an eyebrow. "Really?"

I repressed a sneer. What was the good of a seven figure salary if a fucking real beer cost a couple of hundred? Not that I'd tasted any since leaving Earth orbit, but the memory of that cold, bitter taste . . . .

"Inspector's an important job, but JBI now needs your deep- space construction knowledge and skills to help build Barnard Station. We are willing to provide a substantial advance that will . . . . Are you listening to me?" The weasel was staring at me strangely.

I blinked. Had I actually dozed off? "Sorry, I'm still time-lagged from the Phobos trip."

The weasel stiffened. "Lack of attention can kill you out there. I expected that your years of experience would have taught you that. I expected better." He pursed his lips, just as Ms. Eliot had back in the second grade when I'd pissed in her potted plant.

"As I was saying, you would receive triple your current salary from the time you accept the job until you return to Mars orbit. In addition, we will provide a substantial advance that will allow you to set up a nice investment fund before you depart."

"Just where is Barnard Station?" I wondered how I could have missed that minor point.

"Didn't I mention that?" the weasel said. "It's on Amalthea — Jupiter's third moon."

He told me it was going to be a weather station, but I didn't buy that. With Amalthea taking eleven and a fraction hours to orbit, and Jupiter rotating every ten hours, I couldn't see how any information it gathered would be useful.

One thing I'd learned about JBI was that nothing was ever what it seemed and everything they did served at least two other purposes. I was certain this station would be no different.

* * * * *

First order of business was to make a quick trip to Bradbury station to talk to Julie. I owed her that.

"Jupiter's pretty far out. I'll be gone for over two years." Unmentioned was the risk I might not survive. We both knew the risks inherent in our jobs.

Julie sniffed. "Well, for sure I'm going to miss you and your boozy kisses. Been a lot of fun, Phil. You're a nice guy to pay so much attention to an old bag like me."

I smiled. Julie was five, maybe more, years younger than me and was whipsaw thin. True, the leathery skin and bleached hair made her look older, but most Mars rats were like that — too much surface time and too little medical care.

Of course I was no prize myself, what with my ruddy nose and a body covered with thousands of tiny hemorrhages from the pressure pops. Without my clothes I looked like a mad tattooist had attacked me.

"You aren't that old," I replied. "And you're mighty pretty to boot." That got me a smile and a quick peck on the cheek.

"So, you going to do it?"

That was a good question. I was still on the cusp of a decision. On the one hand JBI was willing to pay top dollar for my experience and that kind of money doesn't come often. There was the adventure as well — being out there on the edge of the frontier, out there in the shadow of the biggest damn planet in the universe, fighting radiation, magnetic storms, static, and who knew what else? It was a challenge, something nobody had tried before. God, I remember when I loved that stuff.

But that was a long time ago. Where was the point when I'd stopped taking risks without a second thought? When had danger stopped being an addictive drug? At what age had I lost my willingness to put my ass on the line? Was that why I was hesitating? Was I scared of taking a chance?

Then there was my recent discovery of Julie. Would she still be here when I got back? Would she still be interested — or worse, still alive? Such certainties were not assured on Mars. She had no reason to expect me to survive either, especially since what I was going to be doing was at least as risky as prospecting.

Trajectories

"I don't know, Jule. My fifty-first is coming up. Maybe I'm too old for this."

Julie took my hand. "You're as old as you let yourself be, Phil. I know a lot of younger guys who don't have the guts you do."

"I appreciate that, Jule. But two years is a long time."

Julie smiled, crinkling the creases around her eyes, and patted my hand. "Don't bullshit me, Phil. I can see in your eyes that you couldn't turn down this job if you wanted to. That's what I like about you, by the way."

"But I'll be gone for two years," I protested. Suddenly, being away from her for that long seemed something awfully hard to bear.

"Two years isn't that much," she replied. "That's why I'm going to mark my calendar for the day you're due back. Might even bump for a bottle of that Earth beer you're always yammering about. Go, take the challenge and come back safe."

And just like that, I knew she was right.

* * * * *

The seven-month trip from Mars orbit to the Jupiter system was as expected — too long and very boring. So far I'd lost forty-two million in poker, won sixty in craps, and lost five in a no-holds-barred game of bridge. I'd watched every piece of entertainment, read every book I was even remotely interested in, and had exhausted every topic of conversation. Too soon, all I wanted to do was get away from the crew and the two insane idiots who wanted to work deep in Jupiter's atmosphere. One of them, who appeared otherwise quite sane, said he was going to help build some sort of ship or station that would float in Jupiter's seas. Sounded crazy to me, but was building a weather station on Amalthea any less insane?

The crew and passengers threw me a combination fifty-first birthday party and Christmas celebration as we swept past Earth's orbit on our outbound swing. For the hundredth time I wondered if I was doing the right thing.

* * * * *

We looped Europa, twisted past Io, and swung to dock at the JBI station in orbit around Jupiter. From Europa, Jupiter appeared the same size as Mars from Deimos but the view from the station was far different. From here Jupiter was a huge ball, its clouds roiled in striated bands as the giant wheeled around every ten hours. It was hard to believe the other passengers would soon be far below, mining the dark clouds to build JBI's industrial base. Better them than me, I thought. Give me good clean space and a clear view any day.

* * * * *

The engineers started briefings and training as soon as we arrived. I couldn't believe the level of detail they'd put into the project plan, every step timed to perfection; did they really expect we could stay on the predicted critical path? I'd done enough deep space construction to know that something always went wrong, something the plans never accounted for. That's why they had people like my crew doing the work instead of using some stinking robot. No machine could adapt as quickly as a human and come up with a make-do solution from whatever was at hand.

That's why I sweated answers from the engineers for every contingency I could imagine.

"We've put in slack for unforeseen circumstances," they pleaded when I begged more time to think up other possibilities. They seemed to think that adding a fudge factor was a way to overcome an unpredictable problem.

"You're paying more attention to the schedule than the work," I objected. "Can't we go over this one more time?"

"Impossible. You've got to launch on schedule," they insisted. "The pallets are already on their way."

Pallets of structural material had been launched from Europa orbit months before and were now taking their long spiraling path toward rendezvous. They'd been sent out at timed intervals so that each would arrive at the appropriate moment in the construction schedule. I tried to picture the train of pallets orbiting Jupiter, a long line extending millions of miles and failed. The whole idea seemed too complex, too dependent on chance, even though it saved precious fuel.

"The pallets are using the same orbital mechanics as we are," Rocks assured me. He was the geologist on our team as well as our adhesives expert. He was hauling a few experiments along with him. Like JBI, he never did one thing without accomplishing something else. "The math is so simple that they can get pinpoint accuracy, even at astronomical distances. Don't worry; everything has been worked out to the ninth decimal place."

"Right. But it's the tenth decimal place that has me worried," I grumbled, but the project engineers were right. We had to leave on schedule.

* * * * *

The transfer bus braked to lose some of our orbital speed from Europa, which dropped us toward Jupiter, which made the bus go faster so we could finally match orbits with the tiny speck that was Amalthea, one of Jupiter's smallest moons.

I had to admit that they'd done a good job outfitting us. The suits were first class, shielded against the worst of the radiation this deep in Jupiter's belt. As a safeguard we'd all been sucking down anti-rad drugs since we broke Mars orbit. The drugs made me edgy and gave us all the trots for the first couple of weeks.

Pham Ra's welding gear was the latest and greatest. Had a honking big capacitor-driven arc welder, a nice acetylene rig, and enough cold-tempered adhesives to stick Amalthea permanently in place. That gear was going with us in the bus. No way would I trust a pallet to deliver it, orbital mathematics or not.

I'd insisted that Pham Ra be on the team to handle the welding that needed doing after Rocks and Xavier finished blasting holes for the so-called weather station's base.

First priority upon arrival was erecting the inflatable habitat where we'd live until we dug a permanent home. We'd have about five days to get set up before the first pallet arrived with the construction materials.

Adapting to the moon's slight gravity — a few thousandths of a gee — wasn't difficult. Things didn't fall very fast, but otherwise it was just like working on any other moon where the horizon was always too damned close.

Our construction site was at Amalthea's planet-facing pole that constantly pointed down at Jupiter. The first thing we did was install pitons for the hand lines we'd need to get around the job site. They ensured that we didn't bounce too much and lose work time.

The pallet containing our first two months of supplies had plowed a long ditch in the dust that covered every surface. Because of the static charge it had acquired in transit, the pallet looked like nothing more than a huge dust ball by the time we arrived. Cleaning off the dust added hours to the unloading, time that wasn't accounted for in the engineer's precious schedule. They never warned me about the dust.

While Pham and I dealt with the dust ball, Rocks and Xavier went to work unpacking their explosive charges. Soon after we saw geysers of exploding regolith shooting into the sky, curving up and behind us. At eclipse the debris stream would sparkle and glow as they impacted other pieces of junk in the inner orbits and contended with the fierce electrical storms. Somebody else would have to contend with the extra dust in orbit for a year or two.

Rocks and Xavier had made a decent sized hole near the "north" pole. The blasted hole revealed an aggregate rock mixture ideal for tunneling. The depth would provide some shielding against the constant rain of charged particles and larger chunks of rock Jupiter threw our way.

We could have lived in the inflatable for the eight months we'd be working, but the guys who would arrive on the bus that was taking us home — the engineers, technicians, and scientists who'd be installing the equipment — would be here longer and needed better accommodations. That was why we made the hole in the wall of the moon's crater.

Once they got the hole done, Rocks sprayed the interior with sealant and we pressurized the place.

*****

The second pallet soft-landed on the backside, slap against the side of Mons Lyctas. Took us a day to move it to the construction site.

Jupiter's huge presence felt far different at the Amalthea work site. The old man rotated overhead, an immense presence whose enormous weight bore down, diminishing everything else to insignificance. It was hard to believe that something that overwhelming was nearly two hundred thousand kilometers away. "Ignore it," I told the crew, but mostly to reassure myself. "It's not going to fall on us."

I spotted the Great Red Spot coming out of the darkness shortly after we'd anchored the pallet in place. Rocks keyed on through the cable linking us. "Great view, eh? We'll see that every eight or so hours. That's the differential between Jupiter's rotation and our revolution."

I was starting to hate the damned suit. All of the radiation plating made movement extremely difficult. It took such an effort to move my arms and legs that a day's work was exhausting. The tethers were always in the way, but we couldn't avoid using them lest an overzealous move throw us off the moon.

The dust was a continuing problem. Unless we grounded ourselves, the dust adhered to everything. "It's Io," Rocks explained. "She's spewed out ions into Jupiter's plasma torus and filled the entire magnetosphere with charged particles. The rain of particles imparts a positive charge to the dust."

Trajectories

And Io must be the reason there was so much sulfur around, I reasoned. Even with clean filters, the habitat still stunk to high heaven. And if Xavier makes one more bad fart joke, I thought, I will throw him out the airlock.

You'd think that at 122 Kelvin the cold would be a huge problem. Actually, the heat generated by our bodies was the greater enemy. Because of the heavy insulation, the radiators on the back of our suits couldn't radiate heat as fast as it built up from our exertions. As a consequence we had to take breaks every four hours, sit around for an hour and a half, and then work for another hour. Six hours was the max time we could work in the bright reflection from Jupiter's day-lit side before it got too dark. That gave us a half hour to undress.

A huge pallet of steel uprights slammed down sixty kilometers off target, giving a lie to Rocks's boast about pinpoint accuracy. "Maybe the magnetic fields perturbed it," he guessed.

"Or maybe blasting the holes shifted Amalthea's orbit," I countered. Probably untrue, but at least it was an explanation. Whatever the reason, it proved the engineers hadn't planned for everything, and that miss worried me.

Regardless, it still meant that we had to schlep the eighty-meter beams halfway around the moon. The negligible gravity meant that even though two of us could carry each beam, they still had the same mass. Also, they were awkward to handle, refusing to stop their forward motion whenever we paused to set our tethers. After the third overshoot we were better able to estimate when we had to put on the brakes.

I checked the schedule after we wrestled all nine beams to the site. Thanks to the screwed-up pallet, we were already a half-day behind schedule.

We began mixing the adhesive with regolith and dust immediately to form the basis for our Amal-crete.

"Welcome to the exciting world of 2151," Xavier said as he hefted a shovelful of dust into the mixing ball. "All the freaking high-tech and I'm digging ditches. I can't believe it."

"You're probably JBI's most expensive ditch digger," I shot back. "Now get to work. We've got to keep up with the schedule." Xavier told me where I should keep the schedule, but he kept digging.

Pham Ra and Rocks had rigged a counterpoise to erect the girder while Xavier and I injected catalyst to the Almal-crete. The first pour was difficult since the -crete didn't want to come out of the ball. We had to scoop it out and pack it around the beam, pressing it down with our boots. We lost time having to clean off the boots before it hardened.

Setting the beam perfectly upright proved to be another problem. Due to its flexibility the beam wiggled like a piece of spaghetti. We wasted two Amal-crete mixtures before Rocks glued on legs to stabilize it while the pour hardened.

By the time we got all nine of the uprights in place, we'd used up five percent of our slack time and were a full day behind.

Before we could weld the beams together I had to climb along each girder and check the alignment with the other three. If there were more than a ten percent error in measurements we'd have to readjust positions. The plan allowed for a full day for that, not nearly enough time, since we'd have to blast the upright free, clean out the hole, and reset the beam. If we had to do more than one we'd waste even more time. Time lost at this stage was important, since most of the construction's unforeseen problems were still ahead of us.

I threw a loop around the first girder to hold my boots against the flange. I intended to walk up the narrow beam to the spot where I'd take the first measurement. No great deal to remain horizontal in this slight gravity.

Halfway up I made the mistake of looking around. Jupiter was wheeling overhead as it rotated, as was Amalthea. The combination of the three axial movements invoked a stomach turning reaction so I stopped being a tourist and got to work.

Walking a beam isn't much to someone used to working the high steel, but when that thin rail is attached to a flyspeck of a moon, it gets scary. Suddenly I wasn't climbing from Amalthea; I was balancing on a rail between her and Jupiter with nothing more substantial than a thread holding me in place. At that, despite my years of experience as a high jack and despite the certain knowledge that nothing could happen to me, I panicked.

I wrapped my arms around the beam and closed my eyes until the involuntary shakes stopped. Concentrate on the job, I kept telling myself. Just keep your mind on the job and don't look down, up, or out, for that matter.

I inched to the mark and, with a huge effort of will, pointed my laser at the third girder to my right, aiming at the target disk at its tip, holding the button for a few seconds and then pressing the record button to capture the reading before pointing at the next. Then I turned and climbed up to Amalthea. The whole time I could feel mighty Jupiter beaconing at my back.

The next climb required an effort. There was no way I wanted to walk down toward Jupiter. Despite the impossibility, I worried that if the loop broke I would fly off and be pulled down into Jupiter's stormy maelstrom, freezing before I hit the atmosphere and roasting after, ending up as a super-compressed lump of carbon and steel at the bottom of that deep gravity well.

Thank God the readings were within limits and we didn't have a single do-over. We'd won back a day from the schedule.

*****

The fourth pallet contained some personal messages along with project material. Somehow they'd rendezvoused to add a pouch of greetings from home as well as news and entertainment chips. Hearing from friends and family was nice, but it was one-way communication. Because of Jupiter's intense electromagnetic fields, radio communication was impossible even using the latest filtering and compression techniques. That meant that, until the bus arrived to take us home, we had no way of sending our replies.

The lack of communication made me wonder how this so-called weather station was going to inform anyone of its readings if radio wouldn't work.

There were three letters from Julie in the pouch. The first two had been made while we were on our way out to Jupiter and the last shortly after we'd arrived at Amalthea.

She said was going out on another prospecting trip, this time to the Valles Marineris, to look for ice caves. There was big money for finding one. Every station and habitat needed water and squeezing it out of Mars' sub-surface was an expensive process. Mining water from the ice caves required much less effort.

The Valles was the most likely location for caves, she wrote, and her partner thought he knew the best place to find them. At the mention of a partner I felt a pang of jealousy. Out in the Valles they'd be sleeping together, sharing meals, sharing danger, and be constantly together. I knew from past experience that a lot of feelings could get tangled up when you're sharing those things. Would Julie weaken, take up with him instead, I wondered? She said she'd wait, but two years is a long time.

High Jack

Damn, why had I ever left?

*****

Pham Ra welded the cross members in place as fast as we could move them from the pallet. He worked so fast that we drained the power and had to wait so the capacitor could recharge. Luckily, there was plenty of free electricity this close to Jupiter.

There were eighteen cross braces ringing the base. The topmost one was twenty meters above the surface. I worried constantly as I watched Pham Ra bobbing around, his movements highlighted by blindingly bright arcs. It couldn't be easy, hanging on with one hand, blind to everything because of the filters, and trying to burn a straight bead with one hand in practically zero gee. That he could do it was admirable, that he could do it so well was nothing short of miraculous.

Pham Ra signaled for more line as he began scooting along the crosspiece to reach the unattached end. Rocks unclipped the welder's tether and pushed it along. Suddenly a bright arc shot from the machine to Rocks's suit. Rocks jerked and then started to float, held in place only by his tether.

I got to him as fast as I could and reached him only slightly before Xavier. The suit was dead — no readouts, no lights. Somehow the electrical discharge must have scrambled his systems.

"Quick," I shouted, forgetting that no one could hear me. I took hold of Rocks's arm and began scooting toward the habitat, forty klicks away. Xavier was hanging on and doing something with his own suit. The extra mass didn't slow me much once I got it moving.

When we reached our base I noticed that Xavier had been sharing his air supply with Rocks, that is, if Rocks hadn't been fried by the discharge.

I let them go through the airlock first and then scrambled in with Pham Ra, who'd followed us. Xavier already had Rocks half out of his suit. "What happened?" Rocks asked. "Everything shut down and I couldn't move."

Luckily he wasn't harmed. I wish I could've said the same about the suit. Somehow the static discharge we'd rigged gave the welder an open pathway to the suit's controls and the discharge had fried most of the electronics. We had some spare parts, but not enough to replace a full suit.

Losing one suit meant that three of us would have to share suits. Sure, we could rotate, but it still effectively reduced how much we could work by a quarter. I did some fast calculating and figured we'd fall a day behind each week. So much for the overly optimistic schedule! Even if nothing else interfered with the job we'd still use up all of the allowed slack time.

Getting the job done on time was important. Sending a bus this deep into Jupiter's well cost a lot of expensive fuel. That was why they'd devised the pallet train. If we didn't finish the job by the time the bus arrived, there'd be eight of us living in a habitat built for four. Not only would this stretch supplies beyond their limits, but it would force us to wait another three months before the next bus arrived for the other crew. JBI would be pissed, Xavier's wife would probably divorce him, and who knew what Julie might think?

I had to figure out how to keep on the schedule.

* * * * *

Thankfully, it only took three of us to rig the decking supports. These were light sulfur-based plastic troughs. Each one didn't have much strength, but once anchored to the uprights they'd provide a stable base for the strong thermoplastic we'd be pouring for the decks.

Pham Ra and I started slapping adhesives and putting the light plastic materials in place, building a spider web of flooring that we then carried to the uprights where Rocks could attach them. Pham Ra and Xavier shared a suit since Rocks was the glue man.

The tethers were a pain in the ass, so we stopped depending on them. We'd learned that so long as you shuffled along with one boot under the lines you could stay on the surface. If we were carrying a load, the inertia of the material kept us from bouncing.

Rocks turned and was reaching for the trough when I saw his helmet jerk, and then he was floating free, following an arc that would take him over the moon's too-close horizon.

Pham Ra reacted faster than I did and reached out to intersect Rocks. I thought we'd have two fliers for a moment before I saw that Pham Ra was holding tight to the other end of the piece we'd just finished. I twisted my foot to entangle the line and held on tight. I thought my arm was going to pop when Pham Ra reached the end of his travel. For a moment it looked as if they were going to miss, but Pham Ra managed to snag Rocks's boot. All of the sudden there were two masses on the end of the very long beam I was holding, swinging it through a long arc.

I shuffled over to where they'd hit. "What the hell were you thinking?"

High Jack

I said as I plugged in. "Of all the fool . . ."

Rocks pointed. "I got distracted, damn it. Look!" I followed his finger, wondering why he was so damn interested in another one of Jupiter's moons when I realized that it wasn't a moon at all, at least not a natural kind.

The fifth pallet raced across the face of Jupiter. It had missed us by at least a kilometer. "It's too early," I said absently and wondered if my calendar had gotten screwed up. Maybe we weren't on schedule after all. No, that couldn't be; we had four independent clocks running and all agreed. Something else had gone wrong.

"Time for a conference," I announced and waved everyone back to the habitat.

* * * * *

According to the plan, the fifth pallet contained more adhesive and another ten days of rations — air and food. I did a quick check to see what was on the following shipment — just more structural material and, worse for us, no supplies.

A quick inventory showed that we had enough air and food to last us for fifteen days, twenty if we stretched it. So long as we didn't exert ourselves the air could last us another thirty days. That should be sufficient until pallet six arrived with fresh supplies.

But that meant losing twenty days off the schedule, using up all our slack time.

"Maybe we could snag the pallet with a line before it gets out of reach," Xavier suggested. "Do we have enough line to do that?"

Rocks looked up. "Even if we did the line wouldn't have enough tensile strength to brake the pallet. It'd snap,"

"How about jumping on it there and throwing the supplies back down," Pham Ra said, only half seriously. I considered that, but each throw would impart more velocity to the pallet, sending it even further away along its elliptical orbit. "And how would you plan on getting back?" I asked. "Even if I were to let you try to do such a stupid trick."

Pham Ra shrugged. "It was just a suggestion, boss."

"Well, unless anyone has any other brilliant suggestions let's prepare to hunker down until pallet number six arrives."

* * * * *

Things got pretty grim while we waited. Worse, every ten hours we could see number five passing us, ever further away and doomed to become just another object in the Gossamer Ring.

The air started to take on a distinct aroma. I was afraid of what the increasing concentration of sulfur might be doing to us, but Rocks assured me we'd run out of oxygen long before it could do much harm. Cheerful guy, but didn't say a thing about fart buildups.

The water was getting cloudy from too many passes through the recycler and our bodies. The food supply had dwindled to a point where we were opening the last resort survival rations, which were all tasteless goop of different consistencies.

Adding to my frustration was knowing how far behind we were falling. Knowing how that would add time to our presence here on Amalthea didn't make the situation more bearable.

We played poker, bridge, and other games so many times they no longer were a challenge. Rocks always folded on a pair, regardless of strength. Pham Ra always went for the finesse, and Xavier couldn't figure out how to capitalize on a doubles roll no matter how many times he tried.

Rocks and Pham Ra fought over the last biscuit, but I put a stop to that quickly and split it four ways. Had to watch our figures, I said as I doled out the pieces to my shamefaced crew.

"Time for number six," Rocks announced one day as we were debating whether to have fried goop or just eat it straight out of the can. Pham Ra, Rocks, and I suited up while Xavier started planning dinner.

We expected the pallet to impact somewhere on the surface. Rocks still had confidence that it was going to land exactly where predicted. After the prior miss I had my doubts.

But even at that I was surprised at what greeted us at the impact site. Pallet six was floating a few hundred meters above the surface.

"It's trailing us," Rocks said when he recovered from the shock. "Must be moving only slightly faster than we are. Look, you can see it getting closer by the minute."

At the rate it was moving we had a few hours until touchdown. Amalthea's gravity was so slight that only the pallet's relative speed would make it stick.

"I think we can make things easier for ourselves," Rocks said. "We aim it toward the site before it lands by pushing it to the side."

"We'd need something to stand on," I replied. "How about putting a small charge on the side?" We still had some explosives left.

Too risky," Rocks warned. "Too much and we might push it further away. How about a rocket of some sort? We have anything like that?"

"I could use what's left in the acetylene tank," Pham Ra suggested. "That might help a bit." He turned and shuffled off to get the tank, not waiting for me to give the OK. That's what I like about my crew, nobody stands on ceremony when they have a great idea.

After attaching some tethers, Rocks and Pham Ra jumped up to the pallet that was continuing its slow-speed approach. By the time they had the tank lashed in place, the pallet was within fifty meters.

After checking to see that the safety lines were firmly anchored, I waved the pair to give their pseudo rocket engine a try. Pham Ra cracked the valve all the way open.

I don't know why I expected to see an immediate result. I couldn't see the gas flowing from the tank nor notice any change in the path of the pallet. Considering the mass of the pallet and that of the escaping gas, an immediate result would have been nothing short of amazing.

But it didn't take long before the safety lines loosened. I took a step toward the work site until the lines tightened before I tugged again and took another step. Rocks and Pham Ra pulled themselves back down and picked up the other lines to help. Our little improvised rocket had already shifted the pallet's landing site significantly.

By the time the pallet finally touched down — landing would have been too dramatic a word — we were almost at the habitat's entrance. That positioning would save us a lot of time in transferring the supplies.

Fresh air, decent food, and replacement filters for our life support were the first priority, and we had a celebratory feast of canned ham and reprocessed veggies. I never tasted something so good.

"Happy birthday, Phil," Rocks said as they toasted me with clean bulbs of water. I had forgotten already. December 13th was my birthday — fifty-two and counting — and I all wanted was to get back to bed.

"Let's you and me climb into our suits, go outside," Rocks said with a smile after checking his chronometer. "I've got a surprise for you."

Curious, I went along and looked where Rocks pointed. It took a minute for me to see them. Both Europa and Io were coming around Jupiter's horizon. They were so close they were bright balls — Io's golden globe and Europa's cold steel. "If you stick around for an hour or so, you'll see Ganymede as well," he said enthusiastically.

"Thanks, Rocks," I said. Although his heart was in the right place, I didn't think it was that big a deal. Hell, I'd been watching Metis and Andrastea race backwards every day. They were just moons, after all. "That's enough celebrating, boys," I said when we got back in.

"We're twenty days behind schedule with no slack time left. We've got to haul ass if we want to catch our bus home. I just hope you all haven't gotten all fat and lazy while we've been laying around."

We went to work immediately. Xavier figured out how we could set up an assembly factory at the seventh pallet, which thankfully had actually landed where the engineers intended. The factory would let us assemble all of the deck components before we had to move them to the site. By moving three complete assemblies at once we'd save three or four days.

Actually we did better than that. By the time we'd emptied the pallet we had shaved our schedule so we were only fifteen days behind.

Pallet eight had more mail, but nothing from Julie. I worried that something might have happened to her or that she'd found someone else to share her life. The logical reason was that she might still be prospecting in the Valles and out of touch, but no matter how many times I told myself that, it was the other, worse, possibilities that preyed on my mind.

* * * * *

Xavier was our first injury. He was trying to muscle a structural member into place instead of letting momentum handle it, and caught his leg between the upright and the piece, twisting it. The suit took the torque all right, but Xavier's leg didn't.

We immediately elected Xavier to be the house bitch, responsible for cooking, cleaning, and ensuring that the sometimes-balky life support unit continued to keep us alive.

The rest of us tried to do the work of four, but this time there was no rotation of duties. Pham Ra, Rocks, and I had to do all the work outside. Eventually, because we were getting exhausted by the extra work, the schedule suffered. It didn't take long before we were eighteen days behind and falling further with each passing day.

Most of the rig's structural skeleton was done but we still hadn't started setting the decks. That would be done after we applied the wall sheets from pallet number nine.

I took another look at the plan. It called for us to pour the plastic and wait for it to cure before pouring the next. "What if we poured the second mix right away?" I suggested. "That would shave half a day off of each deck — a total saving of ten days."

"Heat buildup," Rocks replied. "When that stuff sets it throws off a lot of heat. Might buckle the structure — weaken the plastic floor supports."

That was a problem all right. "Wait a minute. It's what, a couple of hundred degrees below freezing out here, isn't it?"

"Kelvin," Rocks replied dryly. "But the walls radiate too little to cool the stuff."

"Not if we attach some sort of heat sink," I shot back. "Look, we've got some extra wall panels. Shouldn't take more than two days to lay them on. That way they'd help absorb the excess heat and promote rapid cooling."

"I don't know if they'll pull heat off fast enough," Rocks answered. "But we could give it a try during the next daylight."

Pham Ra spoke up. "How about if we rigged lights? That way we could work while we're behind Jupiter."

I hesitated. That might work, although pushing ourselves despite the suits' heat buildup could be dangerous. But it might be worth the risk. If the idea worked, we might, just might be able to get the job completed on time.

Maybe.

* * * * *

The bus arrived on schedule. We threw a party for the new guys who'd install the equipment inside. The habitat was pretty crowded with us, the four new arrivals, and the pilot of the bus, but the bottles of The Old Man's Best beer they'd brought along made it tolerable. The beer wasn't nearly as good as my memories of Earth's brew, but it sure tasted good.

"Nice job. Any problems?" the new crew chief asked as he inspected the gleaming rig. He was like most Jupiter workers, a burly bear of a man who looked more construction worker than engineer or scientist.

"Completed on time and as planned," I replied, unwilling to admit that we'd actually been attaching the final wall sections as the bus touched down.

I thought of Xavier's broken leg, pallet five's missing the mark, the twenty days of bad air and food rationing, the constant presence of Jupiter hanging over our heads, the engineers' lousy, optimistic plans, the daunting, unrelenting schedule, the sleepless nights, and the stupid mistakes we'd each made along the way. Yeah, that and wondering if Julie would still be waiting when I got back to Mars.

"No," I replied modestly. "It was just like any other construction project."

A MATTER OF TIMING
by Maya Kaathryn Bohnhoff

This next story takes us on a journey not just through space, but through time.

The concept of "buying time" is a common one. But what if it became a reality?

Maya Kaathryn Bohnhoff is a New York Times bestselling author of fantasy and science fiction, a founding member of the Book View Cafe writer's co-op and, with her husband, Jeff, performs and records original and parody music.

■■■■■■

Bud's Worry Wart is rumored to be the best hangout in Rippletown. It's dark, cool and dotted with potted plants fashioned from genuine plastic. It's long on ambience and short on glitz. Those who want glitz frequent Aurora Boreyahoo just down the street.

Bud is a cheerful being. Big, slow, smiley — always happy to give out free drinks to whoever can spin the best fabric. There's a game room, a dance floor, and a little promenade café, run by Bud's wife, Uweuwe, but the Wort's claim to fame is the storytelling. And of all the storytellers who frequent the place, Sal Pal is perhaps the favorite, if for no other reason than his promise that fully fifty percent of his stories are true. Whether that means half of his stories are 100 percent true or half of any given story is true is unclear, but his audiences enjoy the speculation. It takes little to set Sal off on a wild tale, as Koosh Mafootz discovered one evening when he made the rather unimaginative observation that it seemed there was never enough time.

Sal Pal blinked his inordinately large, black eyes and asked, "Why don't you simply go out and buy time?"

Their mutual friend, Pim Nakky, paused in the act of snorkeling his ale and gurgled: "A poor pun, Sally."

"I pun not. I am deeply serious."

"Ah," said Koosh. "I suppose you can direct me to a time broker who will arrange for me to be at the weddings of four daughters marrying on the same day at opposite ends of the galaxy?"

"Gack! What bilge!" Pim set his ale pail down on the table with an ear-rending bang and signaled their serving sentient, Astrid. "You have to be in four places at once?"

"Two. The triplets are marrying a Denebian Moluk (heaven help him), and the eldest is betrothed to Sal's cousin Vinnie."

Sal Pal said: "And what is time but a cosmic commodity?"

"Ah. Which you have no doubt traded in during your long and multi-faceted career," suggested Koosh.

"I have, indeed. I was, at one time, in the employ of the Supra-Glutinus Empire—"

"You were in the Supra-Glu?" interrupted Pim Nakky.

He paused to hurl his ale pail across the bar at the unresponsive ser-sent. She/he/it ducked, then moved languidly to clean up the mess.

"Atrocious service! You never mentioned that before."

Sal Pal's silky, black brows ascended to form a broken semi-circle above his equally silky, black eyes. "No? Well, it wasn't the most pleasant of positions."

"I should think not," said Koosh blandly. "I've heard the mortality rate of Supra-Glu employees is astronomically high. I wonder you survived."

The ser-sent arrived at their table, a wrap-around smile on its serpentine face. "Exsscuse please," it said sweetly and touched the tip of its tongue to the top of its snout in salute. "I seem to have missed your initial request for sservice."

"I trust my second request did not miss?"

"No ssir. You wish-sh?"

"Another pail of ale — a different ale. This stuff is bilge!"

Astrid's crest stood straight up on its glistening dome. "That stuff is Bud's finest! It has won copious awards including, ssir, the coveted S-slake S-suprema. How dare you label it bilge?"

"Pardon me," apologized Pim. "I'd no idea it was prestigious bilge!"

The ser-sent's crest bobbed rapidly up and down. "Well, ssir! The fault cannot be with Bud's Pale Ale, since it has been unanimously judged superior by those who know. But, ah!" The ser-sent's head darted forward on its long, slender neck, bringing it eye to bulbous eye with Pim Nakky. "I perceive, sir, that you are Navakian. And it is well known in these cultured parts that Navak is a world of sssavages. Therefore, sir, I do not doubt you find our superior brew repugnant. Your primitive palate is unable to appreciate it. I will bring you a pail of our cheapest ale post haste."

Astrid turned and sidled sinuously back to the bar.

"Damn Xssthni," muttered Pim. "They're so . . . ssens-sitive . . . So, Sal, tell me, when were you in the employ of the Supra-Glutinus Empire?"

"During the reign of Gobbitz the Large," said Sal.

"Ah, you were a youngster, then."

Sal nodded. "A mere incub. Relatively inexperienced, but adventurous and already gaining a heady reputation as a monger."

"I'm sure," said Koosh and smiled sweetly at Astrid, who had already returned with Pim's ale. "I'll have another of the House bilge, please. I seem to have an affinity for it."

Sal waited patiently for his companions to get settled and send the ser-sent on its way before beginning his narrative.

* * * * *

In the second millicent of the reign of Gobbitz the Large (said Sal), the great monarch ran into a spot of trouble. Specifically, he ran into Nemuria the Delightful, Empress of Chirk.

Nemuria the Delightful was everything her name promised, to judge by Bitzy's impassioned ravings. She was beautiful, graceful, and skilled at making a male feel rather more than he was. The Empress of Chirk was also a bad risk, for the simple reason that there was an Emperor of Chirk. And this Emperor rather liked to think of himself and his delightful consort as an unbreakable set.

Bitzy had formed the same opinion about himself and the lady, but at the insistence of his High Council, he attempted to conduct the affair with the utmost discretion. Unfortunately . . . .

* * * * *

Sal paused for a long sip of his Sarcesian Sidewinder, savored it, tamped the ice with the Slurpoon™ and eyed his audience.

"Unfortunately . . . ." repeated Pim.

Koosh gazed disinterestedly across the bar.

"Well, as I said," continued Sal, "Bitzy was feeling rather more than himself. He was feeling especially clever. And Bitzy, bless him, was never clever."

He sipped again, savored again, tamped again. Then he began to stir.

"Well?" asked Pim. "What happened?"

"Nothing good. As I said, Bitzy was peeling his oats—"

"Peeling what?" asked Pim.

"His oats," said Sal patiently. "It's a little saying I picked up on Earth."

"And what is an oat, exactly?"

"An oat is a grain fed to certain herbivorous livestock and small children. They peel them so that the husks will not lodge in the teeth."

"What does de-husked grain have to do with Bitzy's libido?"

"It's just an old saying, Pim. I don't pretend to know how it originated. However, it implies one is feeling rather full of one's self. Gobbitz the Large," Sal continued, "was feeling so consummately full that it had his High Council quite concerned. He tended to be obstinate at the best of times and under the influence of Nemuria the Delightful he was downright arrogant. They urged him to caution, but he would merely laugh bombastically and regale them with accounts of his cleverness in trysting with his lady friend."

"Absurd!" interrupted Koosh Mafootz.

"Yes, and the High Council told him as much. They were in dire fear that their unjustifiably fearless leader was going to embroil them in an interplanetary war with their most fearsome ally. Besides which, it was an election year and none of them wanted the public to think them incapable of managing their monarch."

"No! I mean it's absurd that the Emperor should confide his peccadilloes in his High Council."

Sal nodded. "I agree. But the Glutinus government prides itself on strict adherence to written procedure. Procedure dictates that — and I quote — 'all Imperial affairs are to be reviewed by the High Council.' And this was, after all, an Imperial affair."

Koosh buried his proboscis in his ale pail.

"At any rate," continued Sal, "Gobbitz the Large had begun to think of himself as Gobbitz the Incredibly Clever, and was cavorting about earth and sky in pursuit of the Delightful. He once invited his ladylove and her fearsome husband aboard the Imperial yacht to watch the Glutinus Cup. While the Emperor of Chirk was enjoying the race, Bitzy was enjoying the Empress."

Sal sighed dramatically and shook his head. "It was a tragedy looking for a place to unfold and inevitably it found one."

"Excuse me," interrupted Koosh, "I have an appointment for an ear wax in twenty declins. Do you think the tragedy will have unfolded by then?"

A Matter of Timing

"Perhaps if he was allowed to continue without interruption?" suggested Pim Nakky.

"I apologize . . . . So, our lovers are doomed to discovery?" Sal nodded dolefully.

* * * * *

It happened (said Sal) that Nemuria expressed to her Imperial Consort — Fro-erd the Serious — a heartfelt desire to learn the award-winning spiritual disciplines of the Mak Laen Order. The Emperor agreed immediately, for the Mak Laen monks had just received the coveted Bemmy award for best meditational broadcast and their current leader had been nominated to receive the Glutinus Peace Prize for his unprecedented work in dredging up celebrities' alien past lives. His "How To" book, Regression for Dummies, had been on the best-seller list for decades.

The Queen's monk was a reclusive fellow, never seen without his Veils of Purity. He was also a stickler for discipline, insisting that his pupil train at all hours of the day and night (mostly night). This began to disturb the Royal consort. There came a moment when the guru, who had come upon the Emperor and Empress bathing in their private bubble fount, insisted that she come away with him to engage in a regression.

"But surely, Mak Laen," said the Supreme Chirk, as his beloved rose from the bath waters wreathed in foam, "it can wait until we have bathed!"

"No!" cried the guru. "It cannot wait! For every act of regression there is an auspicious moment. This is the moment. I — I mean, it — cannot wait!"

And with that pronouncement, the gargantuan guru grasped the Empress' delightful hand and hurried her from the bath. "But, your Veiled Immensity," protested the Emperor. "She can't go like that! The Empress has no clothes!"

The monk stopped and peered at Her Naked Highness through his swathe of purity. Then he turned his gaze to the Emperor.

"What is a naked body to a being as pure as myself?" he asked dolorously. "To me your wife is pure spirit. Unaware as I am of her body, how am I to care if it is naked?"

The guru departed with his disciple, a glistening froth in their wake.

The Chirkian Monarch was mightily affected by that speech.

The more he thought about it, the more ashamed he felt. He decided that he owed the monk an apology. He dressed and set off from his bath, following the little trail of bubbles left by his beloved.

The trail led to the monk's chambers, from which came the most indelicate of noises. The Emperor could not imagine what discipline could involve such exertions. He had a servant ring the gong, but got no reply. So, he had the servant open the door and admit him to the chamber.

* * * * *

"Shoo! Go away! Can't you tell we don't want to be disturbed?"

Sal Pal blinked his extraordinarily black eyes and gazed from Pim Nakky's scowling face to see Astrid skulking away from their table.

"Sorry," said Pim. "I hate it when they pother around like that — lifting glasses, shuffling napkins, eavesdropping . . . . So, the Emperor enters the chamber—?"

Sal was sipping again; savoring, tamping, and stirring again.

"I take it," drawled Koosh, "that our dear Emperor was in for a shock."

"Well, he discovered that the disciplines his wife was learning had nothing to do with either meditation or past lives. Indeed, she seemed to be studying regression of an entirely different sort. He also discovered that her instructor was no monk at all, but Gobbitz the Large of Glutin. You can imagine his surprise."

"I cannot," said Koosh.

"It was profound. And its profundity was all that saved Big Bitzy from swift demise. While Fro-erd the Serious was riveted in shocked silence in the door of his wife's bedchamber, Bitzy managed to escape through the adjoining room. He smuggled himself out of the Palace in the laundry and made his way to his Imperial yacht, which was orbiting Chirk. It sailed immediately for Glutin."

* * * * *

Naturally (continued Sal), when the Emperor recovered from his shock, he delivered a stern lecture to his wife and made her write "An Empress does not do things like that!" one thousand times on the mirrored wall of their bedroom. Then, he slipped into his gleaming battle togs, changed his name to Fro-erd the Foul Tempered and set off with a full war fleet to wreak his revenge on Glutin.

Meanwhile, poor Bitzy arrived home to find trouble stalking his own corridors. Actually, his wife was doing the stalking, a Glutinus battle hatchet in hand. It seems she had heard the Empress of Chirk was enlisting the services of a Mak Laen guru. She had immediately contacted Mak Laen headquarters to retain one of her own. It would never do to let Nemuria get a monk up on her, and it would give them something new to chitchat about at cotillions.

She was bemused to discover, in the course of her conversation with MLHQ, that no guru had been dispatched to the Royal House of Chirk. Her feelings went somewhat beyond bemusement when she discovered an empty package from the Courtly Clown Costume Shoppe in her husband's closet and, amid the wrapping paper, a description of the costume: "One Mak Laen Monk, Four Veils, extra."

Well, the Empress of Glutin (Kaet the Shrewd, by name) quickly put these discoveries together with her husband's absence and came up with a most unacceptable scenario. She was waiting for him when he arrived home, hatchet in hand. She threatened him with murder, then with divorce, which on Glutin amounts to the same thing. The only difference being who would serve the decree. Kaet could no doubt arrange her own widowhood but, if she preferred to be a divorcee, it fell to her closest male relative to effect the divorce in the most expedient way at his disposal.

Poor Bitzy was frantic. He did the only thing possible. He came to me and asked me to buy him some time. Obviously, he needed enough time to turn his wife's temporal envelope back to just before she found the incriminating package in his closet.

This posed no insurmountable problems. Such a maneuver merely required buying exactly one day and eight hours local from someone. I found a novice mendicant from an obscure marketing order who was eager to make a little extra money. He was just as eager to skip the several days of recovery time necessary after the carousing he had indulged in while out of sight of his monastery. I drew up a contract for the required time and he signed.

At midnight that same evening, the contract went into effect. Kaet the Shrewd slipped back in time, the muddled mendicant slipped forward, and Gobbitz the Terrified slipped a package from his wife's favorite couture into his wardrobe. In the package was a gown of indescribable splendor with a complete set of baubles set with precious stones. Among the folds of the gown he tucked a tiny card that read: "To my dearest, Kaet. I saw this splendorous garb and imagined how it would hug your incomparable frame. I saw these jewels and thought of your gem-like eyes. Though the splendor of these draperies is eclipsed by the glory of yourself, I beg you to accept them as a token of my love, my passion, and my fidelity. Indeed, I can scarcely wait to see you attired in this humble gift."

Well, just as before, the Empress went into her husband's wardrobe searching for an oversized shirt to wear while having her knees painted. And, as before, she found a mysterious package. Only this time the discovery made her ecstatic. The fact that there was no temporal ghost for the gown was completely overlooked in the giddiness of the moment.

"Temporal what?" inquired Koosh.

"Ghost, dear fellow," returned Sal. "When one experiences a temporal recursion, there is a strong sense of déja vu."

"Day-jah who?" asked Pim.

"An Earthism meaning 'I've been there'. Apparently, when one experiences this sort of repetition, one feels as if one has already done these things or said these words—"

"Because one has!" exclaimed Pim brightly. Koosh made a rude noise into his ale.

Pim glared at him, then turned back to Sal. "Ignore him, Sally. Please continue. Temporal ghosts, you said."

"Yes. You see, during a temporal recursion, one expects the events to unfold in a certain way. Any deviation from the original pattern may cause anything from niggling disorientation to a psychotic episode. That was why there was no wrapping paper."

"Now wait." Koosh held up a digit. "There was wrapping paper in the original package. Kaet found the receipt therein."

Sal nodded, looking as if he might award his Utzian friend a gold star for cleverness. "Precisely."

"What do you mean, 'precisely?' You said—."

"I said there was a temporal ghost. As you surmised, it was a ghost of the wrapping paper in which Kaet the Shrewd found the costumier's receipt. The gown simply took the place of the wrapping paper. Rather than adding a time eddy for the gown, I minimized the chronological ripple factor by substituting one object for another — a frothy piece of fabric for a frothy piece of wrapping paper. The card replaced the receipt and the total effect caused Kaet such rapture that any sense of the recursion was lost."

"So, Bitzy's troubles were at an end," sighed Pim.

"He thought so. In fact, he was pleasantly overwhelmed by his usually aloof consort's warm response. She immediately tried on the gown and, since her designer had known her exact measurements, it splendidly hugged and caressed every voluptuous one of them. She was dazzling, and so was her appreciation. I was with His Imperial Hugeness when she displayed herself for him. The mere memory makes me blush. I slunk from the room unnoticed."

"Ah . . . ." crooned Pim grinning from ear to lop ear.

Sal sighed deeply. "Well, Bitzy was in seventh heaven for about a day and a night."

"Seventh heaven?" asked Koosh dubiously. "Ah, wait . . . an expression you—."

"—picked up on Earth," Sal finished in unison. "Correct. A most appropriate saying, for he behaved as if he had stepped across the Divine Divide into the Supernal Realm."

*****

Bitzy had discovered a captivating new lover right in his own Palace (Sal continued). One attainable without subterfuge. He forgot Nemuria completely. Unfortunately, he also forgot that a Chirkian battle fleet was on its way to Glutin to wreak vengeance on him. By the time he remembered, his time had nearly run out.

He quickly called his War Chief and ordered the Glutinus Fleet assembled.

"Pardon, your Imperial Vastness," said the Chief, "but I'll need the paperwork."

"Paperwork?" grunted Bitzy. "This is a matter of life and death — mine!"

"I'm sorry, your Greatness," commiserated the Chief, "but you must have your Council Act of War form Thirty-five dash SW before I can summon any vessels. And, of course, it's required that you consult the Divine Authority and get Their approval, as well."

"Forms!" snorted Bitzy. "I'll get the forms later. Go raise the fleet!"

"Sorry, your Grandness," insisted the adamant commandant, "but you must produce a CAW35-SW before I can even submit a Defensive Battle Fleet Requisition form FR-D5."

Bitzy went immediately to his High Council and demanded an Act of War. They informed him they couldn't even consider such an Act until they had seen all pertinent environmental and economic impact reports and a letter bearing the DA's approval. The Environmental Agency was summoned first. Its prognosis was not good.

"I can tell you, right up front," said the Envirolord, "that a war would have a serious impact on the surface of this planet. I don't suppose you'd consider holding it somewhere else — an asteroid, perhaps?"

"It's too late for that!" snarled His Highness. "The Chirks are on their way!"

"Well, in that case . . . ." The Envirolord shrugged. "We'll have to issue a full report. Should take about a year — and I can't guarantee clear sailing. When the environmental groups get wind of this, they'll read you the Environmental Riot Act. That could take about two days — with all the amendments."

"But we'll be under siege by then!" roared Gobbitz the Large. "Sorry, no ENV168, no CAW35-SW. No CAW35-SW, no war. You'll have to surrender."

"Surrender!" shrieked Gobbitz the Panicked. "If I surrender, you'll have to live under the rule of Fro-erd the Foul Tempered!"

The Envirolord shrugged again. "So it goes."

Bitzy's interview with the Econolord went no better. He was assured that a home front war would devastate the economy if not properly prepared for, and that it would take roughly two Glutinus years to make the adjustment to a wartime economy. Then, of course, when the peace groups got wind of it, they'd have to read the Emperor their own Riot Act (which was fully as long as the ERA).

Poor Bitzy was at wits' end when he came to me, worn to a sigh from endless days of bureaucracy, and endless nights of Kaet the Suddenly Insatiable.

"What can we do?" he wailed. "I don't have time to run impact surveys and file reports and justify expenses!"

"How much money is in the Imperial Account?" I asked.

He scowled. "You know the answer to that. My funds . . . er, that is, my wife's funds are limitless."

"Could you convince her to part with some of them?"

He smiled wearily. "No problem. How much?"

"I'm not sure what a project of this nature will cost."

"Er, what nature is that, exactly?" asked my Lord.

"What you need," I said, "is a lot of time, correct?"

A Matter of Timing

He nodded, brightening. "So, you'll just buy me some, right?"

"Now, my dear Emperor," I cautioned, "before you get your hopes elevated, please bear this in mind: previously, I purchased one day from a single sentient. To give you enough time to file your reports and procure your Act of War, I'll need to buy roughly two years Glutinus for every sentient on Chirk, plus every member of the swiftly approaching battle fleet. That's approximately . . . . " I did some quick calculations. ". . . four billion five hundred million temporal units of two years Glutinus — give or take a few million . . . . Let's say, five billion even."

Bitzy paled. "How much will that cost?"

"That depends on the rate of exchange. For example, a Glutinus year is roughly twice as long as a year on Earth, but it's only half the length of a Hapi-nu year. So, if I bought time on Earth, I'd have to buy two Terran years for every Glutinus year. If, on the other hand, I bought a Hapi-nu year, it would cover two Glutinus years with time to spare."

His Immensity's broad brow furrowed adorably. "But, isn't it two Chirkian years we need to buy?"

"No, dear Emperor," I explained patiently. "You are the one who needs the time. You need to keep the Chirks occupied for two Glutinus years. If you bought Chirkian years, you'd only have one-point- five years Glutinus to work with. Before you could even raise your fleet, we'd be overrun with Chirks."

"Oh, I see," he said, which of course he didn't. "This sounds like it could be very expensive. I don't suppose we could make time payments?"

"I doubt it, your Largeness. What would you use for collateral?"

"Ah," he said. He stared into space for a moment, then assumed a look of stern resolve. "See to it," he ordered, and marched from the room straight to his wife's boudoir to arrange for funding.

A servant arrived within the hour to give me a message. "Mission accomplished," he said, then looked at me askance. "Do you understand the message, sir?"

"Oh, yes," I assured him. "Perfectly." I couldn't contain a chuckle. My Lord was not only ready for battle, he had already won his first military engagement.

"Well, that was the entire message," said the he-servant. "Oh, except that His Imperial Majesty humbly begs your pardon for not delivering it in person. He said that, although negotiations were successful, the strategy meeting will run quite late, after which, I believe he said, he would have to take a nap. I may have heard him wrong."

I smiled and patted the servant on the shoulder. "When His Imperial Majesty awakes from his nap, give him my regards and tell him I won't let him down."

* * * * *

"How could you be that confident?" asked Pim, signaling for another ale.

Sal waggled his empty glass and Pim had Astrid refill that as well.

"I wasn't confident," Sal admitted. "But, for Bitzy's sake, I had to sound confident. I went to Hapi-Nu first, but the Nus weren't selling. They're a stingy lot. Wouldn't give me the time of day, let alone sell me a whole year. Reprobates." Sal shook his head. "Their lives are one continual party. They gamble, drink, eat, belch a lot and trash each other's tents. They spend so much time in semi-comatose states that they'd never even miss a year or two. But sell? Never. Their miserliness was appalling."

"Well, you know what they say," said Koosh blandly. "No Nus are good Nus."

"What did you do?" asked Pim.

"I continued my search, of course. His Imperial Rotundness put a fast, sleek corvette-class ship at my disposal. I'd had it custom-painted a vibrant shade of red, which being a high visibility color, drastically reduced the insurance premiums. I stopped only where I thought I stood a snowball's chance in hell (another Earthism — don't ask me what a snowball is, or hell either, for that matter) of buying some time. I came up empty at every stop. No one was selling."

"A timeless journey, eh?" asked Koosh, and was ignored.

* * * * *

Finally (said Sal), I set the timer on the corvette to arrive at Earth just as the population was cresting five billion. I like Earth very much and must admit I stopped there more for a soul-restoring respite than because I had any hope of accomplishing my mission. Terran culture was so primitive at that point, they had neither a world government nor a central Divine Authority. They were still bumbling along in small national units, playing cat and mouse with world peace, and with only an inkling of the potential for global unity.

All of this would make striking any kind of deal difficult. It would be nearly impossible to find one person or agency to speak for the entire planet. Still, the fact that Earth's population was a rough match for Chirk's made it attractive. I decided to put some effort into finding a central authority.

I wasn't sure where to turn until I happened to hear of an organization called the United Nations. One headquarters for this council was in a nation called the United States. Promising, I thought. But I went to UNHQ only to discover that the power of this organization was strictly limited by the interests of its national components. The name "United Nations" was mere wishful thinking at this point in their history. I wished them the Deity's assistance in growing into their ideals and looked elsewhere.

In this same neighborhood was the power center of these United States, which had the reputation — to use the vernacular — of being a "super-power." This large Palace was humbly called "The White House" and was the abode of the Emperor of the American Continent. They called him the Potus.

I went to the Potus' Palace, but could get nowhere near the fellow. How he ruled without being available to his people, I'll never understand. At any rate, one of his staff (a man wearing the most amazing collection of tiny ribbons on his chest) informed me that the real power in the US was something called the Pentagon.

I suspected I had stumbled into some bizarre occult network. More so, when I discovered that the Pentagon was not a person, but a place, and actually shaped like a pentagon. Reconnaissance revealed however, that this was not a cultic center, but the seat of a vast military colony. It was many times bigger than the American Emperor's Palace. The amount of money so obviously lavished on it made me hopeful it was the power center I sought.

When I entered the cavernous place I was informed that Visitors were forbidden to pass beyond the anterooms into the inner chambers. Only those with the appropriate badges were allowed into the Sanctum.

There was an information desk along one wall where I politely asked to whom one would speak about making a substantial purchase from the government.

"What do you wish to purchase?" asked the young male behind the desk.

"Several billion temporal units," I replied. "Enough to last five billion persons about two years . . . Glutinus," I added.

His smooth brow wrinkled in thought. "That sounds like you want the

Deeowee — Contracts Administration."

It seemed I was on the right track. I reached the grand offices of this agency around sunset, discovering that Deeowee was actually DOE — an acronym for Department of Energy. My elation at this discovery sagged, for the place seemed empty. But, Terrans are nothing if not considerate of visitors and I discovered a large placard listing the contents of the building. On it, in white letters was what I had hoped to see — Contracts Administration. The coordinates were listed beside the name.

I experienced some confusion upon entering the ContAdDep, as it was referred to on a plate beside the doorway. The few people about were working in cubicles made of cloth-covered panels that swayed dangerously when anyone walked by. I immediately recognized it as a cloister and wondered how the poor ContAdDep monks ever found their cells in that ghastly maze.

I turned my attention to the broad outer corridors, which were much more opulent. I looked for nameplates. Important people on Earth have nameplates that tell others who they are and why they should be feared and respected.

I discovered a corridor containing the cells of the Assistant ContAdDep monks — all empty. But at the end of the corridor I found it — the cell of the Head Contracts Administrator. His name was Ira Schwarzbaum, and he was in.

He was engaged in a rather peculiar task. On the wall across from his desk was a circular hanging composed of varicolored concentric circles. In the center of the object was a two dimensional stationary image of a large satellite dish.

Mr. Schwarzbaum sat with his feet propped on his desk hurling tiny missiles at the image of the dish. Occasionally, one would impale it and lodge in the hanging beneath. More often than not, they would simply smack the wall and fall to the floor. It reminded me of the mate selection ritual of the Phtui.

Eventually Mr. Schwarzbaum ran out of missiles, so I cleared my throat. This is the way polite Terrans get each other's attention. It has a variety of meanings. For example; it might mean, *I wish to interrupt*, or *Please let me through*, or *That was the stupidest thing I've ever heard. Please don't say it again.* In this instance it meant *I'm waiting in your doorway. Please invite me to come in.*

A Matter of Timing

He did invite me in, rather hastily pulling his feet from his desk.

A sheaf of papers and some writing utensils hit thefloor.

Mr. Schwarzbaum cleared his throat (which meant, I am embarrassed to have appeared so clumsy), and picked up the fallen articles.

"Please excuse me," he said. "I was — uh — thinking."

"Indeed?" I glanced at the tracking dish. Another of the little missiles lost its hold on the paper and fell to the floor with a tiny thump. "Is this a method of choosing an item for procurement? I am always interested in new ways to select materiel."

Mr. Schwarzbaum laughed. (I've always found human laughter so difficult to interpret.) "Not exactly. I'd like to procure it, all right, but . . . well, money is an object."

I was surprised. "I thought these United States were quite sound financially."

"Oh, Uncle Sam is doing fine. I'm just a poor relation."

"Excuse?"

"I'm just a government employee, Mister . . . ah . . . ."

"Pal. Sal Pal." We shook hands. "Call me 'Sal.'"

"Sal. Okay. Anyway, a piece of equipment like that is currently beyond my means."

I looked again at the image. "Pardon, but what would a private being do with such a sophisticated device?"

"Movies," he said.

"Movies?" I repeated.

"Yeah." He smiled, looking like an over-sized incub. "From all over the globe. Literally all over. Spaghetti Westerns from Italy. Godzilla movies from Japan. It'll pick up transmissions that aren't even intended for public consumption. When they put a station on the Moon, it'll pick that up. This thing could pick up broadcasts from outer space, if there were any. Plus, it sits on a little flatbed tank-tread, so it's portable. You can move it anywhere a tank can go. And it's got a telescoping mechanism that will allow it to rise to a height of thirty feet. And on top of all that, it only weighs 150 pounds and comes with a camper adapter. Pretty neat, huh?"

"Pretty neat," I agreed (though I'd understood little of what he said).

"Anyway, I can't afford it."

"Ah. Too bad. How much currency does the purchase require?"

"It costs a pretty penny, believe me."

I was not familiar with that denomination and said so.

He glanced at me strangely, then said, "I'm sorry. You're not American, are you? I should've realized — your accent . . . ."

I nodded pleasantly. "You are very observant. No, I am not American."

"A pretty penny, in this case, is about fifty thousand dollars."

"Quite pretty, Ira . . . . May I call you Ira?"

"Sure, Sal. Now, what can I do for you? You didn't come up here to listen to me gripe about a toy I can't afford."

"I would like to discuss a purchase. A substantial purchase."

"Of what, exactly?"

"Time, Ira. I would like to buy some time."

"Who's time?"

"Yours and about five billion other beings. I am authorized to pay a substantial amount of any currency you desire. Of course," I added, glancing at the satellite dish, "there would be a bonus for the negotiator of the deal."

Ira folded his arms and looked at me steadily. I could tell he thought I was joking. He was probably unable to accept that I could command so much money. I was, after all, only a youth.

A slow smile crept up his face and he waggled his finger at me. "You must be a science fiction buff," he said, "in town for the convention — right?"

Science Fiction, I recalled, was the dominant literary art form on this world (which disposes of the popular notion that humanity is a backward species). The recollection encouraged me considerably.

"Yes," I said. "I buff Science Fiction greatly."

"Yeah? I knew it. Me too. What's your favorite SF flick? Mine's still E.T."

"SF flick?" I repeated. I fired up my Library implant and checked the Galactic Compendium aboard my vessel. He was referring to a visual art form. "I am not familiar with E.T.," I said honestly.

His eyes protruded. "You've never seen E.T.? Sal, you've got to see E.T.! It's a classic! You'll love it. Look, why don't we grab a pizza, then go over to my place and watch it? I've got a big screen TV, VCR, the works. It's almost as good as going to the theatre."

Reasoning that this ritual must have something to do with negotiating a deal, I accepted his offer.

Ira's abode was quite large for a single sentient dwelling. He called it a "Victorian." He also called it a "money pit." (There was no entry in the Compendium for this term.)

As he suggested, he got a pizza, which turned out to be a type of food. Quite tasty. There was also a local ale, which was mildly intoxicating. I was quite hopeful now — becoming intoxicated is a standard phase in negotiation rituals on many primitive worlds.

The movie was wonderful, if only two dimensional. ET was as fine an actor as I've seen in any trivie. I did wonder how, since the Terrans had by then only sent manned vehicles as far as their own Moon, they had managed to obtain a leading man from Grzaz Three.

I asked Ira this and he laughed uproariously. Then he explained that E.T. was a true story, chronicling the Extra-Terrestrial's sojourn on Earth.

"Ah, then he returned to make the movie?" I surmised. "The Grzazzi are so busy with their terra-forming business I wonder he had the time. But that's just like them. A finer species it's hard to imagine."

"Oh, yeah," Ira agreed. "It's hard to imagine, alright."

After E.T. we watched several other "classics": Plan Nine from Outer Space, Star Wars and Star Trek. The first of these Ira thought uproariously funny, but I saw few redeeming qualities in it. The picture was not only two-dimensional, it was colorless. And the Extra- Terrestrials were portrayed by humans that were not even in costume. I excused my new friend's enthusiasm for this flick as the result of imbibing too much beer, but I was determined to humor him. When he grinned at me and cocked both thumbs upward to indicate his enjoyment, I echoed the gesture. All part of the negotiating process.

It was the Star Trek movie that gave me an idea as to how I should open formal negotiations. It involved time travel and saving the planet Earth by rescuing a couple of aquatic mammals called whales from certain doom. If I thought of Bitzy as a whale, the plot assumed striking parallels to my own mission.

"Well," said Ira, at last, "which did you like best?"

"Oh," I effused, "all were absolutely thumbs up! But I think I enjoyed Star Trek most. The mission of the heroes reminded me of my own assignment."

"Your . . . . Oh, right. Buying time, you said."

I nodded. "Precisely. In both cases, the stakes are high — the survival of an entire world lies in the balance. In both cases, time is the only remedy."

"Sounds like a good story."

"Oh, it is," I assured him, and told him about poor Bitzy's debacle. Of course, I left out the sordid details of how the whole thing got started. By the time I finished the tale, Ira's eyes were watering profusely, and he was trembling with strong emotion.

Excellent, I thought and pressed my case. "So you see," I said, "my Lord Gobbitz and untold millions of innocent Glutins will die if I cannot buy enough time to complete the pre-hostility paperwork. It is my life's greatest challenge," I added somberly.

He was impressed. "I'm impressed," he said. "That's quite a story. One of the best I've heard . . . . Okay, who put you up to it? George, right?"

"I know no one named George, Ira. His Imperial Highness Gobbitz the Large put me up to it."

"Hmm. You're not going to give up, are you?"

"Not until I have achieved my goal. I must save my Emperor from the Chirks."

"Right. So tell me, what happens to poor old Bitzy if these jerks get him?"

"Chirks," I corrected. Then, I made my face expressive of such sorrow, I nearly shed real tears. "Bitzy's fate is too horrible to contemplate."

The fact was, if Bitzy was toppled, not only would I lose a dear friend, but my job would go down the wormhole with him. Reason enough for depression. "My fallen Emperor in the hands of Fro-erd the Foul Tempered . . . well, he's better off dead. The Chirks are such . . . punctilious people."

"Punctilious?" Ira's eyes watered some more. Then he rubbed his chin and looked at me over the top of his wire-rimmed goggles. "Okay," he said, "I'll bite. How much will you pay?"

"How much is time worth here? I'm afraid I could get no information on the current rate of exchange from your stock market."

Ira pulled out a pocket computer and did some quick calculations. "Let's see, last I heard, we were worth about eighty-nine cents apiece. That was when I was a kid. Given inflation . . . oh, let's say . . . about two hundred dollars per life. Average life span about one hundred years — give or take. That's two bucks per annum. How many years, you need, pal?"

A Matter of Timing

"Four should do nicely, Schwarzbaum."

"Four times two is eight, times — how many?"

"Five billion."

"Ah, yes. Five billion . . . . That's forty billion dollars on the nose."

I tried not to show my relief lest he think his figures were too low. I nodded soberly and sighed. "Yes," I said, "that is only fair. What currency? When and where would you like it deposited?"

"Pronto, shweethaart. ASAP. Deposit forty billion US dollars to a Swiss Bank Account under the name . . . . " He paused. "Sham Shpade." He waggled his eyebrows.

I waggled mine in return.

"Done." I intoned. I withdrew the contract from my inner pocket. "The contract will take effect at midnight tomorrow."

Ira's eyes protruded again. "Contracts? You have contracts?"

"Of course. I am a reputable being, Ira, and a fully certified and licensed Purchasing Agent of the Supra-Glutinus Empire. Would you care to see my credentials?"

"Yeah. Let's see your credentials."

I produced them — license, certification, and charter from the Throne of Glutin.

He studied them thoroughly, shaking his head and smiling. "You're good," he said.

"Thank you. Now, if you would be so kind as to examine this contract with equal thoroughness, I would be most pleased."

He did examine it.

"Now, wait a minute!" he exclaimed after a moment. "How did you do this? This contract already has my name and the amount of purchase printed on it. I just calculated that a minute ago."

"It should be correct. Is it not?"

"No! I mean, yes — it's correct, but, how did you know the amount ahead of time? I calculated it entirely at random."

"I didn't know it in advance, Ira. It was recorded as you gave it to me."

"Recorded? By what?"

"This." I reached into my inner pocket and produced my Buyer's Buddy™ Legal Tablet.

"Wow!" he said and reached for the tablet. His hand stopped and hovered an inch from it. "Uh, may I look at it?"

"Certainly." I handed it to him.

"Wow!" he said again. "This is some computer. How many megs does it have?"

"Megs?"

"Memory."

"Oh, of course. It comes standard with two hundred thousand of what you call terabytes. But, this is the expanded module. It has significantly more — five hundred, I believe."

"WOW!"

I relieved him of the tablet and put the stylus into his hand. He gazed at it his longing for it evident.

Ah! I thought. A techno-junkie.

"I perceive you are taken with my Buyer's Buddy™," I said aloud. "Shall we add one to your commission?"

"My commission?"

I pointed to the fourth clause of the contract.

He read the clause. "The satellite dish? That's my commission?"

"This small item is easily added." I indicated the tablet, into which I slid the contract. "One BLT," I instructed it, "extra fees."

The working light flashed on and off. I handed the finished contract back to Ira.

He checked the addition and shook his head. "This is impossible."

I was immediately on guard. "There is something wrong?"

"No. Yes. I—" He stared at me. "I could almost believe you."

"Ira, I assure you I am as good as my word. Everything I have said and done is — how do you say — on the up-up."

"Up and up," he murmured, staring at the contract. "Yes, up and up."

"You got here in a space ship, right?"

Yes."

"Uh-huh. Big, old starship named Enterprise, right?"

"No. A little red corvette named Looceel."

He stared at me again, then burst out laughing. "You're great, Sal. This is the best practical joke anyone's ever played on me."

I was unfamiliar with practical jokes, so I could only gaze at him sincerely.

He shook his head, still laughing, and signed the contract.

A Matter of Timing

I signed my own name, then smiled and shook his hand. "Thank you, Ira." I rose to go.

"You're leaving?"

"It gets late," I said.

"Right," he said, and escorted me to the door of his house. "Watch the loose boards," he said. I could hear him laughing as I made my way down the front path to my rentacar. A very jovial fellow, Ira.

I arrived on Glutin the day before I left and pried Bitzy away from the Empress. He was grateful beyond measure for my effort and I was now wealthy to the same degree. I quickly invested the money in some off-world real estate . . . just in case.

Bitzy eagerly lost himself in battle preparations — he had Psycho-social surveys to run, Economic Feasibility data to collect and analyze, Environmental Impact reports to file. He was almost gleeful in his attention to this process, looking forward to the confrontation with the Chirk fleet.

He made every effort to keep the whole affair out of the public eye. I hated to be a prophet of doom, but I knew the social activists would catch on. Still, I kept my mouth shut. I also remained silent about an even more immediate danger. And why? My fondness for Bitzy. I wanted him to grab as much happiness as he could before the inevitable happened.

* * * * *

"He's doomed," said Pam sadly. "Didn't you buy him enough time?"

"Oh, more than enough, Pim. The studies were done, the reports laid before the Council, the Divine Authority was approached for final approval. All was in order. But, as I feared, the peace groups got wind of the war and demanded a public debate.

"Bitzy was confident. He went on public tri-vu to confront the head of the Peace and Freedom Coalition. He swayed the public considerably with his tale of impending doom. The war, he explained, was to protect the Peace and Freedom of every male, female, and incub within the Empire. He got ten popularity points up on the PFC."

"Then, what happened?"

* * * * *

Well, first of all (said Sal), the PFC reluctantly revealed the reason that the Peace and Freedom of every male, female, and incub within the Empire was jeopardized in the first place. TV sets snapped off all over. Bitzy lost the debate. Then, there were the studies. They were damning.

Trajectories

Poor Bitzy had them done without once considering the outcome. He never even bothered to read them. To him they were a mere formality — something to satisfy the data pushers. Unfortunately, they revealed the obvious: any war hosted by Glutin would devastate the environment, disrupt the economy, and traumatize every sentient on the planet. Surrender was eminently more practical.

The debate between Bitzy and the head of the Home and Garden Society was particularly devastating. Poor Bitzy, trying to rally his fellow Glutins to patriotic fervor, called them to defend their home world.

"Friends!" he exhorted. "Our planetary pride is at stake! What would you rather be — free Glutins, or just another bunch of Chirks?"

"I'd rather be home for dinner!" someone heckled.

Bitzy ignored him. "Think of it, friends! On one side of the balance is life as you know it. On the other—" he shivered dramatically. "—a life of oppression under the heinous Emperor Fro-erd the Foul Tempered. With a name like that how nice could he be?"

"How nice was the Empress?" shouted the heckler.

"Ask yourselves," Bitzy persevered, "what are a few holes in the ground compared to freedom, prosperity, and a good-natured Emperor like me?"

"You ever had to reseed a lawn?" yelled the heckler.

"Please, sir. That's hardly germane—"

"No, wait," said the Chairman of the H&GS. "He's got a point. You ever reseed a lawn?"

Bitzy was flustered. "Well, uh . . . that is . . . the Imperial lawn will suffer with every other Glutin's foliage."

There was a tiny smattering of applause from a few loyalists.

"That may be," persisted the H&GS Chairman, "but have you ever had to reseed it?"

"Well . . . no."

And that was that. The Chirks arrived, the Government expeditiously surrendered and Fro-erd the Foul Tempered became Emperor of the Supra-Glutinus Empire.

*****

"So, poor Bitzy ended up at the mercy of Fro-erd the Foul Tempered," sighed Pim.

Sal shook his head. "Would that he had. But, no. As I feared, Bitzy faced a far more deadly nemesis — his dear wife, Kaet the Shrewd.

"It seems that his Imperial consort began to wonder why Glutin was under attack by their usually amicable ally. While her spouse was negotiating his surrender, she was having a bubble bath with Nemuria the Delightful. In the course of their bath, Kaet the Shrewd asked, 'Oh, by the way, dear, what was this war business all about, anyway?' Her fellow Empress and bosom friend burst into tears and informed her of her husband's infidelity.

"The two ladies then proceeded to exchange notes on the ensuing events. What they discovered was satisfactory to neither of them. Kaet was furious that Bitzy had taken a mistress and his mistress was furious that he had re-taken his wife. And . . . . " Sal sighed deeply, " . . .both of these ladies had fine, strapping male relations."

"Ah!" cried Pim, in distress. "Death by Divorce! Poor Bitzy!"

"Well?" drawled Koosh. "Don't keep him in a twitch. Which one got him? The brother of Delight or the sibling of Shrewdness?"

Sal scooted his Sarcesian Sidewinder along the table in a trail of dew. "That is not certain," he said. "Both brothers pursued him. Both cornered him in an alley near the docking bays that housed the Imperial yacht. Both drew their Lazerblazers™ and fired at once. There was a blinding flash of light and Bitzy was gone. All that was left of him was his lucky wort's foot, which he had never parted with in his life. The brothers divided this artifact along its cloven hoof and presented the parts to their respective sisters as proof of a successful divorce.

"Fro-erd was crowned Emperor. His first official action was to change the laws of Imperial marriage to permit bigamy. His second was to marry Kaet the Shrewd. His third, to change her name to Kaet the Incredible and his own to Fro-erd the Ecstatic. There was some objection to this development, but Fro-erd's temper was still so foul, it died very quickly."

"Just like poor Bitzy," sniffed Pim.

"So it would seem," agreed Sal. His Sidewinder hydroplaned from one hand to the other.

Koosh waggled a digit at him. "You're baiting Pim! You want him to beg you to reveal what really happened to your over-sized, over-sexed Emperor."

"What really happened?" echoed Pim. "Why, he died, didn't he? That's what you said — Bitzy died."

"No, no! He said Bitzy disappeared in a flash of light."

Sal smiled. "So you were listening after all."

"Perhaps I was — just to see if you slipped up on any details — but I will not beg to know what happened to poor, old Bitzy."

"I will!" exclaimed Pim. "How did he escape the assassins?"

"It was all a matter of timing. Pretending to be a fan of Kaet the Incredible's brother, who was a professional wrestler, I met the two kinsmen as they left on their mission. I insisted that they let me buy them a drink. They couldn't refuse, so I bought them each a large crock of the strongest brew available. So strong was it, that neither of them could finish their portion and they went off half-crocked. I was amazed at what half a crock of this stuff could do. They were both wobbling and squinting so badly when they left the bar, I actually had to steer them to their victim — an offer they eagerly accepted.

"I made sure they reached Bitzy at exactly two mins to sunset. Then I politely got in their way for a min and a half. They fired their Lazerblazers at exactly sunset, and Bitzy dropped his wort's foot and disappeared."

Sal paused for a long sip of Sidewinder. Pim stared at him in anticipation, his mouth slit half agape.

"Well?" Koosh Mafootz glared at him across the table. "Are you going to tell us — I mean, tell Pim — where Bitzy went in this extraordinary fashion?"

Sal smiled.

* * * * *

Bitzy went to my corvette as quickly as his stumpy legs would carry him, (Sal explained). I had taken the precaution of buying an extra half hour from a very obliging young fellow who was scheduled to confront a jealous girlfriend at sundown. At precisely that moment, the contract went into effect and Bitzy shot forward out of the assassins' time frame and took off for the ship post haste.

Everyone assumed he was dead. After all, both Imperial brothers-in-law were crack shots and, while Lazerblazers usually leave a little — um — residue, who could say that two fired in unison wouldn't atomize even as large a target as Bitzy? The assassins were certain that was what happened. (After all, they would never have missed the target sober and neither was about to admit to his sister that he'd gone off half-crocked.) So, everyone unthinkingly accepted that wort's foot as proof of Bitzy's demise. I was mortally afraid that they'd take it as evidence that he was still alive.

The foot, you see, was completely unscathed. There was not a scorch mark on it, even though the trash receptacle Bitzy cowered against was burnt to a crisp. Bitzy managed to drop the thing at the exact moment of the time change. It got caught in the temporal displacement just long enough to avoid being fried, teetered for an instant on an anomalous eddy, then fell back into my present.

Bitzy was beside himself. He insisted he must have that lucky wort's foot. He'd gotten it the day he became Emperor and had never parted with it before. I tried to reason with him, explaining that the lost foot had caused everyone to accept his death, even though the usual physical remains were conspicuously absent. I protested that there was no way to retrieve the silly thing since each Empress wore her half around her neck, day and night.

Bitzy was adamant. He had to have that wort's foot and I had to get it for him.

* * * * *

"And did you get it?" asked Pim.

Sal nodded.

"How?"

"How I got it is another story," said Sal, glancing obliquely at Koosh. "A rather . . . delicate story . . . . But that I did get it . . . . Well, see for yourselves."

He pointed a finger at the wall behind the bar. A large wort's foot, rather the worse for wear, was mounted on a tarnished metal plaque.

Pim gaped. "That's THE wort's foot?"

"The very one."

"But-but . . . you said Bitzy would never part with it."

"He would not."

"Then . . . ."

"Then, where is Bitzy?" demanded Koosh.

"Where his customers can complain to him every day about the flavor of his ale . . . or the lack thereof."

Both Koosh and Pim reacted in the most enjoyable way, gaping at Bud as he trundled happily about his business. He looked over at them, smiled his silly loose-lipped smile and waved jauntily.

Sal waved back.

Trajectories

"You're saying Bud is Gobbitz the Large, Emperor of the Supra-Glutinus Empire?" Koosh's eye sockets were straining unhealthily.

"Ex-Emperor. The very same."

"I don't believe it," said Koosh, poking a digit at Sal's stately nose. "And I'm going to check up on you, believe me."

"Bud will corroborate every word."

"Hah! You've either blackmailed him or he's in your debt."

"Well, I did save his life several times over, but he repaid me elegantly. Through him, I got a plum position with For-erd the Irresistable. Bitzy also introduced me to my wife, Vara. If that weren't enough to cancel the debt, he got us a great deal on our retirement villa. A truly conscientious being, our Bud."

Koosh muttered something scathing in Utzian and stuck his proboscis into his ale pail.

"So, a happy ending!" sighed Pim.

Sal nodded. "Yes indeed. Bud is happily married to Uweuwe and has seventeen lovely incubs."

"Ah-hah!" gurgled Koosh suddenly. He lifted his head from the ale pail. "But there is one loose end."

"Is there?" asked Sal, blinking his pupiless black eyes.

"Your young Earthie, of course. What happened to Ira Schwarzbaum?"

"You know, I'm not sure," admitted Sal. "During my last visit to Earth I was rather pressed for time. I didn't really have an opportunity to look Ira up. However, I do know that he is a very wealthy man — at least, when he uses the alias Sham Shpade."

Pim stood, smiling. "On that satisfying note, I shall depart. A fine story, Sally. We will see you tomorrow evening?"

"Depend on it."

Koosh and Sal sat in silence until the ser-sent appeared out of the chrome-dappled gloom to offer Sal a message.

"Your wife, ssir, is ready to be picked up at the Beauty Bar."

"Ah, thank you, Astrid. Well, Koosh, I shall be off." He rose, donned his red driving cap, and left, waving gaily to Bud. The ser-sent swiveled to return to its duties, but Koosh forestalled it by stepping deliberately on its tail.

"Par-don?" it said.

"Tell me, Astrid, how long have you known Bud?"

A Matter of Timing

"Long enough to ask him to ssit on beings who squash my tail with their clumsy appendages."

Koosh ignored the threat. "Do you know what he did before he bought this place?"

Astrid gave a slippery shrug, then grinned. "I suspect he was incarcerated in an asylum on some nice assteroid." It took a glance about, then lowered its nose and its voice. "Do you know what he says he was? An Emperor!"

"I had heard that claim advanced," mumbled Koosh.

Astrid shook its crest. "These past-lifers. All alike. Always claim to have been the Emperor of the Universe. Funny, I've never heard one claim to have been cook on a garbage barge . . . or even an ordinary sent like you or me." The huge eyes rolled toward the bar. "New customers! Look like hot-tippers, too. Ssee ya." It slithered away, leaving the end of its tail under Koosh's foot.

Disgusted, Koosh got up and moved to the bar. He stared for a while at the glued-together wort's foot, then, giving in to temptation, he called Bud over.

Bud came, his big, loose smile ready and a cask of ale inhand. "Koosh!"

"Bud . . . . Sal just told me a story."

Bud nodded. "He's great, that Sal. The best."

"Hmm. So he says. Tell me, Bud, have you ever gone by the name 'Bitzy?'"

"Sal's the only one who calls me that," said Bud.

Koosh brightened. "I see. Well, tell me this: Have you ever been an Emperor?"

"Is that what Sal said?"

Koosh nodded, starting to smile.

"I suspect he's right about that. My memory is a little soft in spots. Sometimes I remember clear as gel and others—" he shrugged hugely. "Doctor says temporal displacement can do that."

Koosh drooped.

Bud was gazing purposefully at his empty ale pail. "Like a refill on that, Koosh?"

Koosh Mafootz glanced again at the mounted wort's foot. "No, I don't think so, Bud. I have to go see a man about some weddings."

SEEDS

by Mary A. Turzillo

Kapera's friend Annie was always coming up with new schemes, new adventures. Her latest one involved a starship, a "heavily enabled" computer, and having their personalities uploaded into new bodies.

Simple, right?

Mary Turzillo's 1999 Nebula-winner, *Mars Is no Place for Children* and her Analog novel *An Old-Fashioned Martian Girl* are recommended reading on the International Space Station. Her poetry collection *Lovers & Killers* won the 2013 Elgin Award. She's been a finalist on the British Science Fiction Association, Pushcart, Stoker, Dwarf Stars and Rhysling ballots. *Sweet Poison*, her Dark Renaissance collaboration with Marge Simon, was a Stoker finalist and won the Elgin award for 2015. *Mars Girls*, which gives more background on Annie and Kapera, comes out from Apex in 2017 She's working on a novel, *A Mars Cat and his Boy*. She lives in Berea, Ohio, with her scientist-writer husband, Geoffrey A. Landis.

■■■■■■

"He got the braking system all figured out for me," said Annie. Annie and Kapera were sitting around drinking the best fake coffee available on Mars. "I have a perfectly good starship. We should do something with it."

"Who got it all figured out for you?" Kapera asked.

"Bruce. I told you about Bruce. He's got such a cute butt, and eyelashes to die for. Plus he's brilliant."

Kapera said, "Annie, Bruce prefers men."

"I'm sure he's willing to experiment," Annie said, although Kapera suspected that she hadn't taken that into consideration. "Anyway, you want to hear how the Chrysalis is going to make history?"

Annie was full of wild ideas. She had inherited the Chrysalis, a starship that might or might not work, from a crackpot Face on Mars cult. She had been leasing it out to rich people who wanted to use it (while still in orbit around Mars) for role-playing games. But she was always coming up with new schemes for adventures on it. Go to Titan. Surf Saturn's rings. Hell, go to some Kuiper-belt object and bring back — what? Annie always had an idea. Usually the idea somehow was supposed to lead to increased contact with the opposite sex. Though only twenty in Earth years, she was a rich widow, and looking for a good man, or at least a hot one.

"So what's your idea this time?" Kapera wriggled her foot and attracted the attention of the very realistic robotic kitten she had designed.

"It's a starship, right? So, we need to take it out and seed an extrasolar planet."

"Wait a minute. The Chrysalis is a huge, massive starship. It would take it a couple hundred thousand years to get anywhere."

"It is. But listen, it has a really great drive, and if we stripped it—"

"What do you mean a really great drive?"

Annie rolled her eyes. "I think it's a third generation Bussard ram-jet."

"Yeah, that's probably it." Kapera was wondering how somebody could own a starship and not remember what kind of drive it had. Oh, wait. This was Annie, as she styled herself now. Used to be Nanoannie, but thought the name her parents gave her was too childish. Next year she'd probably adopt another new name.

"Anyway, so what we do is strip it down to just the engine and a very well-shielded small cargo compartment. We equip it with a heavily enabled computer, radiation-shielded to the max—"

"A computer to take humanity to the stars? How is that supposed to excite me?"

"No, listen to me! You always think I'm stupid, but I'm just a blogal thinker."

Kapera was the smart one, and Annie was the pretty one, although truth to tell neither of them was spectacularly pretty. And Annie wasn't that stupid, just poorly educated. Or maybe selectively educated.

"Global thinker," said Kapera.

"Yeah, that. Anyway, we provide it with a really really radiation hardened computer and the DNA programs for a couple of thousand zygotes. Then when it gets to the target planet, the computer sends directions to build the zygotes."

Kapera didn't know what to wonder at more, the fact that Annie was able to remember a word like zygote, or that she had forgotten what her starship's drive was and how to pronounce the word global. That was Annie. Maybe that frizzy-haired head contained the brain of a genius. Or maybe helium kept her skull inflated. Could it be both?

"Who, pray tell, is going to raise these zygotes so they don't die instantly upon being manufactured?"

"Well, the computer will build artificial wombs—"

"Out of what?"

"Stop asking niggling questions! This would work!"

"And what happens after they get born? Even if you gestate them to adulthood, they won't have a clue how to survive."

"That's the glory part. The computer will construct two synthetic people to care for them. Little people, about half the size of us so they don't use as much of the available resources, only strong and smart and nearly immortal."

"Synthetic people?"

"Like the Lameeyas they use for guard in the prisons. Only nicer, of course."

"Nicer. Sure."

"Look, we could do this. The Chrysalis isn't as popular since the Facers opened that orbital theme park. Definitely heavy competition. Stupid religion, but they know how to make money. I want to do something for humanity."

"So how the heck are the robots going to get enough matter to build the zygotes when they get to the extra solar planet? I know the tech exists, but if you're talking building babies, you need massive amounts of organics, and—"

"That's the genius part. You know about the magnetic shielding for the Chrysalis?"

"It was never implemented."

"Well, suppose you just let it shield the ship for the first half of the journey. For the second half — are you ready for this?"

Kapera didn't know whether to she was going to have to stifle laughter or pop her eyes at the audacity of — what was this new scheme of Annie's?

"Look, I already talked to Bruce about this. He said it would work." She leaned forward. "Half-way through the journey, you start using the magnetic shield to gather particles of interstellar dust. Gather them in a magnetic bottle about, oh, say a kilometer behind the starship. The mass will accumulate and slow the ship down. So it's accumulating needed mass and acting as a brake at the same time."

Kapera still didn't know whether to laugh or scratch her head. "Bruce did all that number crunching? What's in it for him?"

Annie crossed her legs and looked at Kapera from under her eyelashes. "He's interested."

"In you? Annie, I told you—"

"He really is. I'm sure you're mistaken about his orientation."

"Annie, the last guy you got all hot for turned out to be an AI. He wasn't even instantiated, just a program running on a network somewhere in the Mars cloud."

"Well, all I know is that Bruce ran the numbers and he's in, sweat equity just doing the engineering part. Or organizing it."

Kapera secretly liked the idea, though she knew it needed work.

She just wished Annie would keep her romantic life out of it.

* * * * *

Refitting the Chrysalis took about a mear, and that was okay because the launch toward the exoplanet, Ygdrasil, would need to be when Mars was in Southern winter. Meantime, Kapera and Annie spent most of their daytime hours having their personalities uploaded to the computer's memory, so that it would be uploaded in turn to the two synthetics the Chrysalis would carry and eventually deploy.

"Should we edit ourselves? I wonder if the robots really need memories of my episode with leukemia." Kapera was relaxing into the reception chair. Their parietal cortices and their thalami had already been scanned. Their personal memories would be radio-transmitted. The old MRI method was obsolete, but the young women still needed to enter a hypnotic state in order to access older memories. Personality traits were easier; they were encoded in surface physiology and had already been read with acoustic imaging.

"They aren't robots. Stop calling them robots. They'll have nice warm flesh on them. At least it will feel like flesh." She grabbed a hunk of Kapera's upper arm.

"I'll call them robots until the day I die, and then my synthetic self will call herself a robot."

"See you under an alien sun," said Annie.

"You mean my robo self will. I'm staying right here, all cozy on Mars."

Annie slapped at her. She dodged.

* * * * *

"Shit!" synthetic Annie exclaimed as she rubbed her head, which she'd bumped on the carapace lid above her. Dreams. She tried to catch hold of her dreams. Oh shit! She was artificial life now! Did artificial girls dream? Well, apparently they did. She dreamt about Kapera's brother Sekou again, a bitter-sweet dream, making blithe, simple love to him, then holding him in his arms as he died.

She threw her carapace open and staggered out. There! There was synthetic Kapera's assembly carapace. She threw the lid open and shook her friend's flaccid form "We're here!" she screamed with her synthetic, natural-sounding voice.

Kapera's eyes snapped open in terror. "Oh shit! Where the hell are we?"

Annie calmed down a bit. "We're — we're in the Chrysalis. I think we're about twelve light years from Mars, but —"

"Well, check it! Check the displays."

Annie rolled back her eyes and checked her internal displays, just the way they'd programmed her. She shook Kapera again. "We're in orbit around Ygdrassil! We made it!"

"We did? I guess we did."

"Why don't we just land?" Annie asked.

Kapera rubbed her eyes. They were, however, perfectly clear, unlike human eyes just arising from a few centuries of sleep. "Cause if the planet is hostile to life, it's harder to get away again. We're going to build a colony in orbit first."

"Oh. You didn't mention that."

Actually, Kapera remembered, they had discussed it. Several times. Over a period of months. Annie had a tendency to forget details, especially details that were inconvenient or difficult. "Who cares? We really did it! We're robots!"

Annie's voice went dark. "No, Kapera, we're not robots. We're — artificial life. Nano life. Assembled."

Kapera closed her own eyes and checked her displays. "Okay. The Chrysalis has been here about a century, living on solar energy and gathering material from the upper atmosphere of the planet. The lucky thing is that it found a couple of tiny moons and disassembled one of them for further material. Otherwise, it would have taken millennia."

"It actually destroyed a whole moon? I mean, just blew it out of the sky and absorbed it for its own nefarious purposes?" Annie sounded somehow titillated.

"If by nefarious purposes you mean assembling us and our offspring and an orbital colony to sustain us, it did. I didn't know it had that much initiative, but this is one stone smart computer."

"Excellent! Brilliant!" Annie's eyes glistened with excitement. "Are there vids?"

* * * * *

Kapera had a different take on the environmental impact of disassembling a moon, however tiny, but she kept it to herself.

"No, Annie, no astronomical snuff flicks. Anyway, the assemblers just finished us, and now that we're activated they're starting on the embryos."

"The embryos! Oh my God. Diapers! Lullabies! Bedtime stories! Suppose my mothering programming got corrupted!"

Kapera rolled her synthetic eyes.

Six at a time. Annie's parenting tutor back on Mars had been another of her romantic targets, and this one had apparently liked Annie, although maybe he thought of her as an interesting specimen rather than a potential date. Anyway, he had said two women would be able to take care of sextuplets, and after the children had started to talk, AIs would be able to supplement the raising of the seed children.

Now the first set of six were six Earth years old, the second set were four, the third set were two, and Kapera and Annie had started the synthesis on the fourth batch. That meant that in a few months, there would be twenty-four sets of little feet stampeding the station.

But then the computer messed up. Big time.

"They's corrupted," said Annie. "This batch won't even live to neonate status."

Kapera, though usually the practical one, said, "Could we just leave them in the artificial wombs a few more months?"

Annie shook her head. "Nope. First of all, we don't have time to have the computer build another set of wombs. Second, this batch is missing their brains. Seriously. They're anencephalics."

"What?" whispered Kapera. "How could that happen?"

"Anybody's guess. Maybe they're all from the same Mars mother and she had some defect we didn't catch. Did you check? Maybe when the computer rebuilt the zygotes, it made a mistake. Shit, shit, shit!"

Trajectories

"What can we do?"

Annie was tearing at her synthetic hair. She had a sizable bald spot above her left ear from this activity. The computer could synthesize new hair, but she hadn't had time to lie down for the requisite fifteen minutes to get it implanted. "We have to flush them, Kapera. What did you think we'd do?"

Kapera was trying hard not to cry. Her original program had included functional tear ducts and all the mechanisms of rage and despair, because after all, the children would have to have a model for their own emotions, and also would thus learn empathy. Kapera had always been the sensible one of the two, but she was also very empathic. "They're living children!"

Annie scrutinized her friend's face. "Kapera, you sentimental idiot, we covered all this when we went into it. They aren't living children, they're zygotes, and they are incapable of becoming human beings."

"We can't just flush them." Kapera sat down and buried her head in her hands.

"Recycle," said Annie firmly.

Kapera continued to cry, and Annie could see she wouldn't be much help.

"Anyway," Annie continued, "This will give us a little rest until the next set hatches."

In the end, each of the misprogrammed neonates had enough brain matter to function as insects, so they were bioengineered as flutterbies, a new type of universal polinator that the orbital colony's garden could well use.

* * * * *

Synthetic people can be programmed so that they never tire. But they can become extremely bored. So Annie proposed that the fourteen-year-olds should put on a play to entertain Kapera and herself. Annie was in charge of it, and she wrote a script that was a copy, from memory, of a Tyrielle La Nausicaa five-sense drama she'd audienced several times during the time before the launch to Ygdrasil.

"Why?" said one of the boys, very surly.

"Because we said," Kapera said. "We're here to help you learn and grow, and we think you'd learn a lot from playing the romantic lead in—"

"In this stupid story! It's all based on what you're calling Mars history, and we only have your word for it that Mars ever existed!"

Seeds

"Sanjay," she said reasonably, "You've watched thousands of historical recordings of Mars. How else can you explain how you got here, and who you are?"

"You haven't been paying attention, have you?" The corner of Sanjay's mouth twitched.

"What?"

"I don't want to kiss Elspaith."

"Then what do you want?" Kapera asked doggedly.

"You're ruining the whole pageant!" Annie shrieked. "We can't rewrite the whole —"

"I want to kiss Leon," said Sanjay.

Kapera looked helplessly at Annie.

Annie tore at her hair some more, then sat on the floor and beat her fists against her head. After awhile, she stilled and looked up at Sanjay. "Wait. This might make the whole plot more interesting."

"You're the dramaturge," Kapera said.

*****

Later, as Annie slammed around their headquarters and tried out lines of dramatic dialog, Kapera said, "We never thought to omit homoerotic orientation in the genetic background of the seeds. But then, it's a human variation. Why should we exclude it?"

Annie stopped in the middle of a flowery love speech and stared at her. "Because we want them to reproduce!"

"Let's survey the group and see how prevalent this is. If there's too many we'll have to talk them into reproducing some alternative way."

Later, surveying the second batch, who had now turned twenty, they found that asexuality was also included in the mix.

"You know that guy Dmitri from the fourth gen? The one that I think might be Sister Farseer's son? He's really hot."

"Annie, you changed his diapers!" Kapera found Annie's obsession somehow disturbing.

"But he's an adult now. Twenty-five in Earth years. You think he might go for a somewhat synthetic girl?"

"No, I don't. I think he'll go for one of the other Facer spawn. In fact, I see him with Rachael Sphynxeye a lot."

Annie sagged. "You know, I really miss sleeping. Do you think we could reprogram ourselves to be able to sleep?"

Trajectories

"We had enough sleep while we were waiting for our personalities to be downloaded into the synthetic bodies. Why on Mars or Ygdrasil would you want to waste literally hours a day sleeping?"

"Just an hour or so, every so often?"

"Why?"

Annie sighed. The sigh was purely psychodrama, since she didn't need to fill her synthetic lungs with extra air. "I miss dreaming. I used to have such lovely dreams."

About the time they were building a scout ship to investigate moving the children from the orbiting colony to the planet's surface, Kapera and Annie were sitting drinking some sort of tea-like beverage Kapera had taught the computer to manufacture.

"You were right," said Kapera.

"About —?"

"About men, Annie. You were always the hot-pants, but now I sort of want a boyfriend."

"Told you so, Kapera. Well, I suppose you could reprogram the computer to make a live fully-grown guy."

"Be serious, Annie. The computer can only make zygotes. We have to let them mature in the synthetic womb. It would be just another seed child. And he might not fall in love with me, even after the twenty-odd years I'd have to wait." She stifled tears. "And I want somebody my own age, an equal, not a, a toy!"

"Well, now you understand my obsession with Chang Sphynxeye."

"Chang Sphynxeye?"

Annie smirked.

"What, you actually vibed with Chang?"

"Yep. And there have been others. They always think it's a little weird that I'm so short, but I go out incognito in elevator shoes and they don't realize I'm one of the two original Caregivers." She leaned closer. "They think I'm a dwarf, eighth generation."

Kapera propped her head on her fist. "This can't end well."

*****

"Turk Sphynxeye and Farseeing Triumph Sphynxeye can't get married!" Annie shrieked. "They're half-siblings!"

"Yeah? You tell them that. They keep talking about how much they have in common. They probably got that line from one of the five- sense

Seeds

dramas you remembered from Mars. Or wait: was it one of the ones you actually wrote?"

The seed children had their own five-sense dramas now, of course. Since they'd moved the colony to the planet's surface, they had a lot of their own Stuff.

Annie was uncharacteristically quiet for a few moments. "Kapera, we have to tell them where they came from. I mean, really where. About how so many of Sphynxeye's wives and offspring donated their genome patterns."

Kapera said in a tiny voice. "Okay. We'll give a speech. Tell them there's a new taboo against marrying somebody with the same last name."

"I'll give the speech," said Annie calmly. "I'm much more presentational." She was wearing a fetching new pink unitard, Kapera noticed. It wasn't clear if she had hijacked some of the computer's precious time, or whether it was from the sewing craft guild one the seed children had started.

She looked no older than had her original model on Mars. And possibly not much wiser.

The speech about the new taboo did not go well. About thirty per cent of the seed children had the last name Sphynxeye. Back when the project was getting underway on Mars, the Facers had said they were going to donate zygote patterns with pan-Martian diversity. The truth came out when Annie and Kapera examined the documentation on the zygotes more carefully — too late. And now large number of the couples who had already formed pair-bonds and in a few cases had children (perfectly normal, thank the stars), had that last name in common.

"We shouldn't have trusted people who worship the Face on Mars," said Kapera.

"But they told us the zygote patterns were from Mars-wide populations."

Out in the audience, somebody was yelling, "Who died and made you God?"

*****

"I feel old," said Kapera. She was wearing a nice new scarlet dress Annie had had made for her for Landing Day, and she didn't look particularly old.

"We are old. How many generations of seed kids?"

Trajectories

"I've lost track. The computer keeps spitting them out. And the colonists seem to have no trouble reproducing."

"I still miss dreaming," said Annie. "And men. I'm too recognizable: there aren't any other people half the size of normals. I can't mingle with the population any more. When I flirt, they say it's creepy."

"Then you shouldn't flirt. Just remember our originals on Mars probably married and had families. That will have to be enough for us."

An alarm sounded.

"One of the synthetic wombs is in labor," said Annie. "You go catch the kid this time. I'm going to see if this damn computer can come up with a five-sense drama that doesn't bore me silly."

*****

"I hate this halo," said Annie. "It makes my head look fat."

"Deal with it," said Kapera. "There's a price to pay for being a goddess, and your worshippers await you."

Two years ago at this time there had been almost a hundred thousand waiting for the syntho-girls to appear on the balcony of their cathedral and bless them. Today, there were only a couple hundred.

"They're getting tired of us," said Kapera.

"Goddesses get old."

"We need to come up with some more miracles. Do you think the computer might be able to synthesize chocolate goddess candies?"

"Even I would get religion if it could do that!"

"And maybe we could tell them we need some healthy young men as acolytes to provide special worship to the goddesses."

"Annie, that could be dangerous."

"Yeah, but what's life without a little risk?"

*****

The revolution started on the other side of Ygdrasil. Bashmeti Sphynxeye III had uncovered records that suggested that the syntho-girl goddesses had been mere mortals back on Mars. Or maybe Bashmeti had made up the records. He revealed that one of them had been going incognito and trying to hook up with normal, non-immortal males. Good looking ones. Bashmeti Sphynxeye, who had, from inbreeding, inherited an unattractive underbite, might have been jealous. He'd been turned down as temple acolyte in favor of one of the Cayce clan.

"We should tell the computer to manufacture guns," said Annie. Kapera

"

had forgotten what guns were, but suddenly remembered.

"Annie, these people are almost like our descendants!"

"We didn't donate any zygote patterns ourselves." "It doesn't matter! We can't threaten their lives!"

Annie shrugged. "It doesn't much matter. The acolytes are defending the courtyard of the cathedral. They somehow invented gunpowder and they've got some badly designed weapons to go with. Odds on, they'll start shooting into the crowd."

* * * * *

The revolution didn't last long. There were only a couple hundred acolytes, and the crowd had discovered atheism with a vengeance.

The crowd also discovered the computer, which they promptly made into their new god.

Annie and Kapera escaped through a tunnel into the city and from thence fled from the protective habitat into the cold and hostile Ygdrasil wilderness.

* * * * *

Kapera bashed her synthetic head against a rock. It hurt, but she didn't care. "They got the computer! We're helpless here. What are we going to do for power? How long can we live unprotected?"

"Your guess?"

Kapera thought about this. "I don't know. Probably forever. We can collect solar energy, but winter is coming on, and it's getting dark earlier and earlier."

Annie was silent for a while. Carbon dioxide snow fell on her artificial hair and she decided to allow tears to form in her pretty crystal eyes. "We didn't agree to this, did we?"

Kapera said, "I suppose we did. Although the 'we' that agreed never thought about actually experiencing all this."

"It sucks," said Annie. "All I ever wanted was a husband and a —"

"Oh, shut up! You never wanted a husband and a family. You wanted an expensive wardrobe with Terran fashions, and a bunch of boyfriends fighting over you."

Annie bowed her synthetic head. "Yeah. Guess I did."

Kapera looked up at the sky. She had lost track of the constellations and had no idea which way was the earthly, martian solar system. "I wonder what our meat originals are doing."

"Dancing all night at fashionable bars in Borealopolis. Or eating imported chocolates and watching skanky five sense dramas. Or —"

"Listen to us! Our originals are long dead, unless medical science in the solar system advanced far beyond what we know about."

"It might have," said Annie. "After all, it allowed us to be created."

"So our originals are immortal. They're us. And we're here."

"And what happens when our fuel cells run down?" She stamped her titanium-boned leg and glared at Kapera.

"We die, I suppose."

"Is there a real death? Do you think our originals made other copies, and we're out there somewhere?'

"No. Yes. Who knows? It won't help us. The only thing that will help us is if somebody has a change of heart and feels sorry for two syntho-girls from another world."

"And that will happen — when?"

"Not soon. But here's a plan."

Annie cocked her synthetic head at Kapera.

"We bury ourselves in regolith. We power down. And we wait. Somebody will come."

"What other choice do we have?" Then, as they began to dig, "Maybe I'll have another dream. Like the one just before we arrived and came on line."

"That wasn't a dream. That was a hallucination."

"It was a daydream," said Annie. "I've always been very good at daydreaming."

"You've always been good at being delusional."

Then they knelt down in the sand and began to burrow. Annie stopped digging every now and then to whine, but they dug and dug.

Maybe they would learn how to dream again.

FORMAL CHARGES
By Jay Werkheiser

Space is an unforgiving environment. Try to solve a problem when you're constrained by the unyielding laws of physics, by unavoidable delays in communication. Then add a dash of paranoia. That's the setup for Jay Werkheiser's suspenseful "Formal Charges."

Jay Werkheiser teaches chemistry and physics to high school students, where he often finds inspiration for stories in classroom discussions. Look for his upcoming stories in ANALOG SCIENCE FICTION and the Baen Books anthology *Mission: Tomorrow*. You can follow him on twitter @JayWerkheiser or read his (much neglected) blog at http:// jaywerkheiser.blogspot.com/.

■■■■■■

An incoming distress call lit up the comm panel, jerking Brett to alertness. His tether tightened around his waist and gently tugged him back into his seat.

He swiveled his chair to face the open hatch behind him and shouted, "Hey Cap, you better get over here. *Mayflower* called in a radiation alert."

Dave glided through the hatch moments later, bringing himself to a stop with a single precise tug on the frame. Behind him, Ashley held the guide line in a death grip, her hair a mousy brown halo.

Brett strained to see beyond her. "Is Dannie awake?"

"Nothing wakes her," Dave said. "Where's the radiation coming from?"

"They don't know. Their alarms started going off a few hours ago."

"Hours?" Dave's eyes drilled into Brett as though it were his fault.

"They have no control over the thrust our particle beams are providing. Right now, we're pushing them at three gees. Just standing up is dangerous."

"Damn. The Chinese would just love to see America suffer another black eye." Dave said the word Chinese as though it were a curse.

"Any word from the other beamer stations?"

"Not yet."

Dave huffed and turned to Ashley. "How serious is this, Doc?"

"They brought meds to help with symptoms just in case the radiation shielding doesn't work as well as expected."

"Will it work?"

"Depends how bad the radiation is. Rate and type matter a lot." She raised her eyebrow at Brett.

"They don't know," he said. "They're not going to be able to do much legwork for us. I double checked our beamer output just to be—"

Dave's baleful glare returned to Brett. "Is something wrong with the particle beams?"

"I don't think so." Brett met Dave's stare. "I picked up a slight drop in power output from a few beamers at the beginning of my shift, but they were still within nominal range."

"And you didn't tell me?"

"C'mon, Cap, you know the drill. We'd never get anything done if we sounded alarms every time a dial drifts. I logged it and kept my eye on it. I figured I'd tweak the plasma temp next time I go out."

"I want you EVA *now*. Go over those beamers with a magnifying glass if you have to. If something's wrong, I want to know about it. Ashley, go with him."

Color drained from Ashley's face. "Outside? Me? Dannie's more experienced—"

Dave shook his head. "I need her to check out the bot programming. And I'm going to be on the horn with D.C. Damn! The media's going to jump all over this."

Ashley's eyes, wide with fear, locked onto Brett's. "I can go out alone, Cap," he said.

"You know the regs. No solos." Dave pushed off Brett's chair, propelling himself out of the command center. He brushed past Ashley on his way out, sending her into a slow spin.

"I hate suiting up," she said.

Brett grabbed her shoulder to steady her. "C'mon, Doc. It'll be fun."

* * * * *

Brett yanked one last time on the tether attached to Ashley's waist, then his own end. Her rapid breathing hissed in his helmet radio. "You're sucking oxygen too fast. Remember your flight training?"

"It's been a while."

"You'll be fine. Ready?"

Her mirrored faceplate turned to face him. "Uh, I can't see you nod," he said.

"Oh, right. I'm ready."

He hit the button to cycle the airlock. His suit bulked up as the pressure dropped. He heard Ashley's rapid intake of breath when he popped the seal on the outer door, but then there was nothing but the peaceful hiss of air in his helmet.

Brett pushed the outer door open, giving him a clear view of the beamer array. Clusters of black nanofiber-composite cylinders, grouped like bowling pins, grew out of the asteroidal rock and towered over his head. Brett stood in the airlock doorway with his head craned upward, imagining what the relativistic beams of fullerene particles would look like if he could see them.

"It's gotta make you proud," he said. "We're sending the first people to the stars."

"The Chinese beat us to Mars."

"Don't let Cap hear you talk like that."

"Think only good thoughts."

Brett grinned. "I can't believe NASA couldn't find anyone better to send out here."

"There are a lot of beamer stations, and not enough gung-ho types to man them all."

A guide line hung between the airlock and the array. Brett tugged on it and drifted outside. The surface dust had been electrostatically removed to prevent damage to the beamers, leaving porous black rock. The asteroid's gentle gravity pulled his feet downward until they hit the ground soundlessly.

"Move like you would inside," he said. "Don't try to walk; pull yourself along the line. If you find yourself drifting away from the surface, let me handle it. *Do not* fire your maneuvering jet unless I tell you."

He was glad to see her glide after him with little difficulty. He gave her a thumbs-up and led the way through the forest of particle beamers. "The nearest anomaly is in cluster four. We'll start there."

He allowed himself to drift to his knees next to the cluster's access panel. He was soon immersed in reading the lithium plasma density, synching the laser pulses, tracing the plasma wakefield ripples behind the laser front. He reveled in the minutia of old-fashioned troubleshooting. The familiar routine allowed him to put his hands on autopilot.

"You almost done?"

"Not even close." He belatedly noticed the nervous quiver in her voice. "You all right?"

"I was. It's just . . . I really don't like being outside."

"Get your mind off it."

"Easy for you to say."

"Think about the vast scales of magnitude we're working with. Microscopic bots collecting raw materials for building-sized beamers, which push a city-sized interstellar ship across light years of space. It's— humph."

"Something wrong?" Ashley asked.

"Maybe." He read the diagnostic data on his handheld again. "The fullerene particles in this cluster are lagging behind the wakefield. The laser pulse is drawing enough power, but the particles aren't accelerating like they should."

"Why?"

"I don't know. I'd better call it in."

"I'm on it," she said. "At least I can do something useful out here."

Brett heard a muffled click as she switched channels. He went to work on the next cluster.

Click. "Dave says you have two hours to finish up," Ashley said. "We have a teleconference with Earth."

"Teleconference? Out here? What about the—"

"He didn't sound like he wanted to discuss it."

* * * * *

Dave and Dannie were already in the command center when Brett drifted through the hatch. He and Ashley still wore the padded undergarments of their pressure suits, and the breeze from the overhead air circulators chilled the sweaty padding uncomfortably.

Dannie swiveled in her chair with a mischievous grin. "Standing room only, chumps."

Brett wedged himself into the tiny room behind Dannie's chair, in the view of the camera. She looked up at him with a smirk on her face. Even sitting, her tall lanky form topped with close-cropped platinum hair reminded Brett of a cotton swab.

"You're cheerful today, Q-Tip." He grinned. "Who're we conferencing with, one of your hacker buddies?"

"I wish," she said. "We're stuck with some DOJ flunky."

"DOJ?" Brett turned to Dave.

"Department of Justice." Dave's face was grim. "Guy named Parker."

"Shouldn't we be talking to engineers?"

"What the hell do you think I've been doing while you were outside?" Frustration tightened Dave's voice. "Administration leaders insisted we talk to DOJ."

"It's an election year," Ashley said. "Everyone's going to be covering their own ass."

"Yeah, well, I got mine covered," Dannie said. "My report on the bot scripting went out a few minutes ago. Give 'em something to read during the lightspeed gaps."

"Does this Parker guy understand there's a fifteen-minute delay?" Brett asked. "Each way?"

"Never met him," Dannie said. "But he has a rep with some of the black hats I know. Typical lawyer type, so—"

The comm light flashed amber, cutting her off. Dave flipped a switch and the primary display lit up. Brett craned his neck to see around Dannie's head.

"I've reviewed your log," Parker said in a flat monotone. "The evidence suggests technician Brett Montgomery willfully neglected his duty to report a station malfunction. Further, said negligence has directly endangered the success of the mission."

"The hell?"

He felt the welcome warmth of Ashley's hand squeezing his shoulder. "You didn't do anything wrong."

"Even if the charge doesn't stick, I'll never get another space assignment."

Parker droned on. ". . . Transmit a statement regarding the status of the particle beam generators. Your statement will be a factor in our decision whether to file formal charges."

He paused, glancing down at his notes. "While I wait for your transmission, I'll fill you in on what we know down here. *Mayflower* is propelled by fullerene particles fired from numerous beamer stations . . . ."

"He is *not* going to explain this to us," Dannie said.

"Does he think we're idiots?" Brett said. "Uh, we're not transmitting, are we?"

Dave glared at him. "No, but pipe down and listen."

Trajectories

". . . Generates a magnetic field for your charged particles to push against. Your beamer station . . . ."

Dannie cradled her head in her hands. "The particle beam's neutral, idiot."

Dave shushed her and muted Parker. "You'd better make your statement, Brett."

"What does he expect me to say? Does it even matter?"

"Just explain what's happening. How the beamers work, what the anomaly was, and what you found outside. Ready?"

"As ready as I'll ever be."

"Okay. I want everyone on their best behavior." He cast a sharp glance past Brett's shoulder at Ashley. He flipped the record switch and pointed at Brett.

"A few of our beamers are losing power during particle acceleration," Brett said stiffly. "It seems the particles are lagging behind the wakefield—"

"Perhaps you could back up and explain what a wakefield is," Dave said.

"Um, right. Inside the beamer, a laser pulse creates a bubble of charge separation in a lithium plasma. We call it a wakefield, and it ripples through the plasma at nearly the speed of light, accelerating ionized fullerenes. Uh, those are soccer-ball-shaped cages of carbon atoms." Brett's comfort level rose as he slipped into technical mode. "The bots make them with lanthanum atoms inside the cage, which adds mass and makes them easier to ionize."

"The final beam is neutral," Dannie added. Dave gave her a sharp look.

Brett nodded. "We neutralize the fullerene beam with a relativistic electron beam so it doesn't spread in transit."

"Now explain to Mr. Parker what's wrong," Dave said. Worry lines creased his forehead.

Brett didn't care how little the stupid lawyer understood. He took a deep breath and continued. "The particles aren't keeping up with the wakefield in some of the beamers. That means they're leaving at a slower velocity than they should. We don't know why that is yet, but I don't see how it can be harming the crew of *Mayflower* in any way."

"That's good," Dave said. Brett watched him stop the recorder and hit the transmit button. Slouching in his chair, he asked, "Anyone have any ideas? It would really help Brett if we were the ones to figure out where the radiation is coming from."

"Parker has a rep for being an overzealous bastard," Dannie said.

"Damn it, Dannie, I need *ideas*."

"If it's only a handful of beams that they're worried about," Ashley said, "why not just shut down the affected beamers?"

Dave shook his head. "I already checked with the engineers at D.C. It would cost them too much thrust, add years to their flight. They don't have enough supplies for that."

"And they're already going too fast to abort and recover," Brett added. "This came at the worst possible time."

"Okay, how about this," Dannie said. "Maybe it's not the beamers at all. Maybe it's the cosmic ray shielding."

Brett shook his head. "I can't see it. The ship's magnetosphere traps a protective plume of charged particles. It worked perfectly on the unmanned probes. The design is foolproof, ingenious."

"Except that the crew's getting cooked," Ashley said.

An amber flash attracted Brett's eye to the comm panel. Dave gave Ashley a withering look.

"Are you sure about that?" Parker asked. He paused as though waiting for an answer.

"He's talking about Dannie's report," Dave said.

Parker must have remembered the lightspeed delay. "I hope you're sure. What about the beamers themselves? Did anyone check them?"

"I knew this was a bad idea," Dannie said.

Parker continued. "Your programmer's had some questionable contacts in the past. If I were you, I'd double check her work. That goes for everyone. Have two different people perform each procedure. If you have a saboteur aboard, we'll root him out."

"Sabotage?"

"What the hell's he talking about?"

"I don't believe it."

"Knock it off." Dave's sharp tone jarred the overlapping voices to silence. "It's the only thing that makes sense. You said it yourself, Brett. The timing can't be a coincidence."

Brett stood in place, stunned. After a long moment, Ashley broke the silence. "Who, then?"

"Plenty of people would love to see America fail," Dave said. "The

Chinese, for one. India's been getting aggressive lately. Or maybe Middle Eastern—"

"That's not what I meant."

Brett swiveled his head, looking each of his friends in the eye. *Who, then?*

"As soon as we're done here, I want everyone back to work," Dave said. "Brett, take Dannie out with you to finish the beamer work. Doc, you're long past your sleep shift. Catch a few hours while you can."

Brett nodded. Anything to keep his mind occupied.

* * * * *

"Find anything over there, Q-Tip?" Brett asked.

"Cluster nine looks good as far as I can tell. I'm not much of an engineer. You could be the saboteur and I'd never figure it out."

Brett pursed his lips behind his faceplate. "Do you really think one of us is a saboteur?"

"Doubt it. You and Dave are too gung ho. USA all the way. Ashley doesn't have the tech skills."

"That leaves you."

"If it was me I'd know about it."

An odd pattern grabbed Brett's attention. The last two laser coevaporation chambers he checked were spitting out low-mass fullerenes. He needed better data, so he sampled the output at the next cluster with his handheld mass spec. Average particle mass was definitely too low. Humph. That didn't make sense. Lighter particles should be easier to accelerate.

". . . hear me?" Dannie's voice rose with concern.

"I'm here," Brett said. "Just trying to work through something in my mind."

"What did you find?"

"I don't know yet. Clusters four, five, and six are shooting low- mass particles and I have no idea why."

"Right in the middle of the array," she said. "Could there be some interference effect?"

"Not likely. Maybe the saboteur figured he could hit more beamers if he stuck to the center."

"Did you find any signs of sabotage?"

"No. Damn it, none of this makes sense. I can't imagine any of us as Chinese agents."

"Maybe it's not the Chinese."

"Who, then?"

"My money's on eco-freaks bent on saving the new world from humanity," she said. "Remember those Greenpeace nutjobs who tried to fly through the particle beams during the first test?" She laughed.

Brett sighed. She wasn't looking at negligence charges, at least not yet. "Let's just finish up out here."

* * * * *

Brett reveled in the warm water sloshing around inside the plastic bag, lapping against his body in the low gravity. The primitive pleasures of warmth and comfort brightened his mood. The hatch to the tiny room opened. Startled, he snapped his head around to see Dave's head poking in.

Brett grinned. "I'm not that kind of guy, Cap. You want a shower, you'll have to wait your turn."

"Where's Dannie?" Dave asked.

"I let her clean up first. She went to her room to get some work done."

"Good." He slipped through the hatch and closed it behind him. "I wanted to talk to you alone."

Brett got a good look at the expression on Dave's face and his smile drained away. "What's wrong, Cap?"

"We've got two new problems."

Brett sighed in resignation. "Hit me."

"Radiation level on *Mayflower* just ramped up."

"Damn. What else?"

"There's a problem with the bot programming."

"But I thought Dannie already went over that." His eyes widened. "Oh."

"It's subtle. I'd have missed it if you hadn't reported in with the particle mass issue."

"What do you mean?"

"Some of the bots are collecting nitrogen instead of lanthanum."

"But why—oh, that explains the mass decrease. Wait. We use laser coevaporation to make our fullerenes, which only works with embedded metals. I never learned how you would do it with nonmetals. Didn't relate to beamer engineering."

"I need you to find out everything you can. Quickly."

"Quickly isn't going to happen. It'll take hours just to find someone Earth side who's reliable. Add in the light speed delay. Unless . . . ."

"Unless what?"

"Ashley is a chemistry whiz," Brett said. "Maybe I'll start with her."

Dave's face twisted. "I don't know if I trust her."

"C'mon, Cap. She passed the background checks."

"All right." Dave didn't sound convinced. "Just be careful how much you tell her."

*****

Brett found Ashley in the lounge sipping a bulb of coffee and staring at her handheld. "Mind if I join you, Doc?" He strapped his tether around the chair across from her.

She peered into his eyes. "What's wrong?"

"*Mayflower* reported an increase in radiation levels."

"I feel so useless." A deep frown twisted her lips. "I'm the only one on the station with the time to get bored. I wish I could be more helpful."

"Maybe you can."

She raised her eyebrows.

"How would you get nitrogen inside a fullerene?"

She rolled her eyes skyward for a moment, her face taking on the slack look of deep thought. "At a guess, ion implantation. Does this have something to do with the beamers?"

"Maybe." He drummed his fingers nervously on the table, wondering how much to say. *This is ridiculous.* "The bots are subbing nitrogen for lanthanum in some of the beamers. Any idea why?"

Ashley's fingers played over the keyboard of her handheld. "Says here you need pretty high temperatures for ion implantation. The lithium plasma's probably hot enough, but I'd expect a low yield. Maybe a few percent of the fullerenes get implanted." Her face brightened. "Hey, I bet that's why some of your beamers are shooting blanks."

"What makes you think so?"

"Because metallofullerenes are a lot easier to ionize than empty ones," she said. "The metal inside donates electrons to the cage of carbon atoms, spreading formal charges across the surface."

Formal Charges

"Formal charges?"

"Electric charges assigned to atoms in a molecule," she said. "The charges on the carbon cage are relatively easy to strip away. Didn't you say the fullerenes had to be ionized for the beamers to work?"

Brett nodded.

"Well, lanthanum is trivalent. Three electrons go to the cage and get ripped away. Nitrogen won't give up electrons. The same energy you needed to remove three electrons probably only buys you one when nitrogen's inside the cage."

Brett's eyes went wide. "*That's* why they lag behind the wakefield. Less charge means less force accelerating them."

Ashley took a long draught from her coffee bulb. "I still don't see the point of implanting nitrogen, though. Empty buckyballs would ionize the same way."

Ionization. That was the key. Brett snapped his fingers. "Not exactly the same way." He was onto something important here, he could feel it. "*Mayflower* ionizes the incoming beam with lasers so their magnetosphere can repel the particles. But the lasers are tuned to metallofullerene ionization energies."

"Oh, I get it. Nitrogen endofullerenes won't get ionized. They'll slam into the hull at relativistic speed."

"Yup," Brett said. "Nuclei moving that fast will go right through the hull and sleet across the crew like hard radiation."

"Great!" A smile lit Ashley's face. "Now we know how *Mayflower* is getting irradiated."

"Yeah. But we still don't know why she's doing it."

"She?" Ashley's smile faded. "Dannie? You think *she's* a saboteur? No way!"

"I don't know." Brett sighed. "Who else could have changed the bot programming?"

Ashley's eyes smoldered. "She's your friend, Brett. You of all people should know about witch hunts."

Anger flashed hot in his face, or perhaps it was guilt. "It's not a witch hunt."

"It's starting to look that way to me."

"That's why no one trusts you."

He regretted the words instantly, but there was no taking them back.

Trajectories

He unclipped his tether from the chair and launched himself from the lounge.

*****

There was one place on the cramped beamer station where Brett knew he could be alone, if only for the half hour it would take Dave to consult with Earth. He lay tethered to his cot, his back barely making contact with the surface. He replayed his argument with Ashley in his head, changing his parting words each time through.

Q-Tip was a flake, sure enough, but that didn't make her a traitor.

So who was capable of sabotage?

If it had been a Chinese mission, Dave would have done it in a heartbeat. He was a zealot, gladly willing to sacrifice himself for his country. Who else on the station had that kind of fanaticism?

No one. Ashley did more than her share of griping, but she could never harm the ship's crew. Dannie's only real passion was computer code.

A knock on the hatch interrupted his thoughts. "Open up. I need to talk to you." Dave's voice was muffled by the thick metal.

Brett pushed the hatch open with his foot. He sat up on the cot while Dave pulled himself into the room and closed the hatch behind him. There was barely enough space for the two of them.

"What's up, Cap?"

"I reported Dannie's programming trick to D.C.," Dave said. He hesitated a long moment. "Reply came back a few minutes ago. I have to put her under arrest and ship her back to Earth on the next cargo shuttle."

"Where do they expect you to put her? We don't have a brig."

"I can put a security lock on her quarters," Dave said.

That was news. "I don't know what to say."

"I need you to back me on this," Dave said. "I need one person on this damned crew I can trust, and it sure as hell isn't going to be Ashley."

Brett winced.

Dave's face fell. "You're against me too?"

"Jeez, Cap. I'm loyal. You know that." *I don't have to like it though.*

"Good," Dave said. "Let's do this."

*****

The lounge was the only room in the station large enough to hold all four crew members. Ashley and Dannie sat together at the table, drink bulbs in hand. Brett heard their whispered conversation come to an abrupt end when he and Dave entered. The deadly silence lasted long enough for his feet to drift to the floor.

"What do you want?" Dannie spit the words like venom.

"DOJ wants me to put you under house arrest, Dannie," Dave said. His voice cracked at her name.

"You *know* me, Cap. You really think I'd mess with—"

"I have to deactivate your access codes and lock you in your quarters."

"No," Ashley said firmly.

"Don't make this harder than it has to be," Dave said.

Her eyes found Brett's and he felt the heat of her stare. "You can't go along with this, Brett. Do something."

"She sabotaged the bot programming," he said.

"No, she didn't." Ashley turned to Dannie. "Tell them."

"Won't make a difference," Dannie said, her eyes defiant.

"Damn it, Q-Tip, we're killing the ship's crew," Brett said. "If you have some answers, now's the time."

"Bot programming is right out of the box," she said. "But why waste my breath? Nobody's listening."

It kept coming back to the bots. The answer was there, if only Brett could wrap his mind around it. "Okay, I'm listening," he said. Dave's head swiveled toward him for a moment, a sharp expression on his face. Brett ignored him. "Why would the bots substitute nitrogen for lanthanum on their own?"

She shrugged. Her life was on the line and she shrugged. Damn her. "Bots are stupid," she finally said. "They just do what they're programmed to do."

"Could it be a simple programming error?"

Dannie sighed. "I know you're trying to help, Brett, but I don't see how a programming error would affect us and not other stations."

What's different about this station? Less lanthanum than the other asteroids? No, but a lower relative abundance. The center of the array would get mined out first. "Could the bots be running short of lanthanum?"

Dannie's head snapped away from him as he spoke, ending with a wide-eyed stare in Dave's direction. Brett saw Ashley draw back from Dave, her eyes also wide. He craned his neck to see what they were reacting to.

Dave had a needler gun aimed at Dannie. "Enough," he said. "I have my orders."

Trajectories

Desperate now, Brett locked onto the first thought that occurred. "Maybe we just happened to run out of lanthanum first." Now that he thought about it, the idea made sense. He snapped his fingers. "I bet that's why the radiation level jumped. Check with the other stations, Cap. See if any of them developed the same problem recently."

Dave's voice didn't waver a bit. "If she's innocent, she can sort it out back on Earth."

Ashley tried to stand, but her tether pulled her back to her chair. She huffed and opened the buckle. Dave's arm jerked in her direction at the unexpected motion.

"Shoot me, then," she screamed. "It's the only way you're going to lock her up."

Brett wondered what kind of needles Dave had loaded. Does he want to kill or incapacitate? *He's a zealot.*

This would not end well.

Before realizing he had decided to do it, Brett found himself in mid-leap. He jammed his shoulder into the center of Dave's back and felt his friend's lungs deflate at the impact. His pulse pounded in his ears. He wrapped his arms around Dave, reaching for the gun.

His inner ears told him he and Dave were rotating as they struggled, but his eyes registered nothing beyond the hand gripping the gun. His fingers closed on the hard surface of the needler's barrel a moment before he felt the jarring impact with the ground through Dave's body.

Dave went limp. Brett lay atop him for a while, panting. He calmed himself enough to notice he was drifting upward from the floor. He reached out to grab the edge of the table and stop his motion, still clutching the gun's barrel in his right hand.

By the time he had himself steadied, Ashley was kneeling over Dave and examining his head. He saw Dannie staring at him slack jawed. "Gotta hand it to you," she said. "You know how to go out in a blaze of glory."

Brett nodded, his breath still ragged. "Well, I figured if I'm going down anyway, I might as well be guilty of something." He turned his attention to Ashley. "He going to be all right, Doc?"

"He'll wake up with a hell of a headache, but he'll be fine."

"So what do we do now?" Dannie asked. "It's not like we have anywhere to go."

"He can't lock us all up," Brett said. "We'll have a few months to talk sense into him before anyone from Earth can get here. In the meantime, *Mayflower* is still taking rads. Can you patch the bot programming without shutting everything down?"

Dannie's face brightened. "Just watch the master."

* * * * *

"It looks like the newspods are touting you guys as heroes," Dave said. Brett couldn't tear his eyes away from the tennis-ball-sized welt on his forehead. He felt his face flush. *He keeps it uncovered on purpose.*

"They tell me the President herself mentioned us in a speech," Dannie said.

Dave nodded, his bruise bobbing up and down. "There's no way the DOJ can prosecute any of you now. You're home free, for better or worse." He released his tether and shoved himself out of the lounge.

"I'm just glad it's over," Ashley said. Brett saw her eyes follow Dave until he disappeared into the command center. "If you hadn't figured out that the other stations were going to malfunction too, we'd have killed the crew of *Mayflower*."

Brett nodded. "I just wonder how the programmers on Earth could have left such a gaping hole in their code. Maybe Cap's right to be suspicious."

Dannie laughed. "Ever hear of Hanlon's Razor?"

"Can't say I have."

"Never attribute to malice that which can be adequately explained by stupidity."

"You're not even a little suspicious?" Brett asked.

Dannie shook her head. "Simple logistics. Once the local lanthanum supply was used up, the bots feeding the center clusters had to travel further than the others. The time lag red flagged the production code. The optimization routine kicked in, decided that nitrogen was the best compromise of mass and availability. Artificial stupidity at its best."

"No one even considered the consequences of letting the bots make that kind of decision on their own?"

"What, that nitrogen atoms would fry the crew? Hell, I wouldn't have thought of that. Would you?"

"You win, Q-Tip. Artificial stupidity it is," he said. "I still don't feel like a hero, though."

"Right place, right time." Dannie shrugged. "That's all it ever takes to be a hero."

Maybe she was right. But he knew that he was just an ordinary guy doing his job. The real heroes were going to the stars; he just gave them the chance to do it. Perhaps that was enough.

TRAJECTORIES OF THE HEART

by Arlan Andrews, Sr.

Arlan Andrews, Sr.'s story takes his protagonist Francisco Navarro from the mean streets of his home on Earth, where his martial arts skills protect him from his harsh social environment, to a tense situation in deep space, where his intellectual and technical skills take precedence.

But will technology alone save the day?

Dr. Arlan Andrews, Sr., is the founder of SIGMA, the Science Fiction Think Tank, which works with the U.S. government and non-profit organizations to provide the unique futurism of science fiction writers for those who need it most.

Arlan began his technical career working as a missile tracking telescope operator at White Sands Missile Range. He worked for AT&T Bell Laboratories on the antiballistic missile program, was appointed as a Fellow in the White House Science Office, and co-founded both a Virtual Reality software company and a biotech equipment company.

Arlan has published nearly 500 stories, articles, columns and other features in 100 venues worldwide, primarily in science fiction, the paranormal, futurism, and the fringe areas of science and folklore.

He also appeared on the History Channel cable presentation of "Aliens and Ancient Engineers" in August 2011.

■■■■■■

Francisco Navarro's heart was pounding wildly as he ran from the *criminales* trying to kill him. Ducking into a narrow alleyway, praying he could find a place to hide, he shivered and waited. "*Hola! Aquí!* Here he is!" the shout came. Navarro's overwrought heart sank. The gang of knife-wielding, chain-swinging thugs closed in on him. Boxed into a dirty alcove between crumbling buildings, he knew there would be no escape. Ten to one, his fists against their knives and chains. But with the certain knowledge of death came a calmness of resignation. Navarro's only course revealed itself: pride required resistance; regardless of the odds, at least there was honor in going out fighting!

He assumed a *keratsu* martial arts position, his hands and feet becoming trained weapons. He would inflict as much damage as he could before dying under the knives. Six of the ugly hoodlums rushed him, bumping into themselves as they tried to squeeze into the strait between the walls. An overwhelming smell of lavender assaulted his nostrils. *Cologne on a punk?* a disinterested part of his mind observed. *Perfume?* But strangely, once close, the assailants just dropped their weapons and grabbed him by the arms and legs, swinging him first this way, then that, slamming him against the ground, then against the sky. *How can I hit the sky?* that same part of his mind asked.

"*Emergency! Emergency!*" the piss-yellow sky shouted at him. "*Debris impact!*"

What the hell is wrong? What are these pendejos *doing? The sky? What is it saying?*

Navarro jerked himself to semi-conscious wakefulness, only vaguely aware that his living quarters were spinning around, stretching his restraint harness first this way, then that, as his semi-conscious brain kept interpreting the inchoate sensory data as a personal attack upon himself. "*Chingáo!*" he shouted, trying to control arms and legs still wildly windmilling to keep his dream-assailants away. Shaking his head, he tried to focus his unwilling eyes on the scene: his three-meter cubed personal universe, optimistically named by the U. N. Unified Colonial Authority (the *Unuks*), the "captain's cabin," an undecorated space defined at its boundaries by impersonal yellowish pleated padding. *Familiar, but my inner ear — and these jerking restraints — tell me we're spinning crazily. That means—*

—*the ship is hit!*

He awoke suddenly, fully. *The controls!* he remembered in panic. *Where are the controls?*

As his conscious mind re-asserted itself, he remembered something he must do. Closing and opening his eyes in a recalled sequence, Navarro *verched* up the ship's built-in display lasers that painted images on his retinas. An enormous virtual desk solidified in the space before him, its polished surface embedded with knobs, trackballs, finger holes, stroke pads — all the paraphernalia he must use to take command of his ship. He sighed; at least now he knew where he was and a little of what was happening. He rolled the virtual trackball until the ship's attitude control engines at long last responded, slowing the three-axis spin to a gentle roll along the long axis, giving himself a little gravity. He didn't like the amount of fuel it had taken to corral the bucking bronco; something was dreadfully wrong, but no sense in using all the ACS consumables until he could figure out what was going on.

"Ship," he murmured, "*¿Que pása?*" He decided not to ask about the lavender; he was well aware of that sensory input.

In English — the official language of Space — the ship answered, "Captain Navarro, sir, we have taken a debris impact, and are knocked off course."

Navarro gulped. *Damn!* This was supposed to be just a milk run from *Lee-Oh* to *Lune-Oh*; just an easy way to spend a week and make a few more payments. He wasn't the adventurous type. Afraid of the answer, he gulped and asked, "How far off course?"

"Captain Navarro, sir," came the reply, "there is no answer to that inquiry. Ship's memory is damaged; ship's external sensors are inoperative; ship's external communications are non-existent."

Oh my Lord Krishna, Navarro groaned. *Me halfway to Lune-Oh, and probably not another soul within a hundred thousand klicks!* Quickly, he scanned the consumables tables. Enough air for a week, water for two, food for three. (*Stupid priorities, those!* he thought.) No air or liquid leaks, shielding adequate for solar flares. *Fine, so I'm stuck here for a week and then I die of asphyxiation. Better check the rest of the ship, see if there's anything back there I can use.*

The video didn't respond, so Navarro called up a *verch* image of the ship and asked for damage reports from all sectors. A solid model of Supply Ship Three floated in front of him, stretching from wall to wall. The "captain's cabin" was a tiny box, the size of a sugar cube in this scale, situated midway on a "backbone" girder along the length of the ship. Splayed off this beam in all six directions was a cosmic junkyard of spheres, cubes, tubes and spines, the kaleidoscopic topology of miscellaneous cargo en route from Mother Earth to Baby Luna. A golfball-sized sphere at the right end was the Low Earth Orbit (*Lee-Oh*) ejector engine, which had slung the SS-3 away from the mother planet. A similar ball, grape-sized, at the left end represented the Lunar Orbit (*Lune-Oh*) injector engine, intended to slow the whole assembly down at the other end and later send it back toward *Lee-Oh*. Simple construction, simple trajectories, simple operations. *And an operator just as simple!* This was the nominal ship condition, as launched.

"Ship," he commanded, "full damage report."

Trajectories

The image reconfigured, based on information from molecular- sized sensors embedded in every cubic millimeter of the ship's volume. The resulting picture was not pleasant. By Navarro's interpretation of the verch image, the "backbone" was now V-shaped, held together only by an indeterminate mass of fused, tangled cargo debris, the *Lune-Oh* engine ball gone, snapped off like a dandelion's boll. "My lord Krishna," he whispered, "this looks fatal." His milk run had been stirred into thick cheese.

Navarro was able to reconstruct the anomaly from the remaining ship's memory of its destroyed radar system: He and the ship had encountered a cloud of unknown cosmic debris, a thickening cluster of tiny silicon particles traveling at nearly right angles to the ecliptic, an ellipsoidal cloud some thousand klicks long that accompanied an asteroid-sized body ten kilometers in diameter. Apparently the cloud of micro-sand had scoured the ship's bottom surface, removing all external sensors on that side and penetrating deeply enough to damage seriously much of the network of subsurface nanoelectronic structures that served as the ship's memory. This had occurred within twenty to thirty seconds, preparing the way for larger chunks of space shit that then perforated many of the cargo containers, along with even bigger rocks that had broken the back of the CS-3. The big one, *El Grande*, he named it, took off the *Lune-Oh* engine, finally missing him by mere meters.

Fortunately! he thought.

He sighed. Maybe *unfortunately* was more appropriate. UN Space Control would surely consider the ship a total loss and not mount a rescue effort. He might be stuck out in space alone, left to die with only a padded cell for final comfort. A quick death was to be preferred over what might be facing him.

* * * * *

Death Itself was of little concern. As his dear mother had taught him back in the ashram in Santa Fe, the transition from this incarnation to the next was an event to be cherished, not feared. "Never resist progress, my son. Death is *maya* — illusion." She had lived that thought, and she had died in certain ecstasy, her failing heart not a bother as she anticipated the next chance to improve herself. "The next roll of the Wheel, my dear Francisco, may be my last" she had breathed raspily, having refused the clinic's proffered rejuvenano injection, "But in you I have satisfied my karma. You take these tiny marvels in your body when you can; but me, I only wish to transition from this plane to another."

She had winced, then smiled and whispered a final time, "Sweetie, I'm going to swim the cosmic courses among the streams of stars." Then she died, with a nine-year-old Frankie Navarro standing beside her, considering the vanished collage of life-forces that had constituted his mother, his guiding light, his teacher. His best friend.

Somewhere behind him a nurse murmured, "Too bad she didn't take the nanos years ago, for the kid. Her generation waited so long to have children, now they're dying so soon, the kids left alone."

"All the goddam drugs in the last millennium, you ask me," an intern snorted as she disconnected the life-support cables. "Who knows what these selfish New Agers did to themselves and their kids?" Frankie had wondered at that concern; his Mom always bragged she'd been born on January 1, 2000 – wasn't that in the New Millennium?

* * * * *

His lack of fear of Death didn't make Navarro any less anxious to stay alive as long as possible. He instructed the ship to inventory and catalog its resources: luckily for him, the primary cargo was a large load of oxygen-bearing compounds destined for one of the colony sites, chemicals easily converted by a mobile autochemlab in the ship's surviving cargo. With even a little recycling, there was enough breathable oxygen for many decades, longer than he would live. And the same for food — tons of freeze-dried consumables for the crews of the lunar outposts. The onboard comp ran a quick simulation of the whole situation. The result: Navarro was the sole inhabitant of a miniature planet, a solipsistic ecosystem requiring minimal conservation and reuse. With no further complications, the planet called Supply Ship Number Three — "Planet Navarro, I thus name myself"— would support him comfortably, if without companionship, for the remainder of his life — another forty or fifty years or beyond, if he could endure it. Suddenly he was thankful he hadn't yet accepted the nearly-mandatory juvenano treatment; his Big Four-Oh was a few years away yet. Stuck in this small space for a hundred years or more was a fate he didn't want to contemplate.

Reading the floating cartoon-like *verch* numbers that spelled out his future, he grimly hoped that his wonderful cargo would be replaced by the *unucks*. Onboard Planet Navarro was food for thousands, and his karma shouldn't be burdened with the deprivation of sustenance from others.

Mama. She had introduced him to the concept of eventual retribution for every misdeed. "There are no accidents, Francisco," Mother had said, "Only circumstances that we ourselves planned before we entered this life."

"Like when my puppy was run over?" he'd asked. He didn't think he'd ever plan to kill his own *Tacito*, his nervous little Chihuahua. Certainly not by squishing the back half of his tiny body under a car wheel, while leaving the animal alive for two excruciating hours until they had returned home.

"Yes, dear. When you lived before, maybe in Atlantis, maybe in Egypt, you might have killed someone else's pet on purpose. Then in between lives, you realized you yourself must suffer; and so poor Tacito had to die." Little Francisco had broken down in tears, falling into his mother's open arms. "You see, my son, now you understand; you have paid for your past sins. That is what we call *karma*. And now you are free of that little bit of badness." She smiled.

Francisco wiped away his tears and stood facing his mother. "Okay, Mama, I guess I understand. But Mama," he sniffled, "what did *Tacito* do in *his* past life?"

"Go and play, Frankie," Mama replied tartly, getting to her feet. "Mama must meditate."

Navarro smiled at the memory; in her own way his mother had recognized the Second Law of Thermodynamics: *There ain't no such thing as a free lunch*. Of course, he didn't think that conservation of energy applied beyond the grave. Or as some wag in the previous millennium had put it, "He who dies with the most toys wins!" But, what if Mama had been right? What if the trajectories of Life and Death do inevitably lead to a balancing? What if there is a universal law of "Conservation of Karma," in which sentience itself is never created or destroyed, only transformed from one state to another? He would think on this matter in depth.

He had a world enough, and, maybe, even time.

*****

In the next twenty-four hours, the ship's computer grew more and more erratic, finally losing all audio response capability. Navarro found he couldn't even access the *verch* or audio. Before the system died, he had been able to locate the manual override control panel behind one flap of padding. But with one engine gone and the other probably damaged, there wasn't much to control. The defunct automatic control system was independent, but using manual only, it couldn't be brought into play for serious course correction.

And with the external video gone, he couldn't even see outside his cabin. Unless he wanted to put on the skinsuit and "visit Evita" — do extra-vehicular activities — he'd never witness the Outside again. He considered this: the skinny itself laid wallpaper-thin on one padded wall, a humyn-sized parody of a double paper-doll. All he had to do was press his body and arms against it, stroke its activation pad, and the mini- molecular sheet would insinuate itself by surface tension all over his body. Including his head; that was the part he hadn't liked during the two days of training to become a "Captain." With no intention of ever using it, he hadn't paid a lot attention to the briefing when the *verch*-linked instructor described the pressurized breathing pack and elimination system located in pads under his feet. All he knew was, this damn thing would wrap him up like an old-time condom and let him walk out in Space for a whole work shift — ten, twelve hours.

Evitas themselves were mostly hearsay, and he wasn't sure they were ever really done anymore, not with surface-accessing minibots to do vacuum labor. He hadn't heard of a real Evita this decade. The Loonies, of course, lived most of their miserable loony lives in near- permanent skinnies, but then their whole nearly-sterile world was vacuum-packed. Navarro had "trained" by *verch* simulation only, and stepping out into the Really, Really Infinite wasn't something he wanted to try yet. But, the thought kept returning: without video all he was getting was a system report from internal sensors. What if there were other parts of the ship, broken off but still close by in the debris cloud that accompanied the ship? What if there were rescue vessels right outside, unable to contact him because of the missing antennas? The emergency-aid tools included a small electronic telescope; once Outside at least he could use it to determine his location, maybe find a rescue ship coming toward him.

The thought excited him. Why not try it? There was nothing to lose, and maybe he could tell where he was, maybe work out some strategy for signaling for help. There was air enough, and the tiny amount lost in each use of the molecular airlock couldn't be measured (he remembered). Besides that, there were thousands of those skinnies, one layer atop another, spread against the wall there, just like those old- time ass-wipe-paper rolls. More than sufficient for daily excursions for years.

"Rama, rama, lama, lama, ding-dong," Navarro hummed as he spread-eagled himself against the body-outline on the padding. With his tongue he stroked a centimeter-square roughened panel on the skinny-half to his right. A brief flutter of angel's wings and he felt himself seal- wrapped in a skinsuit. Other than a pervasive hospital-like antiseptic odor, he felt no changes. Looking down at his body, only the faintest shimmer of transparent material revealed any difference, but thick black soles under his feet had made him at least ten centimeters taller. . An outside observer viewing him would have seen only a short, brown-skinned man dressed in a black stretch bodysuit, with the barest suggestion of a glistening aura swimming near his skin. Within seconds, the on-board instrumentation declared the skinny-suit sealed and operational. Taking the pen-sized telescope from its attach-pad, he smiled. "Let's go Outside, *cabrón*," he told himself, "and see Evita."

A stroke-pad adjacent to the skinny-suit location gave him access to the Outside. To Navarro, it was as if he had been teleported to the other side of the wall, though he knew that the molecular airlock had merely severed a section of wall, rotating him and the "floor" where he stood to the Outside, while taking the outside wall In. "*It's still much too magic to me*," he sang aloud, echoing a fairly new TechnoLudd air still popular in *El Sur*. He was happy to see that, as advertised, the skinny-suit didn't fog up inside when he talked or breathed.

The first view of Outside scared the hell out of him: *El Grande* Itself was still visible, a monstrous black body taking up half the sky, its full size revealed by glints of sunlight from various facets in its rough, metallic surface. It must be just kilometers away, if he recalled the size of it. "Whew, Tacito, I think I just about paid for *your* karma, *perrito!* Like to have got squashed by Big Mamacita, there." For an instant he panicked, worried about the swarm of particles still surrounding *El Grande* like bees around a hive. "No worry, self," he said aloud, for confidence, "looks like we're all orbiting Big *El*, there. Relative motion will keep us safe."

He turned to locate Earth and Moon, figuring that maybe if he could determine his location and velocity, he might somehow slingshot off Big *El* and by some miracle get close enough to be picked up by the Unuks. But Earth was nowhere in the sky; again panic set in. "She's on the other side of Big *El*," he gulped, "has to be." The Sun was not diminished in size, so

Trajectories of the Heart

Earth and Moon had to be around somewhere. Anxious and sweating he looked to the stars — Ursa Major? There! Relief; at least he wasn't in some damned parallel dimension or such nonsense as the spec-phi writers liked to dream up. The Southern Cross — there. Great! The same old Universe he'd known and loved. Something bothered him, he couldn't quite pin it down, but — there was Mother Earth!

A sudden thrill ran through him as the discs of Earth and Moon emerged from behind the bulk of Big *El*, and finally from outside the densest part of the speckled cloud of particles of which he and the ship were two. But something was wrong about their positions. What? He pulled up the telescope and zoomed in on Earth. There, to his satisfaction, the familiar blue and white exposed itself to view. But his mind couldn't register the familiar continental outlines. Mentally, he struggled to adjust the parallax. "My good lord Krishna," he exclaimed to the Universe at large, "I'm looking straight down at the North Pole!"

He stroked up his onboard comp to run some calculations. The answer he got back was impossible — he was a hundred thousand miles out of the Ecliptic! In twenty-four hours, he and his little planet, Supply Ship Number Three, had been taken — by Big *El*? — a distance halfway from Moon to Earth, but at right angles to the orbits of the planets around the Sun! "Holy shit," the thought came, and with it a resigned sadness, "I can't be rescued. No one has ever come this way before." And never would, he sighed.

＊＊＊＊＊

"This one is special, dearest," the Hindu fortune teller had told his mother, back down among his earliest memories. The lady was dark, not blonde and lovely like his own mother, and she was swaddled in layers of brightly colored cloth, with a red dot on her forehead and painted nails on fingers and toes. Her furniture-filled "reading room," stifling with overwhelming strata of incense layers, frightened him; he could barely breathe. And Frankie didn't like her, either, caring little for her prodding and probing, afraid of the continual tapping on his forehead. "Teach him the *kundalini*, dearest Dot," she told his mother, "though the crown *chakra* may remain closed to him, the *manipura*, the forehead, the third eye, this one will one day attain it."

Frankie looked to his mother for support, protection against this strange woman, but Mama only nodded. "Yes, Nani, the *chakras*. Unleash the *kundalini*, let him experience the world as it is, not this horrible veil of illusion!" Mama's eyes glistened with otherworldly visions. Frankie, simply, was terrified.

"The way you access the Universal Power, Francisco," Mama said, "is to feel the nodes along your body. These are arranged along the Rod of Brahma." Frankie did his best to sit still, mimicking his mother's cross-legged stance, trying to ignore the overwhelming odor of lavender incense in their small, Persian carpet-walled apartment. "The base *chakra*, the *muladhara*, is the bottom one. Pay attention, my dear son. The first lesson to learn is one of posture, which we call *asana*." Followed by cross-legged meditation. "We shall now learn *mudra*, or the sacred science of hand gestures." The memories tumbled out, like childhood blocks from a bucket of tiny toys. "*Mantra* — our secret, sacred chant. *Pranayama*. Feel the flow of the Universe from without, from within, Francisco. Breathe the breath of Lives Beyond." Frankie wished he didn't have to breathe the incense.

The sessions had been interminable, at least in Navarro's memory, though his mother's handwritten records indicated just one hour a day. *For five years*, he recalled, *half of my childhood years, nearly two thousand hours of training*. It became a childhood game, his and Mama's: "*Asana, mudra, mantra*," Mama would chant, smiling. "*Pranayama, trataka, yantra*," he would answer with a feigned frown. "*Dharana!*" they would shout together, laughing.

And so, in his early years, Francisco Navarro had practiced the techniques of *kundalini* yoga, how to open himself to the true powers of the Universe. A simple childhood game, with a lasting effect on his life. He still despised even the slightest wisp of lavender, but his mind had a way of causing him to smell it in times of stress. *Like almost getting killed* by El Grande!

When his Mama died, Daddy and Daddy's Wife had taken Frankie away from Santa Fe and into the high-tech hills of nearby Los Alamos Verdes, the military-industrial complex that spent the decades before Cold War Two expiating the original sin of Atomic Doom. In the heady environment of the first Green Lab, where former nuclear weaponeers turned their expertise to peacefully heading off the Resource War, Frank Navarro found his early meditative training perfectly suited for the equally exhausting and exhaustive disciplines of mathematics, computer science and astrophysics.

But after a promising start online with Berkeley-*verch*, something metaphysical had clicked inside him, and his interests swung back more or less toward the burgeoning Post-Millennialist Movement in Santa Fe. There had been an important girl somewhere in that PMM experience, but her face was long lost in the kaleidoscope of memories — sensoweb surfing, *verch* sex, simulated drugs, zip-music, maglev skiing, a typical adultlescent absorption with all the toys of the Third Millennium. And so it was that years later, in early middle age, when the experimental PMM associations all predictably went bust, he'd had to fall back on his bachelor's degree in physics, and wound up doing grunt work as the sole union-required humyn "Captain" on a routine *Lee-Oh* to *Lune-Oh* cargo run, with good pay, minimal responsibilities, and no future.

Especially now, he thought. Safely back inside the cabin, he stroked the skinny-suit to "Off," watching disinterestedly as it flowed down his body, onto the floor and into a waste receptacle for recycling. *How do you recycle something just a few molecules thick, anyway?* he wondered without really caring. He watched with amusement as the thick-soled breather boots osmosed over to a receptacle, disappearing into the padded wall.

The fact of his eventual lonely death ate at him. Not that it was an imminent death, nor necessarily even an uncomfortable one. In the cargo he had sustenance sufficient for a lifetime, many lifetimes. But to be alone for decades, could he stand it? He thought of Mama's awe- struck stories of saints, mystics, ascetics, those who had lived voluntary lives of isolation, all the better spiritually for tuning in to the Voice of God. And there were prisoners, too, locked up in dungeons for fifty years or more, without human companionship. *They* had lived, hadn't they? But then, they always knew that some other living being, another man or woman, was never more than a few feet away, even if they never saw or heard them. Which was better, he wondered? Isolation forced or isolation volunteered? But none of these greats, these Ascended Masters, these noble martyrs in prisons, had ever been sent out away from Mother Earth Herself, had ever died alone in the void between the stars. He shivered at the prospect.

Somewhere in the next few days, he found enough sleep to keep his body rested, even though his mind was feverish. "Can't panic-oh, *mi amigo,*" he talked to himself aloud, just to hear a human voice. He hadn't been able to get the ship to repair itself completely, and the verch and audio were still inoperable; there was no other sound but himself. "Not even a guitar to sing to myself," he complained again. His onboard comp might be configured to output acceptable audio, and even possibly access some of the thousands of entertainment modules such supply ships carried as standard time-killers for their "captains." But he decided to save that for later; one had to have something to look forward to, some kind of anticipated novelty over the decades. He would allow himself, he decided, one new song or one new audio book reading segment every other month. Perhaps the anticipation would allow him to endure the imprisonment. Above all, he had to retain his sanity until, Krishna willing, maybe some year he would be detected by other humans and maybe even rescued.

Using the comp and what software he could download from the damaged ship's memory, he computed his options. A tiny three- dimensional plot emerged forth from the small palmsized flatscreen, displaying the set of probabilities that determined, literally, the possible trajectories of his future. He whistled at the dismaying results. "Somewhere between zero and *nada, amigo*. Achieving capture orbits from where we are, breaking loose from *El Grande*, getting back into the Earth or Moon gravity wells, at our weird inclination, just can't be done. Not even if both our engines were attached and the ship was in perfect shape."

The tiny, broken, virtual spaceship whizzed down first one blood-red path, then another, like a wounded insect unable to find its nest. At best, it shot by the model Earth and Moon across the Ecliptic without a possibility of capture. "And with only the *Lune-Oh* engine, what really is reality?" The red trajectories retraced themselves across the locked orbit of Earth and its natural satellite; unfortunately, both objects were hundreds of thousands of miles away by then. "Like missing the train, *pendejo*, we get to the right tracks but the caboose is disappearing from view." He breathed heavily and blinked his eyes to shut down the *verch*. "No matter what we do, *amigo*, we truly can't go home again. Not even close."

* * * * *

"Had to have been the effects of the gravitation, first of the cloud, then of Big *El*, that pulled me out of my trajectory, then dragged me along with it." The next day, Navarro's mood had improved enough to try to determine what had happened, maybe something to gain some insight about his predicament, maybe something the comp hadn't considered when analyzing possible return trajectories. The comp and the *verch* output showed that an abrupt delta-vee out of the Ecliptic would have smashed the ship and jellied its human cargo. The fact that Navarro was still living was testimony that that hadn't happened, so some kind of fortunate vector arithmetic had saved him, even as it broke the back of the ship.

After a week of Evitas, viewing with the telescope, watching as Big *El* took him ever further from his home, Navarro announced to himself, "Gotta do something, *el self*, before Big *Chingaso* out there takes me so far away from the sun that I freeze." He was lying to himself, of course. His comp told him that adjusting the plumbing of the modified tokamak in the *Lune-Oh* engine would provide enough power and heat for close to forever. But Navarro didn't want to die out of sight of Earth, and wouldn't admit that fear to himself. "One shot we got, *cabronito*," he told his image in the mirror. "To separate from Big *El*, out yonder, and go our own way, back toward El Sol, back to the sun and the sand and the beaches of *Isla Mujeres*."

He'd been in his early twenties when he had found his late mother's handwritten logs in a Santa Fe lockbox, the records of his kundalini training, the diaries of their frequent trips to places mystic and strange. To the hoaxed crop circles in Europe, to many of the megalithic stone circles scattered in magical networks in many lands, to the truly mysterious monuments unearthed from the deep ice in central Antarctica, to the disassembled Great Pyramid where its New Islamic destructors were still selling off its heavy blocks to the foolish infidels. And to *Isla Mujeres*, lying off the Turquoise Coast of Mexico, land of butterflies and palms, ocean and sky. Among his unformed memories, populating his earliest dreams, a young Frankie had matured with the ideal of palm-strewn white beaches as his vision of Paradise. And no wonder: his mother lovingly described the two years they'd lived on that small, primitive island as a complete family. With the love of his mother and the forgotten attention of his father, the first two years of his life had been a child's Paradise.

Her diaries told him that much; his childhood dreams had been real. At age twenty-three, an educated, wiser and world-weary Frank Navarro read his mother's writings and recognized many of his own longings for the love of a father. There had been companionship at Los Alamos Verdes, but no real emotional attachment between father and son. A grown, mature person, he had cried over his discoveries, and over his realization of his losses.

"Still love the beaches, the sand, the surf," *The sex*, his mind filled in, much to his displeasure. Yes, there had been that, too, each time he'd returned to *Isla Mujeres*. The movie-set beauty of the region, his own Latino features set off by his Anglo-inherited baby-blue eyes, had often carried him to ultimate pleasures among the sands and in the turquoise waters.

He tried to shake off the image; *that* was never going to happen again. And without even the *verch* for electronic stimulation, he faced a bleak future there, indeed. *El mano*, he snorted. *Mierda!*

*****

With a silent explosion of fusion power, Planet Navarro kicked out of orbit around Big *El* and headed toward *El Sol*. "*Yee-hah!* We're going home, *compadres!*" Navarro shouted out in the empty cabin. He had wanted to ride out the launch on the Outside, but the thought of those billions of deadly sandicles out there forced him to stay inside. "For one day, *cabrón*, then I go to see Evita!"

In one last-gasp effort, over a period of a week he had disconnected the *Lune-Oh* engine from its end of the broken Rod of Brahama, and had used the remaining minibots to reconnect it to the other end of Planet Navarro, with a breakaway structure that could be blown apart with explosive bolts. This he had adapted from a standard cargo-ejection system the ship carried for emergency use only. He figured that the *Lune-Oh*, hot-rodded up to its maximum thrust, would be sufficient to boost him and the ship away from Big *El* and its fellow travelers, back along the trajectory they'd come in the last fourteen days. The angles and the delta-vee were all wrong to insert him back into the Ecliptic, but at least he might be able to take up an orbit closer to the sun, maybe he would make enough "smoke signals" that Earth would take notice, and someday, some year, they'd come pick him up. He had nothing but time left.

For a day, it worked. Standing outside as Planet Navarro left Big *El*, observing as the plume from *Lune-Oh* splayed its ejection mass in a kilometers-wide plasma plume, he prayed, "Lord Krishna, Mother Mary, Quetzalcoatl, all you gods out there, let this get me close to home is all I ask." In an event that caused him never again to tempt the gods, as he spoke those words, the top half of the broken Rod of Brahma, responding to a full day's two-gee acceleration and the accompanying forces and vibrations, quietly detached itself from Planet Navarro and spun off into space. Navarro was facing backwards and noticed the surge in acceleration as half the mass of his world no longer took up part of the engine's thrust. As he watched in awe, the porcupine junkyard forward of his Captain's cabin slid by, barely missing him. Involuntarily, he tried to jump but his gripping shoes held him securely.

The Broken Rod rotated and slammed into the *Lune-Oh* breakaway section. To Navarro's horror, *Lune-Oh*, now relieved of its burdensome duty of pushing thousands of tons of mass, accelerated, breaking free of the Rod and shooting past him, its forward scaffold structure catching the rear end of the Broken Rod. The accelerating engine and mounting assembly careened out into Space, end over end, away from El Sol, away from Planet Navarro. A dwindling star, the Lunar Orbit Insertion Engine and its accompanying girders twinkled one last time, many klicks in the distance, and vanished forever. Automatic ACS jets puffed silently into space, canceling out the spin of the remaining spine of his home.

Powerless, hopeless, far from home, the one-man planet settled into an orbit of loneliness.

After a day of despondency in the cabin, Navarro visited Evita again and, taking measurements with the telescope, re-computed his orbit: he was still out of the Ecliptic some thirty degrees, his nearest approach to the Sun would eventually be between the orbits of Mars and the Asteroid Belt, far from the reach of the UN ships, possessing an impossible-to-match velocity. His furthest distance from the sun, aphelion, was out toward the orbit of Jupiter. By accessing the remaining ship's memory, he determined that the cabin heating system, working from the still intact tokamak power supply, could maintain a livable temperature inside. He had verified that the remaining cargo containers he now opened by hand-crank contained food enough that he would never starve. The oxygen-generating autochemlab hadn't been damaged by any of the traumas his Planet had experienced. Overall, physically, his animal needs were well provided for.

There had been times in his life that he would have called his present situation enviable: no responsibilities, nothing that had to be done. But there was also almost nothing to do, very little to listen to — he still hadn't had the courage to discover whether the comp would play audio recordings — nothing to read, nothing to *verch*. Navarro eventually discovered, as had many of those ascetics, mystics, martyrs and prisoners that Mama used to speak highly of, that the internal Universe of his memories was opening up.

And along the way, he recalled the happier days and the games of his youth. Kundalini games, meditation times.

In frightened solitude, Francisco Navarro remembered Mama.

*****

The yoga meditation position, *asana*, was a piece of cake in zero-gee. *Prana*, breathing, was also much enhanced in the pure atmosphere of his cabin, kept free of pollution by the system's recycling nanofilters. Navarro was sure that the other steps, dutifully but lovingly memorized in those long-ago sessions in the ashram at the base of the Sangre de Cristo mountains, would come naturally. *What was that Mama had said about the chakras, those nodes in the body that interface with the Universal Powers? What have I got to lose?* He smiled at his predicament, trying to put the unpleasant reality out of his mind. *At thirty million miles perigee, twenty million miles from any planetary body for all Eternity, I'm the most Ascendant Master there ever was!*

Hours later, he was seriously into the meditative state and unaware of self.

Asana. mudra, mantra.

"Posture, gesture, chant," Navarro whispered aloud. Almost involuntarily his body had assumed the lotus position, repeating the secret gestures his mother had drilled into him, as his mind echoed the silent chant he had learned so well.

Pranayama, trataka, yantra.

"Breathe the Lives Beyond, focus on the Third Eye, visualize the Enneagram," Mama cooed softly in memory.

Dharana!

"Concentrate on the Bliss Within, await the Resplendent Void," he whispered in awe. Within him, near the base of his spine, the Rod of Brahma stirred. And from out of somewhere, the faintest whiff of lavender drifted by.

*****

Asana. mudra, mantra. Pranayama, trataka, yantra. Dharana! One year.

Navarro mastered his memories, able to enjoy those of his birth and early life near the Sea, selecting those metaphysical lessons Mama had taught, never suspecting that little Frankie would be practicing them out beyond Mars. Or had she? Was she near now, swimming the streams of stars? Navarro felt the prana as the breath of Life of the Universe swirled

Trajectories of the Heart

within him. Strange energies surged within his genitals, his base organs. The *muladhara* chakra, he remembered. *Things are happening.*

There were chimes.

* * * * *

Asana. mudra, mantra. Pranayama, rataka,yantra.

Two years.

Voices spoke, becoming shrill cries, enticing sirens waiting on the shoals of disbelief, ready to drag him under, should he falter. With *dharana*, their wails withered to the mere susurrus of subsiding seas.

Amidst the nearly-continuous meditations, Navarro discovered that he could move his body from point to point within the confines of his padded Universe, using only his mind. Thus uncovering his first *sidhi*, a predictable byproduct of his kundalini meditations, Navarro found that such levitation meant very little to him. *Sidhis*, Mama had warned, were mere baubles that distract One from the greater treasures ahead, on the Path. *Sushumna*, the central channel, running along the Rod of Brahma, is that path, the Way. With a benign smile, Navarro assumed that "the Truth" and "the Life" were the other two channels, ida and pingala.

He wondered, *And do they converge, Trinity becoming Unity, like Father, Son, and Holy Spirit, when they meet in the* sahasrara, *the crown chakra?*

He smiled again. At least this useless development — zero-gee levitation, what an *oxymoron!* — meant he was on the Right Path.

* * * * *

Asana. mudra, mantra. Pranayama, rataka,yantra. Dharana!

Three years.

By now, Navarro sensed each of the chakras in his body, could almost see the iridescent swirls of extra dimensional energies that flowed into his body from Otherspace as he focused attention — *dharana!* — on each, successively. He began to sense that each of the *chakras* interfaced with different energies, perhaps even different Universes. New odors, new colors, new sounds, new senses that made little sense. Any doubts he had once had, that his solitude might be manifesting as illusory hallucinations, were subsumed in the exhilarating newness.

He was still intellectually curious, but the experiences overwhelmed the curiosity as wonder after wonder came into view, and he witnessed them all with new eyes and newer senses.

Trajectories

＊＊＊＊＊

Four years.

Navarro controlled the rising serpent of the kundalini, sensed its tentative, almost modest, approach to the Rod of Brahma, felt it entwine the pathways of the chakras. Felt the Spirit rise. Emotions, he now knew, could be excised, arranged, displayed, reviewed dispassionately when required. They were never required.

The *kundalini* was his friend, his one companion. And he its.

Each day of existence was pure delight.

＊＊＊＊＊

Five years.

By now, Navarro sensed energy flowing from the multi- dimensional Universe to each of his *chakras*; he controlled the ethereal flow and manipulated the shifting patterns that defined the phenomena. The Hindu fortuneteller had been right all those years ago, he realized. Each of his lower nodes had opened, all the way up to the third eye. Colors, odors, sounds and other unimaginable sensory stimulations poured in as the *kundalini* meditations increasingly sensitized his attunement to undreamed-of energies.

A new being was arising from the psychic ashes of the old. Serpent-fire glowed in Navarro's composite being, and that new being luxuriated in the new-found glory.

＊＊＊＊＊

Six years.

Navarro controlled each *chakra* at will, allowing the sensual flavors of the base chakra occasionally to permeate himself, keeping his physical desires ever so tantalizingly unfulfilled. He ate little; he excreted almost nothing; his bodily functions slowed to unnatural rhythms. Ecstasy bloomed at will, and peace was never more than seconds away. In all this time, he had never attempted to access the comp audio.

＊＊＊＊＊

Seven years.

Navarro, now comfortable with his new abilities, unafraid and unchallenged, allowed the Serpent full range of his body.

Instantly, his consciousness expanded to the edges of his tiny Universe, experiencing a momentary dislocation as part of himself emerged into the

Trajectories of the Heart

Outside. He had vision, but more importantly, Vision. An icily intellectual portion of his mind insisted that he must be sensing the full range of the spectrum, from the sharpness of hard X-rays to the dull thunderings of background radiation that were the mating-calls of galaxies. The newly-awakened sectors of Navarro's consciousness, however, accepted the experience as the birth of enlightenment, the emergence of the soul into its natural element.

Pulling himself back into the cozy comfort of the captain's cabin, Navarro was at peace with himself, a golden aura suffusing the volume of his living space. Soon he would be ready.

* * * * *

"Lord Krishna," Navarro announced to himself and to the Universe one morning eight years into his enforced solitude and rigorous meditation, "I am ready to jump the Wheel, to swim the cosmic courses of the streams of stars." In memory, Mama repeated that phrase, that promise. And he allowed the pungent memory of lavender to flow into his nostrils, finally understanding the *otherness* of that plant's odor, something not expressible in human language. After his years in intense meditation, alone as no human before had ever experienced, Navarro felt himself in touch in the All, the power of the Serpent of the *kundalini* uncoiling itself, each of the *chakras* opening up in their specified sequence. "All but the Crown *Chakra*," he said softly, "and only Krishna, Buddha, and the Christ ever achieved that, and then by direct Divine bestowal." Clad only in a breechcloth, he stood next to the airlock and commanded it to open. He was not wearing a skinnysuit.

For all these years, Reality, to Navarro, had been the deadly void outside his tiny world. In a fugue state of complete isolation, day after unending day of exercise, meditation, contemplation and prayer, endless months of constant chanting and prayers, utilizing every meditative technique and practice he had ever been exposed to, he had conditioned himself totally to immersion within the All.

His tentative meditative expeditions Outside were either a new reality, or total hallucination. Either he was ready to transition to the Infinite Union now, as he believed he would, or else he would die, naked and alone, in Space. He was prepared for either, prepared for both, and sensed that perhaps both choices were in actuality only One.

The airlock wall winked; Francisco Navarro instantly found himself, suitless, alone and unprotected in naked Void. To the left and right he surveyed the wreckage of his small rod-shaped world as the Universe slowly wheeled around. He was at the center of Creation. He smiled; surely Lord Krishna would take him now and he could immediately enjoy the companionship of gods. But a full minute passed and he felt no transitioning to another plane, certainly not the pain of asphyxiation or vacuum explosion. *I'm not dying*, he complained silently, surprised at the negativity of his own observation. Holding up his arms in prayer, he shouted to the Universe, "I am ready. Be as One with me!" Shocked, he *heard* his own voice.

"Not in a vacuum! What's happening?" He blinked his eyes, praying that this was not yet one more of the hallucinations that had dogged his meditative progress the first couple of years. Mama had said that some visions and impressions were merely agents of delay, obstacles to be overcome by faith and proper meditation. Yes, there had been those, by the multitudes: naked women, sultry women, even some attractive men, demons of his lower *chakras* tempting him until he conquered them all by the *mantra* and the *yantra* and unceasing chants and prayers. "*Dharana!*" he yelled, once more hearing himself.

But this was no hallucination, no demon-swarm from resistant physical organs. This was old-time physical Reality. He was still alive in raw Vacuum, and he could hear himself talk! As his heartbeat slowed from its moment of panic, a pale golden glow, at first so subtle as to require intense concentration to see, suffused his field of view in all directions, extending far beyond the half-kilometer of the ruined ship that was his World. He turned, looked upwards and downwards, even toward the Sun. The Glow surrounded him, becoming more visible as he considered its impossibility. Navarro blew breath against one hand, felt its mass and warmth. "Lord Krishna, there is atmosphere here. That's why I can hear myself out loud. Am I already passed over, living in another dimension? Have I exited through a *chakra*?" But the surrounding Universe, beyond the Glow, appeared as dark and unforgiving as before.

Even in utter confusion and disorientation, Navarro dared not return into his cabin, that cocoon of so many years of lonely, enforced meditation. To do so would be a retreat. The gods had given him a new chance, existence in Space itself. He gulped audibly and pushed his bare feet against the ship.

He *flew*.

Trajectories of the Heart

With an increasingly bright golden glow that surrounded him for a half-million kilometers, a tenuous sphere of energy bright enough to register on optical instruments on the Moon and Earth itself, the cosmic dandelion that was Francisco Navarro flew purposively away from the remains of Supply Ship Three, Planet Navarro, and swam among the primal debris of the Asteroid Belt.

"I'm beyond the orbit of Mars, all alone in Space, and I'm alive," he shouted, "is this what Death is, to fly freely in the heavens, to enjoy the marvels of Creation?" Somehow he doubted that the state of metaphysical Death would require breathing and an audible voice. "Mama," he cried, "You were right! We *do* swim the cosmic courses among the streams of stars!" He had never known such joy.

Thud! To his left he felt an impact; soft, not painful, but an impact nevertheless. Willing himself to stop, he examined what first appeared to be something near his outstretched left arm. "What have we here, *amigo?*" A chunk of cratered rock floated nearby. No, not nearby: it was hundreds of kilometers away, but he *sensed* it as though it were close. "My sensory perimeter, my nöosphere, has extended," he said softly, "I flex my hand and stroke the sky."

Withdrawing his *anglorium* — his new name for the golden cloud that now re-defined his interface with the Universe — Navarro willed himself to move. "I wonder why the Ascended Masters never described such a sensation," he thought. Then one of his early observations came back to him: *To get to a place like this, they had to die first! I am the first human to Ascend while still alive, because I became Enlightened all alone, out in Space! No gravity, no magnetic field, uncontaminated!*

Truly uncontaminated? he wondered, *or merely* uninterrupted?

Thoughts rushed by kaleidoscopically; but speaking to himself condensed that chaos into an understandable solidity of focus. Navarro willed himself stopped again. "I tell myself I am stopped, but what is that relative to? The Sun, the Earth? Some external reference point? Can't be stationary relative to everything." The thought of Earth brought back longings he had suppressed for all those years of loneliness. Where was Mother Earth? A new instinct told him where to look. "Near the Sun from here," he whispered, "and less than a hundred million miles. Can I fly—" hesitating to complete the thought, he urged himself forward.

An erotic itching, a near-orgasm, began building along the route linking his chakras, and Navarro willed it to climax. The serpent of *kundalini* uncoiled and sprang upwards.

Navarro cried aloud as first one *chakra*, then another, erupted forth its torrent of cosmic orgasmic energies, catapulting him through sequential cataclysmic explosions of indescribable sounds, sights, impressions, ecstasy upon ecstasy. All he could think of as he gasped was, *Each chakra is accessing a different Universe! These hypothetical centers, these vortices, are the body's connections to each of those seven unused dimensions above our normal four! No one ever thought of that before!* And finally, as the tempo increased to a shrieking crescendo of Realities, *When will it stop?*

Serpent-fire erupted from his glowing body, spiraling in a myriad of red vortices outward in all directions. An explosion of undreamed-of ecstasy expanding in his head, Navarro held desperately to one last rational thought. He thought of Mama, smelled lavender.

Around him, the Universe *changed*.

*****

Darkness.

His tongue licked warm, salty sand, and a butterfly tickled his eyelashes. Navarro luxuriated in the repeated kiss of liquid wavelets as they lightly brushed his feet, then receded, leaving scant seconds to dry in the hot sunlight. He rolled over and sighed. *Like when I was a baby, with Mama and Daddy here on Isla Mujeres.*

Here? *Where am I?*

Jerking himself upright, Navarro washed sand from his eyes and found himself sitting on the white sands of a tropical beach, a turquoise sea reaching to the horizon, lapping at his feet. In the distance, the stark towers and piers of a Mexican naval base confirmed his suspicion. "*Isla Mujeres*, Mother of God!" he swore under his breath, "If this is a hallucination, then, praise Krishna, let me stay here forever!"

He moved down from the beach several meters into the surf, waist-deep, nearly insane with joy at the sensations of grit and water and salt and sun. Waves welcomed him back to Earth, as the mother planet rocked him in the bosom of the world ocean. Finally, smiling, Navarro found his footing and stood erect in the surf, waving both arms in triumph. "I did it, *amigo*! I found my way home!" As he walked back toward the beach, waves washed his legs, the warm kisses of a lost lover.

Trajectories of the Heart

Looking around for the first time, Navarro realized that he wasn't alone — horrified bathers, several dozen of them in a half-circle just meters away, were pointing at him. Some were speaking into their wristers. "*Hola, compadres*, I'm Francisco Navarro, home from Space! Aren't you glad to see me?" But as he waved his arms, Navarro could see that the golden glow he'd acquired in Space was still with him. Dense now, a thick golden cloud, extending outwards many meters, enveloping the nearest onlookers, fading in the distance. "Oh," he said apologetically, "I can see why you're frightened. Please forgive me."

As the crowd backed off in mixed fear and awe, Navarro let himself settle into the lotus position in the shallow water, luxuriating in the caresses of the sea around his chest, the smells of salt and spray. In meditation, his golden aura spread out further and further, driving away most of the frightened onlookers. But a few remained, participating in the ecstasy of Navarro's radiation. Many crossed themselves, knelt, and began to sob in unrestrained joy.

The unceasing surf, warm and sensuous, lapped Navarro's unresisting body, again and again,

He was Home.

Trajectories

THE ADVENTURES OF STAR BLAZER
by John F. Allen

So far we've seen several possible futures, both near and far. John F. Allen shares a retro vision, one in which a man whose voice must remain muted in 1950's America finds himself transported to another reality, where an unexpected path toward heroism unfolds.

John F. Allen is an American writer born in Indianapolis, IN. He writes in various speculative fiction genres as well as working as a comic book writer. John's debut novel, *The God Killers*, was published in 2013 by Seventh Star Press, he has several short stories published in various anthologies, and is currently scripting a seven-issue comic book mini-series for All Knightz Publications out of the UK.

John currently resides in Indianapolis, Indiana with his family.

■■■■■■

August, 1959
Los Angeles, California

"Caution, Brick Sullivan, caution!" the Automaton blared.

A tall, dashing figure emerged from swirling clouds of smoke. He surveyed the room and spotted a prone woman on the floor a few feet ahead. He removed a shiny, full face helmet with a backward facing fin to reveal piercing, hazel eyes, dirty blond hair and a pencil thin moustache. He wore a brown leather tunic with a gold star emblem which consisted of a large gem emblazoned in its center, light gray trousers and black riding boots.

"Never fear A.T.O.M., I'm no stranger to danger," the man replied with a cheeky smile.

He stepped forward, leaned down and pulled the listless woman into his arms. Her eyes fluttered before they opened wide in a panicked expression.

"Oh Brick, thank heavens you've arrived! I thought I'd surely die at the hands of your arch enemy, the space pirate, Dark Kang!"

"Cut!"

The room was flooded with lights and a short bald man smoking a cigar strode towards them. "How many times do we hafta go over this, Wilma, its Ming Ki-Khan, Dark Kang is the villain from last week's episode!"

"I'm sorry, Mr. Goldstein, I guess I'm just nervous," the blond haired woman said.

Goldstein frowned and threw his hands into the air. "That's it for tonight, we'll wrap up tomorrow at 7 AM sharp. Don't be late or you're fired!"

Kofi Zedi watched as the crew dispersed from the set. He'd recently been hired as a production assistant by Ed Goldstein.

Groans from the cameramen and set workers filled the room as they abandoned their posts with scowls and angry gestures. The smoke started to recede, although the residual meandered across the set in thin clouds.

The lead actor, Henry Barlow, released the actress, who fell to the floor with a thud. He stormed across the set to catch up with Goldstein.

"Listen here, Ed, this is the umpteenth take we've had to do with this new broad, and she can't get a damn thing right. Can't we just sound edit her line with Darcy's voice?"

Goldstein stopped and turned. Despite the nearly one foot difference in their height, Barlow took a step back from the shorter man, who stabbed his right index finger into his chest.

"You listen here, Barlow, if you hadna been screwing around on Darcy to begin with, we wouldn't have had to replace her in the first place. And furthermore, I don't give a rat's ass how big of a star you think you are now or how many contracts you have with the big studios, you owe me the last two episodes of The Adventures of Star Blazer and you better deliver, or else."

Barlow narrowed his gaze. "Or else what?"

"Or else I'll sue your ass," Goldstein said as he pulled the cigar from his mouth and blew smoke into Barlow's face.

"You wouldn't dare." Barlow stammered.

"Wouldn't I? You may be rubbin shoulders with some hotshot Hollywood producers, Golden Boy, but you best remember where you came from and not try ta weasel your way out of our contract."

Barlow's eyes widened at Goldstein's threat before the director turned and walked away. "I'll remember this, Ed! One day I'll be walking amongst the stars, and you'll see. I bet you'll be begging me to play lead in one of your crappy, low budget projects then."

"Kofi!" Barlow yelled.

The tall young black man made his way towards Barlow. "Yes, Mr. Barlow?"

Barlow had peeled off his tunic and thrust it and his helmet at Kofi. "I want you to polish the helmet and personally dry-clean the tunic."

Kofi nodded. "Yes, sir," he said before he walked away.

He had been fifteen years old when he'd met Barlow almost a decade ago. His father was a tour guide in Tanzania who happened to have led the safari Barlow had commissioned. On that expedition, his father died saving Barlow's life from a group of gem raiders, in search of a fabled stone called the Star Blazer. It was this story which led to the title of the television program and source of Barlow's newfound status.

In return, Barlow had taken Kofi in as his guardian, used him as a valet and hired him out as a set extra from time to time. Recently, Mr. Goldstein saw Kofi's work ethic and decided to make him a permanent production assistant.

Kofi couldn't really complain, he was treated with more respect than Barlow treated his women, but that wasn't saying much. Nonetheless, he had his own dreams of one day being an actor like Harry Belafonte, his cinema idol. He read Barlow's scripts and sometimes acted out his part after everyone else had gone home.

Once he was off the set floor, he made his way to Barlow's dressing room and closed the door. He knew that the show's star would be "busy" with the new girl, Wilma, and he'd be alone. Kofi put on the Star Blazer tunic and decided not to stop there. Kofi switched out his own slacks and shoes for one of Barlow's extras.

Once he was fully garbed as Star Blazer, he stood in front of a full length mirror and smiled. Of course he knew the idea of a Negro man starring in a science fiction film was absurd; but he was nothing if not a dreamer. Kofi had received training as a child in African sword fighting with the ancient *seme* swords, so he took the prop attached to the uniform belt and assumed a battle stance.

"You'll never take me alive, alien scum!" he said, taking in his reflection.

Kofi blinked as his image in the mirror appeared to shimmer. He had been working for sixteen hours straight and attributed this mirage to being tired. As he turned to walk away, a bright light flashed in the corner of his eye. Kofi turned back to the mirror, which rippled like water in a pond.

My eyes must be playing tricks on me, he thought.

He couldn't believe what he saw and cautiously approached the mirror.

Is this some sort of special effect prop?

The light flashed again from within the mirror's surface. Kofi leapt back with a start, as tendrils of light reached out and grasped him. He struggled to free himself, but to no avail. He started to yell out for help and found himself pulled into the light before he could utter a sound.

*****

The Andromeda Star System
In the distant future…

Sharp pain assaulted Kofi's head. He tried to move, but found himself frozen in place. He strained with all his might and managed to make his eyelids flutter.

"Hey, he's waking up," a voice shouted.

Kofi opened his eyes to the blurry image of a small green face staring at him. It appeared to be a cat of some sort and it sat on his chest.

"Where am I?"

The cat stared at him with a wide grin for a few more seconds before he yelled, "Guys, he's waking up!"

Kofi knew he had to be dreaming because cats weren't green, they weren't capable of grinning, and more importantly, they couldn't talk.

A warm sensation coursed through his body as his ability to move returned. He reached up to grab the cat off of him.

"Hey, whatta ya doin', ya big ape? Get your stinkin' paws off me!"

The cat hissed as Kofi flung the animal away and sat up. The room resembled the set of Star Blazer, only much more colorful and elaborate.

His eyes zeroed in on the cat, and he couldn't believe his eyes. The feline was dressed in a blue jumpsuit, miniature military boots and stood upright like a human. It reared its back and snarled at him. Its front paws were shaped like human hands and it held a large scalpel.

"You take it easy there, partner, I don't want things to get any more ugly than they already are," the cat stammered.

Kofi's mind raced at what he saw. How could this be real?

Trajectories

He heard a soft whoosh and movement caught his peripheral vision before he turned. Three people entered the room through an automated door, much like the ones in the fancy markets in Beverly Hills.

"Sacred Shamkaar, the prophecies have come to life!" a lavender-skinned woman exclaimed. She was strikingly beautiful, with long dark purple hair tied into a ponytail. She wore a black jumpsuit beneath silver gleaming armor. The hilts of two large swords extended above her shoulders from her back.

Behind her, to the left, stood a hulking humanoid creature Kofi estimated to be about seven feet tall. It was bald with dark blue skin and chains wrapped tightly around its massive forearms and wore a skintight sleeveless red jumpsuit and black boots. His face bore a menacing scowl with glowing opaque silver eyes.

On her right stood a simple humanoid creature with skin that appeared to be hewn from solid granite, smooth gray with flecks of white and black. Its face had no features other than large black eyes and a slit for a mouth. This creature stood nearly a half foot taller than the first, yet was equally as massive.

"What the hell happened to me? Where am I? And who the hell are you folks?"

The woman kneeled with a bowed head. "You have been transported from a time long ago and from a faraway galaxy to fulfill a great destiny. You are in the Andromeda Galaxy, we are the Space Sentinels and you are the Star Blazer."

Deafening silence lingered in the air.

"My name is Kofi Zedi. Star Blazer is a character on a television program."

The lavender skinned female slowly raised her head. She placed her fist on her chest before she spoke. "I am Kalamura, former princess of Valkaar, on the planet Burkah. The large, blue skinned warrior to my right is Epic, last of the Titans. The green furred mammal to your left is Booster, of Ailuros. And behind me is Petros, the last of an unknown species. You are aboard our starship, the Helios."

"Why did you take me from my planet and bring me here?"

Kalamura looked to the others and back to Kofi. "Every two thousand years, an anomalous event in the time/space continuum occurs, called the Conflux. We sought to secure and protect the sacred gem. It was prophesized that an ebon skinned stranger from another world would become caretaker of the Star Blazer."

Booster slowly stood to his full one-meter height and approached Kofi. "What the purple princess isn't telling you is that this basically means it's now your job to protect the entire universe from all the forces which threaten it. Of course, we were just gonna chop it up and sell the smaller gems on the black market, but what are ya gonna do?"

Kalamura gave Booster a fierce glare. "What, you want me to lie to the caretaker?"

Kofi's mind raced. This was like elements of the television program had come true.

A thunderous boom accompanied by the entire room quaking snapped Kofi from his reverie. "What was that?"

Kalamura stood and strode past him to a large control panel and a view screen. A huge space ship appeared, the likes of which Kofi could never have imagined. It resembled a naval ship with large wings like a commercial airplane.

"It's the Sojourn! Gar-Lan and his marauders must be aware that we have the Star Blazer in our possession," Kalamura said.

Booster was next to her reading from a smaller screen in another console. "Our shields are at 65%, another hit like that and we're going to be in trouble."

"He's hailing us," Epic said.

The image of the ship was replaced with that of an odd looking creature with red scaled skin, large black opaque eyes and tentacles where a mouth should have been. "You mercenaries think that you could swindle Gar-Lan out of one of the most powerful prizes in the universe? Release the primitive life-form to my custody and I might spare your miserable lives. Otherwise, I will surely destroy you!"

Booster hopped onto the console and stared at Gar-Lan and pointed at him with his humanlike forefinger. "Uh, if you destroy our ship, then you destroy the Star Blazer too, you moron!"

A few moments of silence lingered before Gar-Lan responded. "Prepare to be boarded."

"And what makes you think we would surrender so easily?" Kalamura asked.

Gar-Lan bellowed with laughter. "Because you have no other choice."

Trajectories

The lights briefly turned off only to be replaced with red auxiliary lighting. Nine shimmers of light appeared in the corner of the room and formed into armored figures about six feet in height and armed with an assortment of futuristic rifles, pistols and swords.

Kofi couldn't believe his eyes, first green talking cats, colorful aliens and space ships, now armored monsters materializing in front of him.

The armored figure closest to them leveled his rifle at them. "I am Kal-Dak, second to Gar-Lan. You are to surrender the Star Blazer to us or be executed."

Kalamura had drawn both swords and stood in a defensive stance. Epic's eyes glowed as the chains on his forearms constricted, while Petros morphed his hands into large hammer heads. Kofi looked around and couldn't spot Booster.

"Space Sentinels, strike!" Kalamura yelled. Kofi dove for cover as the melee began.

The invading aliens fired their weapons, which filled the room with bursts of concussive light. Kalamura deflected those fired at her with her whirling blades and plowed forward against her foes. The weapon's fire didn't appear to have much effect on Epic or Petros, who barreled into the armed aliens with their massive bodies.

Something tapped Kofi's shoulder. He turned to see Booster holding two weapons. One was a baton about nine inches in length and the other was a small rifle which he kept for himself.

"Hey Earther, here's your weapon."

Kofi looked quizzically at Booster, "My weapon?"

Booster narrowed his eyes. "Yeah, the sacred energy blade. It comes with the job as caretaker to the Star Blazer."

"But this isn't a sword, it's just a stick."

Booster placed a hand across his face and shook his head. "You really are clueless, aren't you? Try to focus your thoughts into extending the energy blade."

Kofi closed his eyes and concentrated on the weapon in his hands. A surge of energy flowed through him like a current of electricity and a yard of light shot from the end of the weapon.

"Well I'll be John Brown!" Kofi exclaimed.

Booster looked back at him. "Who the hell is John Brown?" Kofi smiled. "It's just an expression from my planet."

The Adventures of Star Blazer

"You Earthers are really weird," Booster said before he leapt out into the fray. "What are you waiting for, ya big ape, you wanna live forever?"

Kofi's smile widened. He'd dreamt of playing this role on stage, and now he'd play the role for real, as he rose with his energy blade in hand and waded into battle with aliens light years from Earth.

Kofi utilized his training in African sword fighting and applied those techniques to his use of the energy blade to devastating effect. He parried the thrust of an alien sword and spun with a slash which gutted his foe. The elaborate katas helped him to better evade the weapons fire and block oncoming blasts with his energy sword. It seemed to almost have a life of its own, as Kofi wielded it.

The others were more than holding their own against Gar-Lan's minions. However, for each wave that fell, almost twice in number replaced them.

"We can't fight these guys forever, do you have a plan?" Kofi asked Booster.

The emerald feline hissed as he fired his rifle and took out another armored alien. "No, just to survive. Gar-Lan won't rest until he possesses the Star Blazer."

Kofi dodged a blast from one alien's rifle and parried a sword strike from another.

"Get down!" Epic yelled, as he shielded Kofi from the pistol's blast.

Kofi looked up in time to see the blue behemoth snatch the pistol from a marauder's hand and backhand him. The force of the blow sent him flying into the far wall. Upon impact, it slid down the wall to the floor in a crumpled heap.

"Are you injured, Caretaker?" Epic asked.

Kofi looked on, still stunned by his near death experience. "No, I'm fine. Thanks."

Flashes of light filled the room as the Gar-Lan's armored minions disappeared from the ship.

"Gar-Lan's marauders are retreating," Kalamura said.

All had been transported back to the Sojourn, including the dead. "Booster, fire up the chrono-engines. We've got to time jump now," Kalamura ordered.

Kofi narrowed his gaze at the lavender skinned woman. "Time jump?"

"Yes, we have to leave this area immediately because the only reason

Gar-Lan's marauders would be recalled back to their ship is if their leader was dead."

Kofi looked on puzzled. "Dead? Who killed him?"

"I did!"

All eyes turned toward the view screen to see the image of a hooded figure staring back at them.

"Who are you?" Kalamura asked.

The person in the image chuckled before they pulled back the hood to reveal a face disfigured with severe burns and lacerations.

Kofi stared in disbelief. "Mr. Barlow?"

Kalamura looked back at Kofi. "You know this man?"

"Yes, he's Henry Barlow. He was my employer. What are you doing here, and what happened to you?" Kofi asked.

"Henry Barlow is dead. I am Kar-Vaak. Our probe detected the energy signature of the Star Blazer within this primitive life form on an infantile planet called Earth. However, it was mortally injured when its terrain vehicle left the hewn path. Due to the frail physiology of this species, we were forced to imbue its mortal coil with Cosmic Cells in order to revive it. I have transferred my consciousness into this being and utilized its base memories in the service of the Shadow King himself, to retrieve the Star Blazer."

"Oh no," Kalamura said. "Malevolence knows."

Kofi gave her a sidelong glance. "Malevolence? Who is that?" Booster sighed. "Who's Malevolence? He's like, only the Shadow King, epitome of evil throughout the known galaxies. A cosmic terrorist hell-bent on ruling the universe."

Kofi swallowed hard. "Well, when you put it like that."

"Princess Kalamura, your orders?" Epic asked, from a control console where he was seated.

"Get us out of here now!" Kalamura barked.

Seconds later, Kofi's skin began to prickle with an intense heat, and his vision blurred. The room appeared to stretch on into infinity. It reminded him of the reflection one would see in a Funhouse mirror. Time seemed to stop for a moment before everything around him exploded in a dizzying array of colorful lights and white noise.

In an instant, everything came to a standstill. The image of the large spaceship on the view screen had been replaced with multi-colored ribbons streaming past them.

Kofi crumpled to the floor and fought the urge to vomit.

"We did it, we successfully completed the time jump," Kalamura said. "We can stay hidden within the time/space continuum, which should keep us out of Malevolence's sight for a while."

"Now what?" Kofi asked.

Kalamura smirked. "Now we make you worthy of the Star Blazer mantle."

* * * * *

Over the course of several months, which seemed like years, Kofi Zedi endured extensive and grueling physical conditioning. He had always prided himself in keeping in great shape, but nothing could have prepared him for this. The training threatened to literally kill him several times over. Yet, he survived.

Surviving had been something Kofi had grown accustomed to and thrived at. From his time as a youth in the wilds of Tanzania, to the concrete jungle of Los Angeles and the vicious social climate of his planet.

"Kofi Zedi, please step forward," Kalamura said.

Kofi stepped up to the alien princess and stood at attention. He wore the Star Blazer uniform, complete with the energy blade and a particle pistol. The helmet carefully secured under his left arm, he held his clenched fist over his heart.

"You have successfully completed the required training of the Space Sentinel Squadron. You have proved, without any doubt, to be worthy of the title Space Sentinel and to serve as our Captain, congratulations."

Kofi bowed his head as the other Space Sentinels assembled on the bridge of the ship applauded.

"Thank you, Princess Kalamura," Kofi said with a smile. Booster sat on a perch near the navigation console. "So, Captain Zedi, what do we do now?"

Kofi smirked. "Oh, I don't know. Booster. Perhaps we'll let the gem choose our course."

The golden jewel once housed in Kofi's tunic had been retrofitted into the ship's central processing unit and formed a unique, quasi-sentient matrix called Star Blazer.

"Hello Captain Zedi," the baritone voice rang out.

"Star Blazer, select a destination along the time/space continuum.

Trajectories

Look for any anomaly worthy of our attention."

"Acknowledged, sir. Initiating coordinates," Star Blazer responded.

In an instant, the Helios and its Space Sentinels crew, led by their new captain, caretaker of the sacred Star Blazer, continued on their journey into the far reaches of space, in search of their next adventure.

IN ITS SHADOW
by Martin L. Shoemaker

It turns out bureaucracies just might be the same anywhere in the galaxy. A healthy curiosity, however, always makes a difference.

Martin L. Shoemaker writes software by day and stories by night. His work has appeared in Analog, Galaxy's Edge, Clarkesworld, Digital Science Fiction, Writers of the Future, and Year's Best Science Fiction.

■■■■■■

Chorin looked over the podlings in the pool. Some of them splashed in the deep end in the dark of the cave, but most had come up to hear Chorin's story. Nearly two eights of podlings gathered in the shallows. The oldest were especially attentive. They could feel the itch of first molt approaching, and they were eager to free their legs, leave the pool, and join in their first hunt. Chorin's hunt stories always grabbed their imaginations.

Chorin was happy he could teach the children. It gave him something he could do for the tribe, so they didn't begrudge hunting for him. Something had gone wrong on his fourth molt. That happened often, and usually the victim was too crippled to live. The tribe fed them, but only reluctantly — when the hunting was poor, very reluctantly.

In Chorin's case, though, the deformity was minor. The one-time leader of the hunt was left with one leg withered, and no forepads on that leg. He could hobble with a stick, but not walk, and certainly not outrun a ke beast. He would be a liability on a hunt, and likely end up dead. He looked down at his mismatched legs, the knobby blue skin of the left contrasting with the pale, unhealthy smooth blue of the right. Maybe, if he lived to see another molt, his new legs would be whole; but in his memory, no Afim had lived to a fifth molt. Already his large eyes were set amid wrinkled, dark blue lids and a wrinkled facial ridge. He looked older than his podmates, probably because as hunters they got the better cuts of ke.

But Chorin still knew more about the hunt than anyone else in the tribe. He could pass on that knowledge to the next generation of hunters. Chorin was a skilled storyteller. He taught not just with words, but with pictures, illuminated by the light from the cave mouth. With roots and petals and ash and mud of various colors, he drew pictures of great hunts, showing the podlings how he and other tribe members lay traps and ambushes for the ke beast. And dominating the pictures was the large gray circle. It was a point of reference in every picture, just as the gray sphere outside was a point of reference in every hunt.

The Afims never pondered the sphere. It had lain in a depression in the plain since long before the Afims crept out of the swamp and took shelter in their caves. They had not yet learned to look beyond the next meal or the next predator. They didn't yet look to the stars and wonder, and they didn't yet think that a perfect gray sphere might be any more noteworthy than the swamp, the trees, or the caves. It was a given in their limited world.

* * * * *

Glora leaned back from her desk and massaged the ridge between her eyes. Her day had been nothing but numbers: eights and eightsquares and eightcubes until her eyes blurred. If she had to look at one more budget report from the Finance Authority, she would rather go through an early molt. As always, the bureaucratic side of her work threatened to completely obliterate the scientific side. She hadn't touched an instrument in over an eightday.

As soon as her computer sensed she wasn't working, it popped up a message. "Message recorded from Nialo Graad. Play / Queue / Auto?" Beside the query was a photo of Graad making a funny face: eyes bulged out like a podling, tongue tip sticking out from his bright blue lips, hands splayed behind his ears to make them look larger than a ke beast's. Glora smiled: her betrothed was in a good mood. That wasn't always true when she worked late, especially since the protests had started. Glora tapped "Play", and the photo was replaced with the recorded message.

"Hoooooo, Swamp Snuggly, computer says you're still hard at work." Glora flushed a deep blue and looked around, happily discovering that the lab was empty. The last thing she needed was for the staff to hear their boss called "Swamp Snuggly". She would make Graad pay for that! "Ferl and Wayon called and asked if we wanted to go get drinks and dinner in the downtown circle. I told them probably not, but they insisted I call and check. You know Wayon: she thinks you work too hard, and she thinks I'm supposed to make you stop. 'You tell her it's time she got out of University Circle for a while!' Yeah, like *she* ever does what Ferl tells *her* to do!"

Glora reached to call Graad and tell him to go ahead with her podsister and Ferl; but he continued before she got the chance.

"Anyway, they left before I could call, and they said we can catch up with them if we like. But I had another idea. I'm going to pick up some slugs and ke, and maybe some vine shoots, and bring them by your office. I figure you could use a treat after such a long day. Then I'll find a comfortable spot and work on the journal while you do whatever you have to do. Then we can take a romantic drive home."

Glora sighed. Graad was putting on a brave face, but he wasn't fooling her. He had grown more worried each day as the protests grew. The Pod of Riyib added members every eighthday, it seemed, and their political power was hard to ignore. Lately all of that power was turned to one goal: shutting down the Sphere Institute.

Glora looked over her desk and out the window to the giant gray Sphere that had rested there since Afim prehistory. Around it for as far as the eye could see, the Ejan Plain was dotted with relics of earlier civilizations that had risen and fallen in the shadow of the Sphere. Much of the area today had become a living museum of archaeology, but by no means all of it. The Sphere still occupied such an important place in the Afim psyche and culture that no government in a century had dared to cut off public access to the Ejan Plain. Whether they saw it as a pilgrimage or a tourist attraction, Afim from around the world flocked to see the Sphere through war and peace, prosperity and depression, sun and cold. And today, they came despite — or increasingly, because of — the Pod of Riyib who massed around the Sphere and waved their flags of protest.

* * * * *

Aknon stood before Riyib and implored the tribe to heed its message. Late in the day, this spot would be in shadow; but for now, it was in full light of Obost, and Arbost had risen above the horizon and was heating the spot as well. Beneath his tunic, Aknon's skin dried nearly to the point of cracking, but he didn't mind: it was part of his duty to Riyib, and a few cracks gave his words a dramatic edge.

Most of the tribe ignored Aknon. They had fields to till, and ke beasts to keep out of the vines. Since the tribe had started cultivating the vines, there were more ke beasts than ever. They lost many vines to the beasts, but the improved hunting made up for it.

But some of the oldest and youngest of the field hands took breaks to listen to Aknon. At first, they listened to mock him. But he asked questions they could not answer, and gave answers they could not disprove. And his certitude and his charm combined to slowly win him respect.

"But what is it made of?" Aknon had a habit of staring right into the eyes of a challenger, discomfiting the target to Aknon's advantage.

He concentrated his gaze right on the facial ridge of young Eja.

"Why—" Eja gulped deep in his gullet, and tried again "Why does it have to be made of anything? It's just the Sphere."

"No, it's Riyib!"

"Riyib, Sphere, who cares about the name? It just is."

"Ah. It's not made of anything. It just is. Hooom. Is it made of stone?

"No, stone can be worn or broken."

"Is it made of water?"

"No, water flows from the sky or the hills into the plain, and flows from the plain to the rising suns."

"Is it made of vine?"

"No, vine grows and dies."

"Is it made of flesh?"

"No, flesh moves and molts and breathes. And dies." Eja's certainty faded with every question.

"Is it made of light? Or dark?"

"No. Light fades to dark. Dark fades to light."

"Is it made of . . . spirit?"

Eja pinched his facial ridge in thought, but said nothing.

"Is it made of spirit? Spirit isn't worn or broken. Spirit doesn't flow. Spirit doesn't grow; and when we die, spirit is what remains, unfaded."

"It—" Eja looked at the Sphere, eyes widening in awe. "It could be made of spirit . . . ."

"It is made of spirit. It is spirit! It is Riyib, the Spirit, the one who

gives us our spirits. Riyib was here before us. Riyib will be here when we are gone. Riyib watches us. Riyib judges us."

Eja was on the verge of persuasion, but still questioning. "But how can we know what this 'Riyib' wants? How can we know its judgments?"

"Listen. Listen with your spirit, as I have learned to listen. Join me, and we will learn to live as Riyib orders."

*****

Glora's computer popped open an urgent message, obscuring her budget report. "Auxiliary entrance reports Nialo Graad in the entry. Identification confirmed. No other individuals in the entry. Grant Access/Deny Access?" Glora tapped "Grant Access", and then pulled back from her desk. No sense trying to get back to the report. Graad would reach her office in a short while. Might as well greet him at the door.

Graad emerged from the elevator, carrying a bag of food and looking weary. Glora rushed up to him, stood on her forepads to gain a little height, and nuzzled his facial ridge with hers. He set down the bag and clasped her hands in his, twining his long fingers with hers as he returned the nuzzle. They stood there like that, gurgling low in their gullets, rumbles of pleasure too soft for anyone to hear but each other.

Finally Glora pulled her face away, because another urge in her stomach demanded attention. "Sorry, Pod Eyes, but I'm famished. You mentioned slugs and ke? I can't smell them."

Graad let go her hands and picked up the bag. "That's because they're cold, I'm afraid. We'll have to reheat them. It was a long walk from the Institute gate." He knew where the radiant oven was in her cove in the lab, so he took the food over to heat it.

"A long walk from the gate?" Glora noticed that his white shirt was stained from exertion.

"I had to park at the gate, go through a scanner, and walk here. You didn't know about the increased security?"

"No. I'm only in charge of the Institute. Why would they tell me?"

"I'm sure it's no big deal, Glora. There are crowds gathered all over the circle, so I'm sure Vin's just being cautious." Graad's tone was soothing, but his eyes were worried.

"I don't care if it's a small deal. If someone's keeping Institute business from me, I'll give him a scolding so hot he'll molt." She tapped the node for central security.

"Yes, Director?" A large, old Afim appeared on the screen. From his dark blue skin and wrinkles, one might judge Marad Vin to be old and unthreatening; but Glora knew him as a cunning security chief who played life like a game of *tacro*, always five moves ahead of the game board. She trusted no one more when it came to Institute security.

"Vin, Graad tells me you've closed the gates?"

"Yes, Director. No vehicles in or out, screened foot traffic only. I was preparing to tell you, but I want to cover the details in person. The Pod may have cyber snoops that we missed. I'm at the main building now, should be there soon."

Vin signed off as Graad pulled the food from the oven. "So much for our night alone. But maybe I'll learn something good for my journal."

"Nialo Graad, don't you dare! Or I'll have Vin escort you out. We can't have you telling the world about our security, not at this critical stage."

"I'm kidding, Snuggles, I'm kidding. I thought a joke would help cut the tension. I'm getting worried here."

"As well you should, kid," Vin said from the doorway. Even this late at night, he looked neat and professional in his gray uniform tunic and breeches. "It's getting more serious out there. Hooom, is that slugs I smell?"

"Graad, dish us up the food. Vin, have a seat and tell me what's up."

"Just a few slugs, Graad, already had my dinner. And I'll stand, Director. Don't want my pads to stiffen up."

"OK, stand then, but explain to me what's going on."

Vin gulped a mouthful of hot pink slugs in spiced sauce. "Hooom, good stuff. Director, have you seen the news tonight? No, you're too busy, I'm sure. The Assembly is voting tonight on Horg Raba's bill to defund the Institute."

Glora's eyes trembled. Vin politely chose not to notice. "So it's done. They're shutting us down."

"No, Director, I don't think so. My sources in the capital tell me Horg doesn't have the votes."

"And you trust these sources?" Vin bobbed in agreement. "So then why the increased security?"

"Because my sources tell me Horg *expects* to lose. He's pushing the issue even knowing he doesn't have the votes to win. But he has enough votes to make a lot of noise. And my men on the Plain tell me the mood there is dangerously deluded. The Pod thinks they're going to win in the Assembly. They're all but celebrating victory already."

"Because naturally that's what Horg has been promising them."

"Hooom, yes, exactly. So when they lose the vote . . . ."

"They'll be disappointed. Angry."

"Outraged. And ready to take matters into their own hands. So before it gets to that point, I stepped up the Institute's security."

"Smart. And you didn't tell me because . . . ?"

"Because you're too fast for me. I'm minimizing traffic on the computers. We've been hacked before, you know. So I planned to come inform you after I finished checking the stations. Then when Graad showed up, I figured you'd find out from him. These slugs from Mother's Kettle?" Graad nodded. "Thought so. They've got the best slugs in this circle."

*****

"Take up your axes, Children of Riyib! Take up your axes and your shields! The heretics think they can keep us from Riyib! They twist the words of the prophet Eja and lie to the people. They enslave your children, and they defile Riyib with their stench! To arms! We fight for Riyib!"

And once again, the plain around the sphere ran blue with Afim blood. Periodic schisms in the followers of Riyib led to periodic wars until one sect stood triumphant. Thus things would stay, sometimes for a year, sometimes for a generation or more. Then new schisms would arise.

But there came a day when the Ejan Plain had been over-harvested and the ke had been over-hunted. The Afim still fought to hold the ground near Riyib; but attackers and defenders both grew weaker by the year. It was a battle that might have ended in the extinction of the entire species, had it not been for Nusa.

Nusa Hau was a commander in the Army of Riyib's Vengeance. He was brilliant. He was a charismatic leader. And he was loyal, in his way. But he wasn't particularly devout, and as the Prophet Boro demanded ever more reckless assaults, Nusa came to feel he owed more loyalty to his men than to Boro. And finally, in the face of a particularly insane command, he broke.

"It's not worth it! Whatever this Sphere is, it's not worth it! We give it obedience, we give it blood, we give it sacrifice, and it gives us

nothing. Nothing! It's not worth the life of one more Afim. Somewhere out there, there are swamps where the vines are still plentiful and the ke still roam. We should hunt ke, not a bunch of foolish Afim. If they want to die for it, let them! But we shall not!"

This heresy could not go unpunished. Boro had Nusa arrested, and ordered him flayed. But Nusa's men were as loyal to him as he to them, and they found wisdom in his words. They rebelled against Boro and rescued Nusa; and Nusa led the army away in an orderly retreat. Boro's remaining loyalists looked at the retreating army and the advancing forces of Aknon's Temple. Most decided to follow the army in haste. The few who stood their ground didn't see the next rise of Obost.

Nusa's people found all that he promised, and more: fresh swamps, juicy vines, abundant ke, clean rivers, high mountains, plentiful ores, stout trees, and defensible territory. It was a golden age for the Afim, as the newly discovered resources fed their stomachs and their minds. King Nusa soon governed a territory longer than an Afim could walk in eightsquareds of days. His descendants grew that to an empire that covered nearly an eighth of the northern continent, finding plants and animals beyond description, and riches they could barely count.

And five generations after, the Nusan Empire returned to the Ejan Plain and slew or enslaved the weary Afim who clung to their claim. The Empire found vines and slugs and ore and rivers and mountains and plants and animals and gems; but in all their explorations, they never found another Sphere. There was only the one, and they had never forgotten it.

* * * * *

The three of them stood on a semicircular balcony overhanging the Institute's main gate. With its walled grounds and security gates, the Institute looked less like a seat of learning and more like a fortress. The layout had been open when the Institute was founded twice eightsquared years ago; but an eightsquared years back, war had once more swept the Ejan Plain, and the Institute was sacked and burned. When the Regents decided to rebuild it, they demanded fortified walls and other defensive features.

Graad stood nervously behind Glora. He had tried several times to talk her out of this, but finally gave up when she snapped at him. Now he rocked onto his forepads and back onto his heels, ready to explode. He was glad that the Institute was walled.

Where Graad was all fidgeting anxiety, Vin was coiled energy and alertness. His gaze bounced across the Plain, never settling on one spot for long. He listened to security reports on his comm, occasionally issuing terse, coded orders. "I wish you'd think about this."

"I have thought about it." Glora had changed from her lab jumpsuit to a formal jacket and breeches. She stood at the front of the balcony, with her computer set up on a post beside her. Part of the screen was filled with feeds from the Institute's security cameras, while the rest was in video call mode. "It's time we showed these people what we've learned here. It's time to wake them up to the real world."

Glora punched in a call to the technicians on the north tower. "Shula, are you ready?"

"Almost, Director." Shula was a young technician, skin still a bright blue, but one of the better minds in the Institute. "The generator is powered on, and we're running diagnostics. We'll be ready on schedule."

"Good, but wait for my command. I'll copy you on the call so you'll know when to go." She disconnected, then looked at her security chief and her betrothed. "Vin, it's time. Contact your friend in the capitol."

Vin entered a call code, and Glora's computer showed another young Afim. "Yes, Vin?"

"Soru, did you get through to him?"

"Yes. Horg has agreed to the broadcast. He thinks the Director wants to make a deal." Glora bobbed once: just what she expected. "His people have arranged a projector on the Plain. He wants everyone to see his success."

"How soon will he be ready?"

"Eightsquared beats. He's just moisturizing. Wants to look good for the camera. We're ready on this end."

"All right. Director, take over here. Soru, patch us in when he's ready."

Glora took a deep breath, then touched the control to copy the output to Shula. Then she waited for Horg.

But the savvy politician did things his way, as usual. Out on the plain, a large projector screen lit up with the logo of the Ejan news journal, and the same image appeared on Glora's screen. A voice announced, "We have a special announcement from the honorable Assemblyman Horg Raba, Elector At Large of the Pod of Riyib, regarding tonight's budget vote for the so-called Sphere Institute.”

A second voice, female, responded as the scene changed to an overview of the crowd in the Plain. “Yes, we have word that Assemblyman Horg and Institute Director Bnoni Glora are near an agreement to revise the Institute’s charter to address issues that concern many of our fellow citizens. A spokesperson from Horg’s office says that if these issues can be resolved, he may support a reduced budget for the Institute under direct Assembly control. Unnamed sources speculate that Horg would be the likely overseer for that task. Not a result the Director would choose, perhaps, but better than a complete funding cutoff.”

The first voice returned. “And now . . . Assemblyman Horg Raba, Elector At Large of the Pod of Riyib.” There were wild cheers from the Plain. “And Bnoni Glora.”

Glora’s computer screen switched to the well-moisturized visage of Horg Raba. In the plain, the camera held on Horg’s image for nearly an eight beat while the crowd cheered again. Then the screen split, showing Horg and Glora. Horg looked subtly larger and more imposing than she did. Glora tried twice to adjust her camera for a more balanced view, but the screen readjusted each time. Horg’s production team were controlling this presentation for maximum effect.

“Greetings, podmates!” Horg paused for yet another cheer. “Greetings, and thank you once again for the chance to represent you here in the Assembly.” More cheers. “Tonight we stand together in defense of the oldest truths in Afim history: the primacy of Riyib, and the inviolability of Riyib’s laws.” There were scattered cheers, but also a low rumble of reverent murmurs.

“For two eightsquared years, these scientists at this ‘Sphere Institute’ have studied Riyib.” Now cheers turned to jeers, but Horg spoke over them. “Now, now. Nothing wrong with their impulse. Nothing wrong. These aren’t the bad days of the last war, when the Klisno forces waged war upon knowledge itself. No, they sacked the Institute, and that went too far. It is natural and proper for Afim to study Riyib. Though these scientists are naïve in their efforts, we understand that Riyib calls to them, too.

“But they go astray. They try to study Riyib with ever more invasive and destructive forces. Oh, Riyib in its perfection remains unmarred by their efforts; but as they persist, they endanger Pod members with their beams and probes and meters. And yet their publications are full of negatives: report after report of what Riyib is *not*, even as they stare blindly past Riyib That Is. The dangers and costs are too high for experiments that always yield negative results. And there is always the possibility that their foolish arrogance will bring forth Riyib's wrath. Before that can happen, the Assembly *must* exercise proper oversight of this work.

"Now some might argue that the Assembly should cut off funding entirely. Indeed, I planned to propose exactly that, before I learned that Director Bnoni was ready to discuss the future of the Institute. But if she and I can overcome our differences and stand before you tonight, then I have hope that we can continue the Institute's studies with proper reverence and respect for history. Director Bnoni, do you have anything to add?"

Glora took a deep breath. This was her moment. If Horg felt he was losing control of the broadcast, he would cut it off. She needed to act subtly, then quickly when she reached her point. "Assemblyman Horg, we at the Institute are very honored by your concerns for our future. We're sure that with proper support, we can see continued success.

"But I emphasize *continued* success, and I have to respectfully disagree with you on that detail. Our results have not *all* been negative, as you can see if you read some of our latest publications. We now have a very sound theory of what the Sphere is: a single super-particle with a relative timeframe velocity of zero."

"A theory—"

"Yes, Assemblyman, a very sound theory, at least according to those who reviewed the publications. This super-particle has a fixed spacetime vector; and until it reaches the endpoint of that vector, it resides outside of our time stream. What we see is only the interface of this super-particle with our local spacetime. If you think in terms of wave mechanics, it's somewhat like a giant photon, though its velocity vector is constrained."

Horg showed only a moment of puzzlement at all the jargon before he fell back on a simple but effective retort: "Yes, but how do you *know*?"

Glora resisted the urge to smile. "Because once we understood what the Sphere is, it was a matter of mere engineering to create another one. Shula, now."

On the north tower, Shula flipped his switch, and also keyed a command to activate a spotlight on the tower. Glora tapped a command, and her camera shut down, replaced by a zoom shot of the north tower as seen by her second camera. Slowly at first, and then accelerating, a gray sphere grew on the flat top of the tower. Unseen by the crowd below, the super-particle generator was already powering down, its work done.

Glora narrated the view from her camera. "We've had success in the lab already, but we weren't quite ready to publish. But with you and our audience here tonight, we decided to bypass normal publication protocols and show you what the Institute can do with proper funding."

The new Sphere was already nearly the size of the original; and it was slowly descending to the Plain below. "We've plotted a very simple spacetime vector for this experiment, since we still have a lot to learn about these vectors. Translated from mathematics, this super- particle's vector starts from a point, grows to a specified size, and then translates through three dimensions to the Plain. There it will remain stationary for eightcubed beats so that the people in the Plain can examine it and confirm that it's exactly like the Sphere. Then it will dwindle back to a point."

Horg had been speechless for perhaps the first time in his career; but he had finally recovered. "You can't do this! Stop it! Turn it off!"

"I'm afraid I can't, Assemblyman. If there is a way to alter the spacetime vector, we haven't discovered it yet. The super-particle simply has to complete the vector traversal."

"Bnoni, you fool, look at what you've done! Not at your blasphemous 'particle', look at the people!"

Glora realized she had been too focused on her demonstration and on Horg's dismay. She looked out on the Plain — and saw chaos. The people gathered there were in a panic. Some shouted and chanted. Some ran up to touch the new Sphere. Some threw rocks at it, and at the Institute.

The projector screen went dark, and the broadcast cut out. But the Plain lit up with new light: flames. Torches and flares and bonfires. Angry shouts came from every direction. The crowd merged into churning waves, waves that moved in different directions as different passions flared. When waves came together, sometimes they merged, but sometimes they clashed, violently. From her peaceful perch above the gate, Glora was certain that rationality had entirely left the Plain.

"Director! Down!" Spurred by uncanny senses, Vin tackled Glora shortly before the first shot rang out. Then he shouted into his comm. "Turn on the electric fence! Lock the gate! All guards, stun loads are authorized. Lethal loads on standby. Best discretion."

Looking through the balcony rails, Glora saw more than a protest, more than a riot. This was insurrection, perhaps war. Gun flares were visible from multiple locations. Glass was breaking. At least one building in the circle was on fire.

Then she saw one very bright flare of light. Glora had never seen artillery before, but Vin had. He and Graad were dragging her inside when the shell struck above the balcony. She saw flames and falling stone, and then she saw nothing.

*****

The Sphere inspired reverence and bloodshed; but it also inspired curiosity and discovery in those inclined to such. In many ways, it sped the progress of Afim knowledge.

The perfection of the Sphere inspired early geometers to contemplate angle and radius and ratio. They discovered pi before they mastered stone construction, and they calculated its value to high precision in the early years of their Bronze Age.

As the Afim spread across their world, they took with them their memories and histories of the Sphere. To an obsessive degree, each branch of the Afim insisted on knowing where they were in relation to the Sphere and how far they were from it. This led to an explosion in the fields of cartography, surveying, navigation, astronomy, and chronometry.

The question of the Sphere's composition led the Afim to explore the properties of all manner of ore and stone and other compounds. While a super-particle was a concept they would not imagine nor describe for another eightsquared generations or more, their efforts did lead them to the rudiments of chemistry. Debate over how to interpret the results led to the importance of falsifiable tests, and from there to the basics of the scientific method.

Much later, attempts to probe the interior of the Sphere led to the science of acoustics, and later still optics. The super-particle did not properly reflect nor absorb nor transmit, leading the Afim to discover diffraction; and then more precise measurements led to the double-split experiment and the discovery of wave-particle duality.

But as much as study of the Sphere advanced Afim science, the Sphere itself remained a mystery. Throughout all their research, their knowledge remained divided into "the Sphere" and "the natural world", a duality that the Pod of Riyib never tired of proclaiming.

Trajectories

And so it remained until the momentous discoveries by the Sphere Institute.

*****

Glora woke in cool, murky water and dim light. A hospital bath?

Yes, as her eyes adjusted, she saw monitors and cabinets and wires and tubes. The wires and tubes were mostly connected to her, though some ran into the water, no doubt sampling and measuring nutrients and other compounds.

Glora's skin felt smooth and tight. She had molted. This molt was years too early, so it must have been a forced molt. Had she been seriously injured? Burned, perhaps? Yes, she remembered flames.

She flexed her limbs, causing ripples in the bath. Arms and legs all seemed fine, save for the tightness that would relax over time. Molt defect was rare in the modern age, especially when the molt occurred under medical care, but it was always a worry. And forced molting, while therapeutic, had a much higher rate of defects.

The door to her room opened, and Glora saw a doctor enter, no doubt alerted by the bath sensors. He leaned over her and smiled. "Good morning, Glora. I'm Dr. Trivin. And how are you feeling this morning?"

"Hungry, I think. I don't suppose there are slugs in this mud?"

"You wouldn't want them. Medicated mud spoils the taste. But hunger is a good sign." He touched a comm on his shoulder. "Ask the nutritionist to prepare breakfast slugs for Director Bnoni. All right, pull yourself up onto the shallows and let me see those new legs."

Dr. Trivin reached out a hand to help her, and Glora pulled out of the mud and up on the shallow shelf of the bath. He probed her legs with his fingers, feeling the springy new bones and the developing muscles.

Finally Trivin bobbed in approval. "Very good, very good. I think you're ready to walk today. In a month, you'll forget these legs are new."

"How badly was I burned, doctor?"

"Oh, it wasn't the burn. It was the masonry that fell on your legs. Crushed them both beyond repair. The burns just finished the job. But we induced molt with no complications, and your new legs grew like a textbook case."

"What about Graad? And Vin?"

"Vin? That old warrior? He's the toughest Afim who ever crawled out of the mud. Now *he* had some burns, but he refused to leave his post until the Assembly got control of the riots. He oversaw the Institute's defenses, and he coordinated with the Assembly Guard to tackle the crowd. He's ex-Guard himself, I'm sure you knew that, so they took him to a Guard Hospital after the battle. Fine with me, I'm not sure I can handle a patient that stubborn.

"And Graad?" The doctor walked over, opened the door, and waved his hand. "He hasn't left this room or this hallway in an eighthday, asking questions and asking to help. Graad, come on in."

Graad pushed in past Dr. Trivin, who wisely took his opportunity to leave them in privacy. Without even waiting to strip down, Graad climbed into the bath and embraced Glora, careful not to crush her new legs. He found her facial ridge with his, and they nuzzled gently.

After many eight beats of nuzzling, their ridges were warming with passion. Glora was not about to indulge that here in the hospital, so she pulled her face away. Graad pulled away as well, looked into her eyes, and smiled. "I thought I lost you. I thought you were gone. But Vin . . . . He wouldn't give up. We pulled you to safety, he gave me a gun, and he told me 'Shoot anyone who comes near her.' Only later did I realize I didn't even know how to use it! Then he went out, and . . . . Well, I don't know exactly what all he did, but he saved the Institute! And he saved you."

"And you."

"Yes, and me. I guess we owe him. Shall we name our first male podling after him?"

The talk of podlings again made Glora aware of Graad's closeness in the pool. *Think of something else . . . . Think of something else . . . .* "So what happened with the riot?"

"Vin's troops collaborated with the Guard to divide and conquer the mob. Isolate a group, pacify them, arrest when necessary, and repeat. Some of them snuck in military weapons — former Guard members, according to the journals — but they were mostly disorganized. The Guard took them down with minimal casualties all the way around. The Assembly declared a state of emergency and martial law in the Ejan Plain and the circles around it. That was — hooom, five days ago, around the time Dr. Trivin triggered your molt. They lifted the state of emergency two days ago, but the Guard presence still dominates the Plain. The Assembly wants no more trouble."

"And Horg Raba? He has nothing to say about the Guard occupation of his sacred Plain?"

"Horg? Horg is here. He wants to talk to you."

"What!"

"He has tried to see you three times since you came in."

"Why? So he can tell me in person that he's closing the Institute? And why would I want to see him?"

"I think you should, Glora. Things have — changed. You should hear him out." Graad's eyes showed just a hint of amusement.

"Hooom." Thoroughly annoyed, Glora felt her ridge cool. Well, she *had* wanted a distraction. "I'm not meeting Horg naked and swimming in a pod. Help me out, and find me some breeches and a robe. And a towel. And I'm not seeing anyone else until I get some slugs!"

When Glora was dried and dressed and seated in her bed, Graad went out into the hall. He returned leading Horg Raba. The Assemblyman cautiously approached the bed. "Director Bnoni."

Glora set down her half-eaten slugs. "Assemblyman Horg. You've come to gloat?"

Horg paled. Glora found it hard to believe, but his usual arrogant charm had turned meek, almost humble. "Gloat? I've come to apologize. You must believe me, Director, I wanted the Institute under Assembly control, but I didn't want violence. I never wanted to see you hurt, never wanted anyone to get hurt. I had no idea those people were armed."

"But you didn't hesitate to rile them up."

"Rile them up!" There was a brief flash of the old Horg arrogance, but he quickly tamped it down. "I addressed my people, the ones who elected me, on a matter that's important to them. *Was* important, I mean. I spoke what was on their minds, the truths they elected me to represent. But you—"

"I showed them a different truth. Scientifically determined truth, as best we understand it today."

"You showed them—" Horg pushed toward the bed, but not far. Graad grabbed his arm and firmly pulled him back. "You showed them tricks to confuse them. I never should've given you a stage for your illusions."

"Illusions? You really believe that, don't you? I show you the biggest leap in science in eightcubed years, and you think it's an illusion." Glora sighed. "What a waste. But I had to try. You had to speak for your beliefs, and I had to show the evidence for mine. We'll always know what the

Institute accomplished before you shut us down."

"Shut you down?" Horg laughed, a bitter chuckle from deep in his gut. "Director, no one is shutting you down. You didn't know?"

"What?" Glora looked at Graad, who stood behind Horg with a mischievous grin.

Horg croaked out another bitter laugh. "You mean you didn't plan it this way? Ha! No, you couldn't. Only Riyib could plan such a disastrous fate. I grew too self-important, so Riyib punished me, using you as the instrument of my downfall."

"Your downfall?"

"My downfall. That *demonstration* of yours . . . . It shattered the Pod of Riyib. You have created more schisms in one day than we have seen in eight generations. I swear there are as many interpretations as there are Afim who saw *your* sphere; and thanks to my own network, it was seen across the globe. Plus more than eight-to-the-fourth Afim saw it for themselves, touched it even!

"Some saw it for what it clearly was: blasphemy of the highest order. But some saw it as another Riyib. Some say your sphere was a trick; but then they ask if Riyib might be a trick as well. Some say it proves that Riyib isn't Riyib at all, merely a messenger, with your sphere another messenger. Some say you are Riyib's messenger. And some . . . ." He dropped his voice. "Some say *you* are Riyib . . . ."

"Nonsense!"

"And worst of all: some say you are right, and they're abandoning Riyib for your 'science'.

"The disputes aren't subsiding over the past eighthday, they're growing. They've turned to violence again in some places. And the Pod of Riyib is splintered. More than a dozen groups have declared themselves the Pod of Riyib, or the True Pod of Riyib, or the Pod of Riyib's Message, or the Pod of the New Riyib, or . . . ."

"Ah." Glora finally saw the political angle. "And if the Pod is splintered, who will be their Elector At Large?"

"Exactly." Horg glowered. "The Assembly has already formally noticed that the Pod is divided, and none of the factions remaining is large enough to qualify for an Elector At Large. I'm still an Elector for my home Circle; but without the Pod, most of my power is gone."

Graad grinned even wider. "Shall I tell her the rest, Assemblyman?"

Trajectories

"No." Horg glared at Graad. "As I said, many Afim believe you're a messenger of Riyib, or some other sort of prophet. Others believe . . . . Well, I won't repeat that blasphemy again. But you have a lot of supporters there."

"Supporters? I'm no miracle worker, I don't want that sort of support."

"As an experienced politician, I can tell you: you can't always choose your supporters. Want them or not, you have them, you just have to decide how to use them. Plus you have those swayed by your 'science'. Plus the Institute and the University support you, and . . . . Well, after your success, and your results that your staff published in the journals the next day, you've gained stature in the Assembly. Not the Institute, you personally. And they're discussing adding an Elector for the Institute; and only one name is being mentioned."

"I see."

"No, I don't think you see why I'm here. You've come into a great deal of power. I've lost almost all of mine, and I'm clinging to what I have left." Suddenly Horg seemed to shrink, almost collapse. "So that's why I came to apologize, to humble myself and beg your forgiveness and your mercy. Once you learn to wield your newfound power, you can crush me if you choose.

"Director Bnoni, you've won. I've lost almost everything. Is that enough? Are you satisfied with my ruin, or do you want me completely crushed?"

Horg trembled slightly. Once he had been larger than life, pumped up with his arrogance, dominating any room in which he stood.

Glora didn't trust him at all, and expected he would scheme to reclaim power if he could; but that day, in that room, he was deflated. He was broken.

"Horg, you ask the wrong question. It proves you'll never understand me or what's important to me." Glora smiled. "Am I satisfied with your ruin? No, Horg, I'm satisfied that today we know more than we knew yesterday. And tomorrow we'll know even more."

*****

The Sphere spurred scientific advance among the Afim, but not uniformly. They excelled in sciences directly related to the Sphere. Their many wars for control of it also advanced sciences such as metallurgy and tactics.

In Its Shadow

But in other sciences, they were strangely deficient. They learned of advanced science long before they felt the crush of population pressure. Due to their life cycle with its periods of return to the mud for molting, they were less inclined to exploration than they might otherwise have been. So though they made great advances in particle physics and beyond, few if any Afim had ever contemplated space travel. Even after the truth of the Sphere was revealed, none of them could imagine leaving it that far behind.

* * * * *

Glora looked out at the apparatus arrayed on the Ejan Plain, and she smiled. This would be a very good day, she was sure.

Glora didn't have enough good days of late. Oh, she appreciated most things in her life. She was proud of her three pods of children, of course. The eldest pod had been through second molt already, and would soon start careers of their own. She and Graad were proud of their podlings.

And she was grateful for Graad. Throughout the years, he had been her loyal support system through all her struggles for the Institute. And though her ridge had grown smooth over time, Graad still found the time to nuzzle it tenderly; and he still could warm her ridge.

And she was proud of what the Institute had become under her leadership; but at the same time, it was the Institute that left her melancholy on most days. She remembered a time when she might not do scientific work in an eighthday; but now she looked fondly back on that time. In her time as Elector of the Institute, she did almost no actual science at all. She might go eight months or more between experiments, and she scarcely even had time to read her team's publications. Trusted aides like Shula did the work, while Glora ensured they had the freedom and the funding to do so.

But not today! Even while she mastered the ugly art of politics, Glora had never entirely let go of the science of the Sphere. And today she would run her greatest experiment of all.

After the Sphere had been explained, new questions arose, and Shula's team answered them. The biggest question was: why did the super-particle remain motionless relative to the planet, even though the planet rotated on its axis and revolved around its star system? They knew it had a fixed spacetime vector, but how could that vector be plotted through more rotations and revolutions than anyone could count? From that, after eightsquares of experiments, they determined that the vector was not in spacetime, but in a new concept they dubbed spacetimepotential. The potential energy of the system affected the vector, and the planet's gravity created a deep well of potential energy. The calculations took Glora an eighthday to understand — time she should have spent on Assembly business — and she still wasn't sure she quite got them. But the result was that the super-particle's spacetimepotential vector was entangled with the planet's, and so remained motionless relative to the planet's surface.

Once they understood spacetimepotential, Shula devised new tools to probe the Sphere. They had first envisioned it as a mere point in space, artificially enlarged due to its vector; but with the new tools, Shula demonstrated that the Sphere had mass, and the mass was not evenly distributed within the super-particle. There was something inside of it. This result was controversial, until Shula performed an experiment almost as bold as Glora's experiment so long before: he surrounded a park bench with a super-particle with a moving vector; and when the super-particle reached the end of its vector and returned to virtual, the park bench had moved with it. In later experiments, Shula used super- particles to transport a ke beast, and then finally himself. As his theory had predicted, he detected no passage of time while he was inside the super-particle.

And with that knowledge, the Institute staff convened a conference to consider the big remaining questions about the Sphere: who had generated it? Where had it come from? Where and when would it reach the end of its vector? And what was inside of it? Their final hypotheses for these questions were all interconnected. The most likely answers were the most fantastic: the Sphere had come from another star, incomprehensibly distant. The creators, whoever they might have been, launched it from far enough away that they didn't realize Obost and Arbost had a planetary system. Perhaps the planetary system didn't even exist when they plotted the vector, and only coalesced later. And so the unexpected mass had altered the shape of the vector, the gravity well changing the potential energy dimension such that the vector turned in an unexpected direction. The vector could not reach its terminus as long as their world existed; and wherever it came from, it had likely been trapped on their world for eight-to-the-eighth years or more.

And what was inside it, frozen in time? They couldn't answer with even speculative certainty. But Glora intended to find out.

In Its Shadow

And so she found time. With Graad's support, she gave even more time to the Institute, time for science for the first time in years. And when she realized the answer, it was almost too simple. But she demonstrated it first with test spheres; and it always worked, without fail. She could open the Sphere at any time.

This time, Glora was more mature and politically savvy. This wasn't a demonstration to prove a point; this was a turning point like never before in Afim history. If she succeeded — and she would! — her culture would never be the same. So she used her power as Elector to clear the Plain and put it under Guard control. She spent eightcubes of credits to spread the word and assure that people understood her plan and had seen the test films. The journals were allowed to report from a cove at a safe distance. The Riyibites protested as they always did; but she and the Assembly did everything possible to calm the populace and control the protests.

And so today she stood in front of the Sphere, with Graad beside her. She had asked him to stay with the podlings in case the Sphere's contents were dangerous; but after all these years, he wouldn't let her face this alone. And in some ways, it was his accomplishment as much as hers. So the podlings were with Wayon, and the two of them faced history.

Beside them, Shula knelt and inspected the generator. "Are you ready, Director? Do you want to make a speech?"

Glora grinned. All those years ago, her speech had led to riots, and the Institute staff had turned that into a running joke. "No, not today. Today I think we'll just run our experiment. Do you have the vector plotted?"

"All plotted. We can activate at any time."

"Then there's no point in waiting. Activate the generator."

Shula pushed the button, and the generator briefly hummed. Then he rose and stood with Glora and Graad. As they watched, a new super-particle appeared, completely encompassing the Sphere. Glora's calculations had shown, and then her experiments had proven: a super-particle could interrupt and terminate the spacetimepotential vector of another super-particle. Yes, almost too simple.

And then the new super-particle faded away; and where it had stood since the dawn of time, the Sphere was gone. There was a gasp heard across the plain. Even having been warned what would happen, everyone gasped. Even Glora, who had *calculated* what would happen, joined involuntarily. The single constant in their society . . . was gone.

Trajectories

In its place was a large airship of strange design. It settled gently to the Plain. After the gasp, every Afim in sight stood in silent awe.

A door opened. A ramp lowered. And six . . . *things* . . . walked down. They were vaguely Afim-shaped — two arms, two legs, a head — but taller. They wore strange baggy clothing that covered them from boot tops to their even stranger helmets. Glora couldn't be at all sure through that clothing, but they gave an impression of being larger as well as taller. When the creatures reached the bottom of the ramp, one of them consulted some display on its sleeve. They must have communicated somehow, because they all simultaneously removed their helmets. Underneath, their skin was in strange colors, from slug pink to ke brown. Though the creatures were tall and strong, their heads were disproportionately small. Strange fibers capped their heads. Their eyes were smaller than Afim eyes, and less round. They had no facial ridges; but where a ridge might be, they had small protuberances, each with two holes on the underside. Beneath the protuberances, their mouths were small, and seemed to be rimmed with small white bits of bone behind muscular lips.

While the creatures looked around, Glora stepped forward, bobbing slightly in a way she hoped they would find reassuring. "Greetings." She spoke slowly and carefully so that they could analyze what she said. "I know you won't understand, but welcome to our world. We are the Afim. And you . . . you bring the answers to our oldest question. And a universe of new questions."

THE GHOST CONDUCTOR
OF THE INTERSTELLAR EXPRESS

by Brad R. Torgersen

It was a great theory — a mission to a world that should be utterly Earth-like.

But theories often give way to unpleasant facts — and unexpected encounters.

Brad R. Torgersen is a multi-award-winning, multi-award-nominated speculative fiction writer whose stories have appeared prominently in the pages of *Analog magazine*, *Galaxy's Edge magazine*, various anthologies, numerous overseas markets, and several on-line venues, such as *Orson Scott Card's InterGalactic Medicine Show*. His first full-length novel, *The Chaplain's War*, was published by Baen books, who are also publishing Brad's second full-length novel, *A Star-Wheeled Sky*, in the near future. Married 22 years, with one daughter, her two cats, and the family dog, Brad is a full-time tech nerd for a big Utah healthcare company, while also serving his country part-time as a Chief Warrant Officer in the United States Army Reserve.

■■■■■■

As planets went, New Olympia was a hopeful disappointment. The right size and mass — to roughly match Earth — it even orbited within the theoretical green zone of its yellow dwarf home star. Alas, similar to Venus, the atmosphere of New Olympia was choking and toxic. A problem that was not wholly insurmountable, given current bioengineering and atmosphere conversion science. But if there ever was to be a truly blue sky on New Olympia — and seas of water to match — these things were very far in the future. Humans had only been working on the problem for a scant handful of years, since the colony boat *Mainfront* arrived — following its two century journey from Sol System.

Caddy Brenton barely remembered the cities of Earth. She'd been single-digit-old when her parents put her into the stasis bed before the flight, and she'd emerged more or less in the same state on the other side — just she and her older brother, Peter. Mom and dad hadn't been qualified for the flight. Too old, according to the surgeons doing the colony screening.

Trajectories

Caddy had begged mom and dad not to make her go. But Old Earth had been dying. Too dirty. Too crowded. Too used-up. Or so she'd been told. The accessions officials for the Emergency Resettlement Project had been taking children — and children only — for their bulk colonist manifests. So, Caddy and Peter were consigned to one of the big boats being built. And launched on a very long, one-way trip.

Strange, Caddy often thought, that twenty decades could pass, without her mind being wise to the fact. Life in the stasis bed had been virtually dreamless. Sometimes, she wished she could get back into the stasis bed, and let twenty more decades pass. Maybe by then New Olympia would be ready for habitation? What good was a new life, if all it meant was being confined to the habitat modules slowly spreading across the surface of the asteroid *Mainfront* had towed into New Olympia orbit? Perhaps her great-great grandchildren would get to rub their toes in the New Olympian sand. But Caddy would not. And this filled her with an almost unutterable bitterness.

That, and the fact that Peter had left.

"Uh oh, I know that look," said a voice over Caddy's shoulder.

She turned away from the observation bubble — aimed perpetually down at New Olympia's rocky, dangerous, altogether inhospitable surface — and greeted her friend Troy.

"Yo, man," she said, waving a hand half-heartedly.

"Blues got you down again?" Troy said, floating up beside her. The asteroid had a tiny bit of gravity, enough to eventually bring everything to rest on the floor, if you stood still. But not enough to make walking possible. Every module and connecting tube was therefore lined with railings and handholds — a person pulled herself through the world, as much as pushed off.

"You might say that," Caddy said, turning her eyes planetward. Even she wasn't sure why she spent so much time here. It wasn't like staring at New Olympia was going to transform the surface any faster. There wasn't even a guarantee that the aerosol pods being dumped into the atmosphere every month — containing hundreds of kilograms of genetically-modified one-celled plants — were going to work. There was only the theory of them working. Just as the *Mainfront* had come all this way on the theory that a roughly-Earth-sized world at roughly the right distance from its roughly-Sol-like star, would have liquid water, and the potential to support an oxygen-nitrogen atmosphere. And Caddy knew damned well how that particular gamble had turned out. Much to her dissatisfaction.

"Just think," Troy said, "We could still be stuck—"

"—on Earth," Caddy said, finishing his sentence for him. "Spare me, please. I see the broadcasts that the *Mainfront* mayor disseminates into the school files. How the skies on Earth are always gloomy. How they're rushing to do for the Earth's atmosphere, what we're trying to do here; before Earth goes like Venus. Everyone walking around wearing masks. Barely any elbow room. It looks awful. But Troy, did you ever stop to wonder how accurate that all is?"

"What do you mean?" the teenaged boy — young man, really, with arms and shoulders thickening and broadening handsomely — said, looking at her sideways.

"I mean," Caddy said, "What if they just tell us that Earth's terrible, because they don't want us to get homesick?"

"How can we get homesick for a place we barely remember?" Troy asked.

"Well *I* remember," Caddy said defensively, still glaring down at New Olympia's surface. "It wasn't that bad when we left. It wasn't like they show it now."

"The way they show it now," Troy said, "is the way it looked two hundred years ago. Two hundred years for the broadcasts to reach us. I bet it's worse, at this very moment, than either of us can imagine. Only we won't see it for two hundred years. Do you really think we'd be better off if we never came?"

"I . . ." Caddy said, then shut her mouth.

Troy maneuvered up close to her and put a hand on her shoulder. "I don't know what to think," Caddy finally said, rubbing her eyes with her fists.

"Peter believed in this place," Troy said, sweeping his arm out toward the planet below. "That's why he volunteered to be part of the first wave of comet-catchers."

"And vanished into thin air," Caddy said.

"Yeah, well . . ." now it was Troy who shut his mouth.

"Sorry," he said, after a long pause. "I know you don't like to talk about it."

"No, I don't," Caddy said.

Trajectories

"But you for sure will want to talk about this," Troy said, fishing a small phone out of his jumper's zippered breast pocket, and using his fingertips to pull something up on the small screen.

Caddy peered at what the screen said. "Scores have been released?" she asked.

"Not officially," Troy said. "But I know the girl in the office who runs the workstation for the testing administrator, and she slipped me the data a day early." He winked at her.

"Dance your way around too many flames," Caddy chided him, "and you may eventually get burned."

She followed up the comment with a fist slugging playfully into Troy's shoulder. He went flying across the module, laughing and rubbing his arm. His phone remained in Caddy's hand, as she looked more closely at what he'd come to show her.

"I've passed," she said, suddenly turning serious.

"Not just passed," Troy said. "The same girl who gave me the scores, told me that they've already been picking names for the next class being trained to run the comet-catchers. Your name is on that list. And a year earlier than you expected it to be, too."

Caddy clutched the little phone to her chest.

"I'd hoped," she said, then allowed herself a small giggle, and a grin. "I mean, I worked hard and I pestered them endlessly to let me try for the next group. So what if I am only seventeen."

"I think the fact you're following in Peter's shoes . . ." But Troy never finished the thought.

Caddy's brother was like a friendly ghost, forever flitting about in the periphery of their vision. Not dead. Not here. Just . . . missing. One of the other comet-catchers had found Peter's ship slowly drifting back into the inner system, gently shoving its captured comet; on pure autopilot. No Peter. No sign of an accident. No evidence at all that there had been any problem. And a log that had been wiped blank, so no records or telemetry to tell what had become of him.

After that, solo missions were off-limits. All comet-catcher ships went out with two and even three people aboard. At minimum. Whatever had happened to Peter, the *Mainfront* executive council determined that they didn't want it to happen again.

Caddy?

The Ghost Conductor of the Interstellar Express

Part of her still felt that Peter was out there, somewhere.

"Hey," Troy said, "remember what I said when I came in here? About knowing that look on your face? Now you've got a different one. I am sorry I brought your brother up."

"No, this is great news," Caddy said. "Peter would be proud of me, I am sure. This is my big chance to get out of here, too. To see the far edge of the system. Being stuck here? It's like living on the front porch of a house I can never enter. I don't want to spend my life doing that. So, if I can't go down there—" She pointed at the planet. "—I want to be out there." Her finger moved off the limb of the world, and aimed for deep space.

"Well, I hope you make it through training," Troy said. "I am sure you'll be the best comet-catcher of them all."

* * * * *

Piloting in the new school was an exercise in learning to think big. Technically, every single person who'd come with the *Mainfront* — both young and old alike — knew how to operate the little shuttles and other vehicles that serviced their budding, single-asteroid civilization. If you understood thrust vectoring in a microgravity environment, and could manage a finite fuel source, there was very little chance to screw it up. The comet-catchers merely amped the equations, because instead of pushing ore cargo or container boxes about, a comet-catcher literally herded an entire cometary body out of its long-period orbit at the edge of the star system, into a short-period orbit which would eventually line it up for an insertion around New Olympia proper — before ultimately being de-orbited at a velocity that wouldn't send the comet smacking into the planet's crust at speeds guaranteed to cause tectonic turmoil.

To that end, each comet-catcher was almost like a miniature version of the *Mainfront* itself: big fuel tanks — both for reactor consumption, and for working mass — and a big, high-efficiency, low- thrust fusion engine. The life module and pilot's globe were small in comparison to the rest of the ship. It was made of as few parts as possible, all machined in the colony's ever-expanding nano-augmented fleet yard. And each prospective pilot — as well as her onboard backup assignee — was trained to make fixes to potential problems enroute.

Losing comet-catchers was not unheard of. The risk merely added to the job's glamour. But the executive council didn't want to sacrifice any more ships or lives than were absolutely necessary. The objective was to bring back water — as much as could be had — for the terraforming effort. Not fill the comet-catcher academy memorial board with names.

"Your objective is the snowball," Caddy's instructor said to them all as they floated in a loose formation around the scale model of the comet-catcher the academy had constructed at the center of its bubble-domed, one-room schoolhouse. There were two dozen in Caddy's class — the biggest yet. With the fleet yard able to build more ships with greater efficiency each year, the comet-catcher arm of the terraforming effort was picking up steam.

The instructor — Chief Pilot Okatsu — pointed a thin stick at the bow of the model.

"Your most delicate piece of equipment is also your most important. The pusher web is stored in its protective cocoon until you need to deploy it. Once it is deployed, it cannot be quickly stowed. The web itself expands until it forms a semi-flexible glove or bowl, roughly one kilometer in diameter. Far, far bigger than your craft itself, but more than big enough to serve as a . . . as a snow shoe for you, when you have to begin 'kicking' your target back home."

Caddy raised her hand.

"Candidate Brenton," the Chief said, pointing at her with the stick.

"Why doesn't the web collapse as soon as it touches the comet's surface?" she asked.

"Good question," Chief said. "I was just getting to that part. The web itself is actually a nanofiber filament that can be electrically charged. When it's left idle, it's like a draw string on your jumper. It hangs loose. When you activate the charge, the filaments in the fiber compress and align in one direction. The web is woven such that the compression and straightening forces the web to assume the shape we want. But it's still flexible — and large — enough, so that when you touch down on a comet's surface, the web should bend without breaking. We want both you, and the comet, to come home in one piece."

Chief pulled up a holo-video above the scale model, showing a sped-up animation that demonstrated what he'd just described. Like a flower blooming, the web unfurled out of the front of the comet catcher, until it was like a wide, shallow cup.

"Now, ordinarily, that web wouldn't stand up to you or I pushing against a single strand with so much as a finger's strength. But taken as a whole, the web will disperse the force of your ship's thrust across the surface of the cometary body, allowing you to manipulate the comet without sinking into it."

As if on cue, the computer animation showed the little ship maneuvering to place the near side of an amorphous comet — lumpy, somewhat rounded in shape — into the business end of its web. When the ship began making sudden movements, the web eventually shattered, and the little ship tunneled its way into the comet.

"Bury yourself like this," the Chief warned, "and you might be digging yourself a grave. I've been on this operation from the get-go — when most of you were still young, and fresh out of your stasis beds. I've lost friends to carelessness. Please don't join their ranks."

Which is not, Caddy thought, how Peter was lost. His ship had come back fine — just missing the pilot, was all.

A tiny prickling sensation went up Caddy's spine.

"Now," Chief continued, "you've all been spending a lot of time in the simulators, and I know it's not much fun. But really, you're going to have to get used to it. You need to be prepared for every possibility, including sudden instrumentation or mechanical error, during your approach. You get one chance to snag a comet the right way. Screw it up, and wreck your web, and it's a long trip back home to get your ship fixed — and we might decide to let somebody else go out in your place. We're too young — as a colony — to be able to afford careless mistakes. The number of comets that need to be harvested for the transformation of New Olympia is immense. But every single one counts. Which means *you* count. Understand?"

A chorus of yessirs echoed around the schoolhouse.

"Good," Chief said. "Now, let's break for fifteen, and then we can start talking about how to work your fuel replenishment electrolyzers. Your comet is not just your target object, it's also your source of working mass for getting yourself back home."

The various candidates split off or split up, veering around Caddy as she remained and stared at the scale model. When the room had emptied, leaving just herself and Okatsu, he stepped closer to her — staring at the little empty pilot's globe.

"I knew Peter," he said quietly. "He had a gift for this work. One of our most productive pilots. Seventeen lifetime catches without a single accident. I am sure he'd have tried for hundreds more."

Caddy wrapped her arms around herself, and rubbed her palms along her triceps.

"It's going to be lonely out there," she said.

"It is," Chief said. "But then, that's part of how we pick you all for this job. Each pairing works in twelve-hour shifts. One of you is resting in the living module, while the other is in the pilot's globe. You will have as much or as little contact with each other as you want. Your file says you like to spend a lot of solo time looking at the stars. And down at New Olympia. Your brother's file said the same."

"I hope I can fill his shoes," Caddy said. "I'm just a little scared, is all."

"You should be," Chief said. "These missions are going to be long, and a lot can go wrong on the way out, and on the way back. You won't follow your comets in — your job is to nudge them in the right direction, then let gravity do the rest — but between the time you leave here, and the time you return for refurbishment and resupply, it might be a year or more."

Caddy nodded her head, absorbing the older, more experienced man's wisdom.

"Sir," she said, "can I ask a question — not related to class?"

"Okay," Okatsu said, fishing a water bottle out of a pocket and taking a drink.

"Was Earth really bad?" she asked. "When we left, I mean?"

The man's eyes lost focus for a second, and he slowly swallowed several mouthfuls of water, before putting the bottle back in its pocket.

"Yup," he said.

"I just can't remember that well," Caddy admitted.

"You wouldn't. You were . . . six years old? When your parents signed you over to us? I was twenty five. Spent my whole life in Japan. If you think things are cramped now — the way we live on this asteroid — try living in a country where people hot-bunked in shoe-box style dormitory structures that make our present living quarters look palatial by comparison. Once the geriatric medicine boom of the late twenty-first century took hold, suddenly people were living far healthier lives for far longer. Global population tripled inside of a generation. They eventually locked the clamps on with mandatory birth control, but by then all the old, chronic problems had come roaring back to bite us. Trust me, Earth is not somewhere you'd choose to live. They're banking on us making these colonies work, so that maybe in another five hundred or a thousand years — however long it takes to crack the bulk transit barrier, or the light-speed barrier; whichever falls first — we can be a safety valve."

Okatsu suddenly began to chuckle. It was a harsh sound.

"Of course, by that time, the colonies might have ideas of their own," he said.

"What do you mean?" Caddy asked.

"Just because Earth wants to send more people, doesn't mean we necessarily want more people. Hell, for all we know, a string of sister ships — to the *Mainfront* — was launched in our wake. We won't know about it until those ships suddenly begin arriving. Do we have room for all the new people? Will we have room? If New Olympia has oceans and breathable air — and land aplenty to fertilize and cultivate with Earth life — that's one thing. But if we're still living on this asteroid, and tinkering with New Olympia's air — the sudden arrival of an additional thousand mouths to feed . . . anyway, this is all kind of political. I'm getting ahead of myself. Us oldsters talk about this crap. You kids don't need to worry about it. Just focus on learning to operate the comet- catchers, then get out there and do us proud. Do *Peter* proud."

* * * * *

"Target body is in the green, plus or minus ten," Caddy said. She was cradled in the simulator's pilot's chair, surrounded on all sides by what was — for all intents and purposes — a working version of a comet- catcher's pilot's globe. The globe itself was a solid piece of transparent, micrometeroid-proof plastic that gave her virtually unlimited visibility in every direction. The chair proper was mounted on a single pole that projected out into the globe, and allowed the chair to pivot or swivel according to the pilot's preference. Presently, the globe was surrounded by a very realistic three-dimensional projection of deep space. A shadow — representing a soon-to-be-captured comet — loomed in the "far" distance. Caddy had her comet-catcher's web fully charged and extended. She couldn't see it, except for the false-color imagery that showed the web superimposed over a different false-color image of the comet proper. Sweat slowly formed across Caddy's skin as she used the finesse controls to gently dial up her ship's thrust. She was approaching the comet at mere meters per minute now. Any faster and she risked impacting too hard. Any slower . . . and her nerves would break. Things were taking too long as it was. She resisted the urge to rush the job.

This was the final phase of simulator testing. Once they passed this, they'd graduate to live ship exercises. Beyond which lay graduation, and promotion to live flight status. But being able to prove she could stick the catch was the biggest test to date.

Peter, if you're out there, help me do this, Caddy thought silently as she watched the proximity sensors. The space between herself and the simulated comet shrank, and shrank, and shrank.

Just a bit more . . .

Suddenly a *bwooping* alarm hit her ears.

The comet-catcher began to accelerate, and drift down.

"What the—" she began to swear, but her hands were already in motion. The heads-up hologram indicated that a thrust unit on the rear of the ship had gone active, and was refusing orders to switch itself off. Caddy's mind went white for an instant, as she realized she was moments from wrecking her web, and even burying the snout of her ship in the foamy, filthy ice on the comet's surface.

Counterthrust, she thought defiantly, and instantly pulled up a tactical display showing the numbers from the malfunctioning unit. She dialed the unit — on the exact opposite side of the axes — to an identical level of thrust, and watched as the ship's dangerously increasing velocity held steady . . . but did not decrease.

"Shit," Caddy said, and realized she didn't just have to combat the effects of the broken unit, she had to correct for the mistake which had already happened. She opened up her forward thruster array and dialed responses by feel. The *bwoop* from the computer continued, as the comet was now dangerously close to the web, and she was still moving forward and down at the wrong angle.

When the *bwoop* was joined by a second, angry *pang* sound, Caddy knew she was in the red zone. She opened all of the forward thrusters up to one hundred percent in a desperate attempt to reverse course. If she could back off in time, maybe she could get the broken thruster taken care of, and take another crack at it.

But then the pilot's globe lit up with warnings about stress failures along the breadth of the web. She was slamming to stern, but with such sudden force that it was not only causing her to pull into the straps of the pilot's chair, it was collapsing the web as well. She tried to dial back the action, but it was too late. The web was in pieces now, and the comet was receding. Unharmed, but also untouchable, now that she'd ruined her chance.

Caddy spat a blue streak of profanity, and slammed her arms onto the rests on either side of the chair.

"Easy," said a voice over the simulator speakers. It was Chief. "Learning how to keep cool in the face of a defeat is as important as learning how to keep cool on the brink of victory. The chances of that actual malfunction happening during a live catch are extraordinarily low. The computer is set up so that a stuck thruster unit has its fuel supply automatically cut off after five seconds. For both the thruster to fail and the computer cutoff to fail . . . well, it's not impossible, but it's unlikely."

"Then why'd you throw that one at me, boss?" Caddy said, slowly peeling herself out of the chair — soaked with perspiration, and very much in need of a shower.

"I've got a mean streak," was all the voice said. "Chalk it up to lesson learned, Candidate. Now get out of my simulator, and don't take it personally. Everybody's getting roasted during Finals Week. Or did you think I'd just let you cakewalk your way to the live exercises?"

Caddy was tempted to make an obscene gesture at the several cameras she knew were monitoring her as she floated toward the neck of the pilot's globe — and the door back to the rest of civilization — but decided she was too tired to make the effort.

*****

Live piloting involved repeats of everything they'd practiced in the simulators, except they weren't using actual comets. They were using scaled-down, inflated balloons which represented comets, with webs scaled accordingly. Captures and other maneuvers were noticeably free of mysterious mechanical glitches — Caddy found it a much more relaxing experience than anything she'd gone through in the sim — and everybody was proceeding through class more or less according to the book.

Outside class, Caddy kept to herself much of the time. But then, so did the others. The Chief had said it: they were each chosen for their comfort in solitude, as much as for the potential aptitude with the ships. And though they all bunked dormitory style, Caddy avoided the eventual pairing off that began to occur, as people realized graduation was approaching, and it would soon be time to go out on a real mission.

Nobody had been told how the crews would be selected. Everybody seemed to be assuming that whoever was their buddy now would be their buddy when they launched in their actual comet-catchers.

But Chief had never made any such promise, and Caddy suspected there might be some rude surprises when the time came for them to leave orbit.

One of their final exercises was not an exercise at all, but rather the passive observation of an in-system capture. For years, comet- catchers had been working in the cometary halo at the very edge of New Olympia's system, diverting comets onto short-period trajectories that would bring them within reach of New Olympia's expanding in-system space infrastructure. So, to complement the comet-catchers working on the edge, an almost identical team of comet catchers worked closer to home: flying out to meet comets as they came in, each of them streaming huge, bright tails of sublimated gas and dust blown off by the solar wind from New Olympia's home star. Those comets were then slowly herded toward New Olympia itself, and prepared for an eventual de-orbit — their precious water being added to New Olympia's gradually moistening atmosphere.

Nobody knew how many comets in total it would take, before New Olympia had enough water for the atmosphere and climate to change dramatically. At present, it was much, much too hot, and composed of all the wrong gasses. With time, and the relentless addition of water, nitrogen, and whatever else the comets brought with them, New Olympia might eventually resemble a world worth growing things on.

During the observation, Caddy and each of the other students were strung out in a line — each of them commanding one of the many pint-sized trainer ships that the academy used for training hops close to home. Being able to see an actual comet — gloriously dazzling, surrounded by its coma of gas and dust — was as exhilarating as it was sobering. The comet was literally huge. A monster. A megaton ball of packed ice and snow, left over from the formation of the system at least a billion or more years in the past. The comet-catcher — the actual one assigned to make the snag — was like a tiny insect compared to the object it was attempting to corral. The web proper was not even visible, having been deployed in full.

"Watch how gently she does this," Chief said over the instructor net, as they waited and watched. The comet-catcher seemed to be barely moving at all as it slowly closed on the comet. Relatively speaking, they were all hurtling toward the home star at several tens of thousands of kilometers per hour. Just matching velocity had taken them over a day's worth of careful maneuvering.

Caddy's pilot's globe display showed the core of the comet, hidden behind the bright gas and dust. The comet-catcher maneuvered toward it like a tiny dust mite wielding a salad bowl on its head. Second by second, the distance shrank. Occasionally, the comet-catcher pilot muttered something into her mic: numbers, or a comment about what she was seeing on her readout. Deadpan tone of voice. Cool as a cucumber, one might say.

Caddy wondered if she'd ultimately be that steady when clutch time came.

Eventually the comet-catcher disappeared into the comet's coma, but there was still a ways to go before the web made contact. Once that happened, the web itself would begin to partially conform to the unique crevices, bumps, valleys, rifts, and other features on the comet's surface. That would allow the web to get a good "grip" prior to the comet-catcher sinking in its fuel reclamation hoses, and beginning the process of tanking up on fresh working mass for the push toward home.

The most deceptive part was the perception of the comet as a solid. Chief had drilled this fact into them over and over again. It might seem solid. It might look like one big blob of stuff on the displays. But if a comet got nudged too hard in any particular direction, the comet's constituent pieces could go flying apart. That would waste the opportunity to bring the comet back to New Olympia orbit, but also create lots of dangerous trash that would eventually need to be policed up — otherwise it could pose a threat to comet-catching and other ships in the future. Even a small, muddy clump of sand, going at the speeds comets tended to achieve, would put a lethal hole in the best craft New Olympia could build.

So, making the snag on the first try — and doing it right — was of utmost importance. Somebody had managed it out on the edge of the system. Now somebody had to manage it close to home.

Caddy was almost unable to breathe as the final few meters were closed. And then happy chimes sounded across her pilot's globe, as the comet-catcher's sensors reported good contact across the web, and the bow of the craft gently came to rest against the comet's surface proper.

Trajectories

Cheers rang out across the instructor net, including those of Chief, who was among the loudest.

"That's how it's done," he said proudly into their ears. "I can't emphasize it enough, Candidates. Slowness and patience win, every time. If you feel like it's not right on the approach, don't be afraid to gently back off, get your attitude and your trajectory right, and try it again. There's no shame in making a second, third, fourth, or fifth try. But you only get one time to screw it up. Then your ship is fouled, and you have to come home. Or, worse, you're too fouled to effect your own extraction, and you're signaling for rescue. And out there in the cometary halo, the distances are often too big for help to arrive in anything less than a few weeks. You don't want to be stuck with your thumbs sticking up your you-know-whats, waiting for others to come clean up your messes for you. Roger?"

Caddy and the rest sounded an immediate *roger* through the net. "Now the long, gentle push to get this thing to New Olympia,"

Chief said. "Which we won't stick around for. Hey, Sarah—" Chief momentarily keyed over to the live net, to talk to the pilot who'd made the successful snag "—thanks for showing the new kids how it's done. Nice work out there. You made it look almost too easy."

"Happy to influence the new generation," said an older woman's voice, followed by the sound of her yawning and stretching. "Right now I am going to let my partner in crime take over, while I go get some sleep. One thing you newbies need to remember: even though this is not physically strenuous work, once you're dialed in and focused on making a snag, everything goes into time warp. Hours will pass in what seem like moments. Muscles will cramp. You will complete the snag, only to discover that you haven't eaten in a whole day, and suddenly you want to eat until your sides split. Don't overdo it. Just disengage, let your partner come up after you — fresh and ready — and let yourself decompress. Good luck after graduation, okay? I will see you all out here."

Caddy and the other Candidates voiced their understanding and appreciation for the comet-catcher's words of wisdom, then they busied themselves for the return voyage home. It had certainly been a day to remember.

* * * * *

"But . . . I graduate tomorrow," Caddy said hotly.

"Graduation doesn't always mean being put on the job right away,"

The Ghost Conductor of the Interstellar Express

Chief Okatsu said. "Not everyone has a ship waiting for them at the end of school. Since we lost one of your classmates to a medical problem at the last minute, you're now the odd woman out. I am sorry. Look, it's not the end of the world. We'll just mate you up with one of the students from the next class."

"Which will be months away," Caddy said, still fuming.

"It can't be helped," Okatsu said. "Nobody flies alone. Not anymore."

Unsaid: *not since your brother disappeared.*

Caddy could feel the hot tears pushing at the corners of her eyes, but she held them back. This was not the time to vent. She'd do that later, alone. When she could throw a pillow. Maybe even kick something. And nobody would see her. She'd worked too long and too hard for this. That things were being delayed at the final moment . . . bad luck. Dumb, stupid, bad luck.

Her breathing slowed, and she momentarily closed her eyes. They were in the main school room, long after the final chime for that day's concluding briefing had sounded. Everyone else was gone to get something to eat, and to talk excitedly about the big day tomorrow. It was just Caddy and the instructor.

She gently rested a hand on the comet-catcher scale model at the room's center — to steady herself.

"Stupid Peter," she finally said, the words coming out in a long breath. "Always leaving a shadow for me to fall into. If he never vanishes, solo missions are still on the books, and I go out as soon as there's a ship for me."

Chief folded his arms — the grip surface on his toes keeping him in place on the floor.

"There was already talk about going to double and triple crews, long before Peter's accident."

"They ruled it an accident?" Caddy said, laughing sarcastically.

"No other way to classify it," Chief said. "Ship returns on auto-pilot, nobody aboard. Did your brother go outside to fix something? Was he in the airlock when it accidentally got triggered? It was like he just . . . left. No indication whatsoever that there had been any problem. But also no record to tell us about the final days leading up to his ultimate vanishing. Your brother is a giant question mark in the minds of all of us dedicated to the comet-catching team. But don't think his story alone, caused us to change policy. We operated solo in the early days because we had so few pilots to work with, and the executive council wanted us to begin retrieving comets immediately. But as the number of qualified pilots began to grow, we knew it was simply common sense to jump to double crews. Your brother's circumstance . . . merely solidified that decision. Since then, we've never lost a ship or a crew without knowing exactly how, and why."

Caddy chewed air for at least a minute. She wasn't sure what else could be said. Obviously Chief was the final say on the matter, and she respected the man too much to begin calling him names, for simply having prudence.

"Look," he said, putting a gentle hand on her shoulder, "getting out there now won't make it any different than if you wait for the next class to finish. I've seen the way you watch the stars, when class is taking a break. I can tell you're searching out there. With your spirit."

"For him," she said. "I don't think I even want to bring him back, I just want to know what happened. What became of him, you know? Not having an answer . . . it's like I can't go out there — doing the job that he did — without trying to find the solution to the mystery. Maybe you're right, maybe it's something I have to let go of. But dammit, he's my older brother, and he was the only family who came with me from Earth. I've been like an orphan since he went away. I just want something to close the hole. Does that make sense?"

"It does," Chief said. "And I'd be lying if I told you some of the other instructors didn't want you off the project as a result. They think you're going to do something stupid trying to discover what became of Peter."

"So why don't you oppose me doing this job?" Caddy asked.

Chief ran a tongue inside one cheek, and his eyes lost focus for a moment.

"Because it's not my right to tell you that you can't fulfill your destiny."

"My destiny?" Caddy said. That was a word she'd almost never heard anyone use before, outside of grand political platitudes from the executive council, regarding eventual human settlement on the surface of New Olympia.

"Yes," Chief said. "Each of us has one. And only we — ourselves — can ultimately figure out what that destiny might be. I tell you not to go out there . . . and it's likely you find a way to go out there anyway, whether I like it or not. People are funny like that. You tell them no, they just redouble their efforts to go ahead and do something anyway. Maybe, as part of the comet-catcher program, at least you're using your instincts for something practical. Besides, I think your brother would be proud of you."

"Thanks," Caddy said, standing up a little straighter. "I'd want Peter to feel proud of me."

"Wherever he is," Chief said, squeezing her shoulder, "I think he is that. Oh yes, I think that very much."

* * * * *

Post-graduation was like an exercise in slow-motion dentistry.

To keep herself from going stir-crazy, Caddy used all the spare simulator time the schoolhouse could give her. In this regard she became a bit of a rump student: someone the new class veered around as they went through the motions.

Everyone except Troy, that is.

How or why he'd gotten into the program, Caddy couldn't be sure.

He'd never expressed the slightest interest in being on the comet-catcher missions. And if his grades actually supported his application — which they clearly had — it was surely by the smallest of margins. Troy had never actually tried for anything in his academic life, so far as she knew. He was one of those guys who seemed content to just sail through things, until he latched onto something that might be popular with the girls.

Which comet-catching definitely wasn't.

"Seemed like the best job of any," he said one afternoon, while they hung around the cafeteria, slurping on trays of stir-fry vat-grown beef, with veggies and noodles.

"I know you," she said, eyeing him across the table. "You're a people person. You thrive on attention. Where we're eventually going . . . you're going to be stuck with nobody to talk to."

"There'll be my partner," he said. "I can talk to that guy." "Assuming 'that guy' even feels like talking," Caddy said. "Look, comet-catching is a lonely job. No joke. You haven't been out there to see what it's like."

"Oh, and you have?" Troy retorted, raising an eyebrow at her.

"I've seen more of the job than you," she responded. "Spent more time around the working pilots, too. We're a quiet lot. We prefer the silence. When have you ever preferred silence to a noisy gaggle of hangers-on, Troy? People you can send into hysterics with your latest joke, or cutting up in front of the teacher? Well, we're not in school anymore. This is serious."

Trajectories

"Hey, wait a minute, why are you throwing cold water on this with me, huh?" Troy said, sitting up straighter and putting his arms on either side of his tray — fists balled defiantly. "I've got just as much right to be here — to take my shot — as you do. The tests said I'm in, so I'm in. Every week I pass the exams and move on to the next phase. Just like you did. And you've never been on a snag before. Not for real. You want to find out if you've got what it takes. And frankly . . . so do I."

"You don't think I have what it takes??" Caddy shot, her cheeks turning red.

"No, that's not what I meant," he said, relaxing his hands. "Look, Caddy, since that day we talked in the observation module — when I brought you your scores — I've been thinking. You're right. Bumming around the colony isn't exactly how I want to spend the rest of my days. I am sure I could get engrossed in the mines, or running some automated milling operation, or even learning to become a medic, or, heck, a surgeon if I felt like it. I think I'm smart enough to do anything I feel like. My parents used to tell me that, back on Earth. 'Young man, you're smart enough to do anything you put your mind to.' Well, this is what I've decided I want to put my mind to. At least for now. If I get bored and decide to change jobs, I am sure you will be the first to know."

They ate in silence for several moments. Caddy didn't really have a good reply to any of that. It was largely the same speech to herself she'd been rehearsing in her own mind — in various forms — over the years. Just because Troy had always seemed too unserious and freewheeling to ever make it on the oh-so-serious comet-catcher team . . . didn't mean she was qualified to tell the man no. Any more than Chief Okatsu had felt qualified to tell Caddy no.

"You ever miss them?" Caddy finally asked, changing the conversational direction.

"My parents?" he asked.

"Yeah," she said.

"Sometimes. It's like, I can never be sure when that feeling is going to hit. It gets me at the strangest moments. I mean, the adults here are all good people and they did their best to finish the job our parents started . . . but I can never quite get over the fact that our parents aren't just far away in space, they're also far away in time, too. While we slept on the trip aboard *Mainfront* they lived out the rest of their lives on Earth. Or did they emigrate to one of the colonies in Earth's solar system? Did they have any more kids? Do we have brothers and sisters who also had kids, and then their kids had kids, and somewhere back on Earth right now, people our age — the descendants of siblings we never met — are looking up into the sky, and wondering about us: the relatives they will never know, other than in name?"

"I never thought about it that far," Caddy admitted.

"I did," Troy said. "Especially after you and I talked, and I could tell how happy you were at the chance to become a Candidate in the comet-catcher business. I realized that if ever our relatives — far, far away, on dirty, crowded, dying Earth — are ever going to have a chance to meet our children, or our children's children, we have to make sure that New Olympia works. That there is an actual, living world for the people of Earth to come to. A place for them to settle."

"Assuming we let them," Caddy said, remembering what Chief Okatsu had once told her.

"Yeah, well, right, assuming we can stop them if we want to," Troy said, correcting her. "If a dozen sister ships to *Mainfront* showed up in orbit tomorrow, who do you think would cast the deciding votes? Which people on the present executive council would try to overrule the decision? Naw. Our best bet is to make sure New Olympia is a huge, wide-open, living planet. Forests. Seas. Life from pole to pole. Enough room for twenty billion human beings, if necessary. We give them enough room they can lose themselves in it, we won't have any problems. In fact, it will be payback for the effort invested in launching *Mainfront* in the first place."

"You make it sound like we owe Earth a debt," Caddy said.

"I think maybe we do," Troy said. And then he went back to eating.

Surprise, surprise, Caddy thought. She'd never realized that happy-go-lucky Troy could think such thoughts.

Then again, with both of them being quickly thrust into the adult world, switching gears into grown-up mode was something Caddy had been forced to grapple with, too. What would the future hold? Assuming she liked comet-catching, would she simply do that job . . . forever? The initial agreement — upon signing as a Candidate — was for ten years of service. But beyond that, what did she want to do? Where did she want to go? Troy had mentioned children. Caddy hadn't even considered the possibility before now. But Troy was right. Unless disaster struck, some day, New

Trajectories

Olympia would be a destination for fresh colonists leaving Earth. Caddy herself might be gone by then, but her legacy might live on. Assuming she found someone with the right components to be a husband. She eyed Troy over the food between them, and didn't say another word.

*****

Deep space was like a literal coal sack. Other than the bright stars glowing perfectly across the sky, no other light source was discernible. Even New Olympia's home star was just a bright, yellow-white bulb, almost small enough to disappear among the other stars.

Thrusting out this far had taken months. Time during which Caddy and Troy traded off piloting the ship. They didn't have a name for their craft. It seemed neither large enough, nor important enough, to give it a name, the way *Mainfront* had a name. They were merely a call-sign on the comet-catcher net. Assigned to rendezvous with a numbered objective which had been identified for them well in advance of their departure. It was their first designated capture. And they'd gambled to see who would be the one to make the attempt upon arrival — with Caddy coming out on top.

Troy seemed to take it in stride, much to Caddy's surprise.

"Less pressure on me," he chided during one of their mid-shift swapouts — when she would go back to the living module and begin her twelve hours of down time, while he went into the pilot's globe and spent twelve hours keeping the ship on course.

Much could have been left to automatic control, naturally. But comet-catcher doctrine was to never leave the pilot's globe empty for more than a few minutes at a stretch. And both Troy and Caddy adhered to doctrine in a by-the-book fashion.

Food was plentiful. The only real concern was making sure the electrolyzer worked correctly once they sank their web into the target comet. That electrolyzer would ensure they had fuel, air, and water for the return trip. Or at least enough fuel, air, and water to get the target comet headed on its way — at which point they would detach, receive new instructions for a new target comet in their relative vicinity, and the process would begin all over again.

It was assumed they could divert dozens of comets before diving back into the inner system, for docking and refitting at home.

Caddy felt herself marveling at the absolute, magnificent solitude she enjoyed during her stints in the piloting globe. With gentle music — the countless millions of recordings from Earth — playing into her ears, she could turn off all the lights and feel like she was practically one with the cosmos. A disembodied personage, floating free through the ether of time and space. She wondered if this was how the very first astronauts — riding alone, aloft, aboard their primitive rockets — had felt. She also wondered if this is how Peter had felt too. Before . . . before whatever took him away.

Which was one thing Caddy had gradually become sure of: whatever had happened to Peter, it hadn't been something premeditated or planned. He'd been enticed by something. Maybe the very nakedness of space itself. Caddy wondered whether on one of those long, lonesome stretches of time, Peter had simply decided to eliminate all barriers between himself, and the cosmos proper. Perhaps he'd felt so completely and absolutely in unison with the quiet blackness surrounding him, he'd stepped to the airlock, and calmly let himself outside. To make the marriage — the man, and the void — complete.

A morbid, and yet also very eerily elegant thought. Or so Caddy admitted on one of her many shifts at the comet-catcher'scontrols.

When at last their target comet presented itself, it was as a massive, dark shadow that blotted out the stars. No beautiful coma this far from the sun. Probably the nucleus had not felt any warmth for hundreds of thousands, or even millions, of years, depending on its actual period.

The capture proper was a thing of held-breath anxiety, yet it yielded no drama whatsoever. Caddy had practiced the maneuver how many times, back in the simulators? And this time there was no mischief- making instructor to throw her a technical curve ball right when she was making her final approach.

* * * * *

The dreams began after the fifth capture.

Not vividly, at first. But gradually growing in frequency and intensity, until — by the ninth capture — Caddy was positively agitated. The dreams were too real, and they were beginning to get to her emotionally. She couldn't make them stop, and they seemed to be directly connected to the fact that Caddy was progressing more deeply into the cometary halo than anyone else ever had in this region of space before.

Nervously, she told Troy about the dreams. The book said every pilot was responsible for keeping her partner fully appraised of any irregularities or issues which might affect the mission. And if Caddy was slowly losing her mind, Troy deserved to know about it before it got too serious for either of them to handle.

"This is where they think your brother vanished," Troy said.

Caddy raised both eyebrows. "How do you know that?" she asked, shocked. "Even I was never told that."

"I sleuthed the coordinates out of your brother's sealed case file, before we left."

"Let me guess: you're in tight with a girl who—"

"No, listen," Troy said. "It's not that. Chief Okatsu pulled me aside the day before we left dock. He asked me to keep an eye on you. I told him I would, but I also asked him if there was anything I should know — something nobody had officially been told. He let me look at the flight forensics for your brother's ship. Where he was at the time of the expected disappearance, and about how deep into the cometary halo. We're entering that general zone now. At least if all my relative calculations are correct. So tell me again, exactly, what happens in the dreams?"

"It's Peter," Caddy said, closing her eyes and picturing her brother's face. "He's in his pilot's suit. He's trying to talk to me, but he's not making any sound. It's like I'm in the pilot's globe, and he's right outside the globe. Only the vacuum of space isn't hurting him. I read his lips. I want to make out the words."

"Is he warning you?" Troy asked. "Is he trying to tell you not to do something?"

"No," Caddy said. "It's like . . . it's just the opposite. It's like he's found something, and he wants me to come see. And every time I unbuckle from the pilot's chair and float to the exterior of the pilot's globe, he vanishes. And then I wake up."

"And it's like that every time?" Troy asked?

"Yes," Caddy said. "It's been like that for at least the past few weeks. And the dreams get more vivid every night. I ignored them awhile back, just because I thought maybe I was simply beginning to feel the effects of us being gone from home for too long — they told us that extreme isolation would do strange things to our sleep cycle. But this isn't just my mind playing games with me, Troy. I think this is something else entirely."

"Except . . ." Troy said, and didn't finish his thought.

"Except what?" Caddy said, grabbing his wrist with more force than she had any right to.

He looked down at her white-knuckled hand.

"Except I've not been having the same experience, Caddy. My sleep's been fine. If there is something about this region of the cometary halo that is specifically affecting you, why isn't it affecting me too?"

"I don't know," Caddy said.

"Well, whatever it is, do you think we should abort and go home?"

"So soon?" Caddy said. "We're due for more snags! What will they say when we return early? God, Troy, they'll take away my flight status! I'll get thrown in the psych unit for sure!"

"Hold on, hold on," Troy said, holding up his hands to placate her. "It was just an idea. But what else can we do, Caddy? What if the dreams get more intense? What if you can't rest? You're no good to us if you can't fly the ship. And the book says I can't fly this mission solo. If you're incapacitated to the point you can't function—"

"But I'm not incapacitated," Caddy said. "I'm clear as a bell when I'm awake. Dammit, Troy, I just want you to know what's going on, okay? I don't want you to be in the dark — and I can't keep this to myself forever. I had to tell somebody."

"Got it," Troy said. "Thanks for trusting me. Okay, look. Let's do this. Proceed with the mission. You start telling everything you know — everything you've told me — to a video log. We won't send the log back home. We keep the recording with us. So, if something really weird happens, there is at least some kind of file they can look at . . . when they recover the ship."

Morbid thoughts, indeed. But Peter's disappearance was utmost in their minds.

"And hey," Troy said, "if I start to notice anything funny with me? I'll be the first to say so. I promise."

"Thanks," Caddy said, and reached over the table to pull Troy into a hug. He returned the gesture for a surprisingly long time.

*****

The ghost came like a moth to a flame. It flitted about, just on the periphery of Caddy's vision. Per usual, when she was piloting, she had all the lights dialed low, and a melodic piece of symphony orchestra music piping gently over the piloting globe's speaker system. The coal sack effect was on brilliant display — a million tiny jewels scattered across an endless ocean of absolute black — but a particular light seemed to be dancing crazily just off to the side. Yet every time Caddy snapped her head to look, the flickering would vanish . . . only to reappear, moments later, on the other side of her peripheral vision.

"Dammit," Caddy said. "I hope to hell I've just dozed off. I can't afford to begin seeing things while I'm damned awake!"

She'd practically shouted the last words, and was shocked by the words that came in reply.

"But you *are* awake, sis."

Caddy froze. The voice was clear and strong, just as she'd remembered in the years since Peter's final voyage.

Suddenly, he was there. Smiling slightly. So close, she felt she could reach out and touch him. Unlike in her dreams, he was clearly inside the piloting globe this time. Caddy's hand shook badly as she reached out for him — hoping to touch his full head of gently wavy brown hair.

"You can't touch me yet," he said — forcing Caddy to snap her hand back.

"Peter . . ." she breathed, feeling the tears flow hotly at the corners of her eyes.

"It's me, sis," he said. "But not like you remember. If you touch me now . . . you'll be transported to where I am. Before that happens, we have to talk."

* * * * *

"Peter, oh God, this can't be real," Caddy croaked, swiping at her face with her sleeve. Surely she'd dozed off at the controls, and the life monitor computer would pick up on the error at any moment, and begin to gently chime her back to wakefulness. But a quick glance at the life monitor told her that all was well. She was as alert as she should be. Nothing was amiss. Except . . . Peter was standing there in mid-air, having a conversation with his kid sister, like he'd just walked into her bedroom while she was doing homework.

"Peter . . . what happened?" Caddy asked. "Everyone has been trying to figure out what went wrong with your flight."

"Nothing went wrong," Peter said. "Everything went exactly the way it's supposed to. Except, I found something out here. Something nobody could have expected."

The Ghost Conductor of the Interstellar Express

"What?" Caddy asked, still desperately wanting to put her hands on her brother's face — to experience the warmth and tangibleness of him.

"I can't explain all the technical details to you," he said. "That would be too time-consuming, and it wouldn't make any difference. Suffice to say that the portion of the star system you're in now, is like the platform for a subway train. Remember those from Earth? You'd go down from street level, and there would be a huge, long tube? It was empty most of the time. Except, every few minutes, a train would come through, stop, pick up people, drop others off, and move on down the track. Well, this part of space is the same thing. It's a waiting area for a galactic train system that stops through every once in awhile, picks up passengers, drops other passengers off, and then goes on its way. Except, I don't think the people who originally built the subway exist anymore. When the train came through last time — when I was out here — climbing aboard showed me nothing but an empty car. And though I've ridden the car through a thousand different star systems by now, I've never seen any sign of anyone who knows how the system was built."

"Aliens," Caddy blurted, still wiping tears from her eyes.

"Yes," Peter said.

"Then how come your whole ship didn't get taken?" Caddy demanded. "Why did your ship come back untouched, without you in it, and all the logs and memory discs erased?"

"It was a sudden thing, really," Peter said, his face making an expression Caddy remembered, from when she was much younger, and her older brother was trying to explain complex things to her — things he wasn't sure she could fully understand. She'd found the expression infuriating then, but it only made her heart break now. She wanted nothing more than to wrap her arms around his neck and pull him to her. "Try to tell me," Caddy said. "I don't care if you think it won't make sense. Tell me everything that happened."

Peter rubbed a thumb along his jaw — he seemed not to have aged a day since he last left home.

"I was comet-catching," he said, "like you are now. And I started having vivid dreams. I didn't understand them at first. But eventually I interpreted them as a kind of waking dream — the ones they say you can control, if you become aware of what they are. In the dreams I was able to take a kind of time and space warp far away from this system. Far away from any systems even remotely close to Earth. I could pick and choose which stars and planets I wanted to see. It was like playing tourist. I began to see other civilizations — built by amazing creatures of all manner and description. It was exciting. I almost began to think it was real. And then, one day, while I was in the pilot's globe — like you are now — it became real. It was like the door to the subway car opened in my mind, and I stepped through it. Ever since then, I've been riding the system. You can't believe the places I've been. The galaxy is alive with different people, many of them far older and wiser than humans are."

"How come Earth never knew about any of this," Caddy asked. "Why doesn't the . . . Subway? . . . Why won't it run to Sol?"

"I think the original builders never got around to building a stop there," Peter confessed. "Back when they were creating the subway, humans didn't exist yet. I don't even think the dinosaurs existed. Earth hadn't gotten interesting yet. That seems to be the key. The subway only stops at places that have something interesting going on — development, technology, signs of intelligent industry."

"If that's true, what makes this system so special?" Caddy asked. "New Olympia is dead as a doornail."

"But it didn't used to be," Peter said. "Long, long ago, there was a civilization on the surface. Advanced enough to build radio telescopes, and begin launching rockets into orbit. But the climate was changing too fast. They never had enough water to sustain the plants, to sustain the biosphere. A little bit like Mars, but a little bit like Venus too. Eventually they died out, before they could ever launch a ship deep enough into space to reach the subway. But the makers left the subway stop here anyway — just in case? Which is where I came in. I happened to be in the right time at the right place, and I climbed aboard when the chance presented itself. And I'm back now. The train is coming through again. I never thought it would be you out here, sis, but I'm glad that it is. I know how much you hated life back home. How much you dreaded being stuck on that asteroid with nowhere to go and nothing to do. Come with me, and I can show you all the places I've seen — the amazing life that waits for us in the galaxy."

Just then, Troy popped the hatch to the pilot's globe. Both Peter and Caddy spun to face him as he floated in. His eyes were so wide, the whites were bright — even in the dim light. Peter seemed to shine of his own accord, like a lamp from nowhere were projected upon him at all times.

"Can . . . can . . ." Caddy whispered to Troy.

"Can I see him?" Troy said. "Yes. Sorry, Caddy, but I've been running a monitor on your piloting sessions ever since you told me about your dreams. I programmed the monitor to wake me up if ever it caught you talking to yourself. I never guessed you'd actually be talking to—"

"A ghost?" Peter said, smiling.

"If that's what you are, then yes," Troy said, clasping the handholds on the side of the pilot's chair. He regarded Peter's avatar warily.

"Peter," Caddy said, composing herself, "if this 'subway' is real, and you could get on, can you not also get off? Stay with us. Come back to the colony. Everyone will be amazed by what you've discovered! You have to tell them! You'll be famous! They'll broadcast the news to Earth!"

Peter's face darkened.

"It's not that simple," Peter said.

"Why not?" Caddy demanded. "Damn you, do you have any idea what you've done to those of us you left behind?"

Suddenly Peter became aware of Caddy's red, damp face — as if for the first time.

"I'm sorry, sis. I didn't . . . I didn't mean to hurt you."

"No, of course you didn't," she said, sniffling. "But why did you have to vanish without a trace?"

"There are certain side effects to how the subway works," Peter said. "Our technology is too primitive. Our data storage is too vulnerable to the wave effect the subway leaves when it passes."

"You couldn't have written a stupid note on a stupid piece of paper?" Caddy practically shouted.

"Who uses hardcopy anymore?" Peter said. "Look, I'm sorry, and I mean it. Sis . . . I've come back. Isn't that all that matters now? You can come with me this time!"

"What about Troy?" Caddy said.

Peter considered the other young man in the globe. "He can come too, if he wants."

"And back home, nobody knows anything about what happened to any of us," Troy said.

"If it's like last time? No, probably not," Peter admitted.

Caddy could see the sparkle in Troy's eyes — he was considering it.

Just as Caddy herself was considering it.

Trajectories

"You said it's not that simple, when I asked you why you can't come back with us," Caddy said. "Explain what that means. Why can't you come back?"

"It's like . . . sis . . . I've seen too much. If you'd been some of the places I've been . . . the subway is an instant transport. It takes mere seconds to jump me tens of light-years in actual space. And each step of the way, I get to meet the other people who are waiting. They know about the subway. They even use it from time to time. They tell me about their worlds. I get to see images, listen to music, hear their speech — did you know there is a universal language that dates all the way back to the builders? The subway itself teaches you the language, if you're patient enough to sit and learn."

"So how come we can't see it?" Troy asked. "Why can we only see you?"

"The subway functions apart from our ordinary concept of space-time," Peter said. "I can use the subway controls to project myself into our space-time for a short while — just as long as the car is at the platform in this system. As soon as the train leaves again — as soon as the particular car I inhabit, goes away — the me that you see, will vanish. But if you take my hands — both of you — I can use the car to jump you to where I am now. You'll leave the comet-catcher behind. No help for it. But once you're here, seeing what I've been seeing, I think everything will make a lot more sense."

Caddy was breathing rapidly, her heart pounding. This was too much for her to accept at face value. Her brain demanded hard evidence, before she'd accept the hallucination that she — and now, Troy — had been thrust into. Still, it was also an answer to her most fervent wish: to be offered a free ticket out of the purgatory of her colonist existence. Away from New Olympia. Away from human beings altogether. Pure adventure. If Peter was right, the potential was practically limitless.

Still, something nagged at her conscience.

"People have been working too hard," she said, her brow knit.

"At what?" Peter asked.

"New Olympia," Caddy said. "The colony. Troy and me, we spent months and months in simulators and exercises, preparing to come out here and do a job."

"It's a boring job," Peter said. "I can tell you that better than anybody."

The Ghost Conductor of the Interstellar Express

"But Peter," Caddy said, "sometimes the things which are most worth doing, are boring. Troy and I talked about this, and I've decided that he's right. Earth is depending on us to make New Olympia into a planet worth settling some day. Those old aliens — the ones who lost this world in the first place — they never had the technology to save themselves. But we do, and though it might take a long time, somebody's got to try."

"There are plenty of people to run the comet-catchers," Peter said, dismissing her words with the wave of his hand. "What I'm offering you is the voyage of eternity."

"I don't doubt it," Caddy said, considering her thoughts as she formed them into words. "And maybe, some day, when I'm old, and I've given my life to making New Olympia a better place than how I first found it, I will want to retire — come out here, climb aboard your train, and take a trip. But now? Now . . . I'm dug in, big brother. Going through Candidate school? Our first snags? Sending those comets back to the inner system? I feel like the things I am doing finally count for something. I've never felt that before. And I don't feel like I'm done yet."

"I don't think I am either," Troy said, nodding his head along with Caddy's words. "You know, you've become a legend, Peter. And I'm sure after we get back and tell everybody about this, you'll become an even bigger legend still. Assuming anyone believes us. I am assuming when you . . . warp out of here, that our computers are going to get wiped?"

"Probably, yes," Peter said, nodding.

"No worries," Caddy said. "We have protected backups for all the programs to continue the mission. But what about our minds?"

"The subway won't do anything to those," Peter said. "I can assure you."

"Well, then," Caddy said, suddenly feeling warmth building in the center of her chest, "I respectfully decline your offer, big brother. Not easily, mind you. I am sure there will be many nights when I will regret not taking you up on this . . . thing you've embarked upon. But there's comets that need catching, and Troy and me, we're comet-catchers. New Olympia needs the air and the water. It won't be fit for man or beast next year, nor in ten years, nor maybe even in a hundred years. But if you're right — and this subway comes through again — I think there will plenty of time for me to make my mark in this little corner of the galaxy. Before running off to see all the rest."

Trajectories

Peter was actually smiling at this point. "I always thought your heart was in the right place, sis."

"And I never stopped loving you, big brother," Caddy said.

Peter turned his attention to Troy.

"You," Peter said sternly, aiming a finger at Troy's nose.

"Yessir?" Troy said reflexively.

"You be good to her," he said. "And be a good dad to my nieces and nephews, understand?"

"But I—" Troy began to sputter.

"Understand?" Peter said again, his finger waving sternly.

"Got it," Troy said, and swallowed thickly. "I promise."

"Right," Peter said. Then he turned his attention back to Caddy.

"I have to go now," he said, his tone turning soft. "The window for me to be here is almost shut. If I had more time, we could talk more. I mean it when I say you can't believe the places I've been."

"I'll get my chance!" Caddy said, tears forming anew. "But first, there's work to be done. Just make sure the damned subway never misses this stop, okay? I have a feeling whole boatloads of people will be coming out here eventually, to take you up on your offer. You'll become known as the ghost conductor of the interstellar express!"

Peter laughed, and ran a finger along his jaw. "I like the sound of that."

And instantly, he popped out of existence. No sound. He just . . . wasn't there anymore.

For many minutes, Caddy and Troy simply stared in silence. Nothing was said. The soft orchestra music continued to play. The sparkling vastness of the coal sack night was everywhere at once. Magnificent, chilling, and larger than any single human mind could grasp.

"Do you think anyone will buy it?" Troy said. "When we tell them?"

"Does it matter?" Caddy responded. "Just us telling the story is going to get explorers scrambling out here to check it out. At first they'll say we're nuts — and maybe they will be right. But if what just happened, happened, sooner or later somebody other than us is going to be around when Peter's train pulls through, and that's when it's gonna get real interesting."

Troy laughed, then swung his way back toward the hatch that led out of the pilot's globe, and back to the living module.

"Leaving so soon?" she said.

"I've still got a few hours sleep to get, before my shift!" he shouted.

"And what about when—"

Suddenly all of the electronics onboard fluttered, and died. Only to come back to life ten seconds later.

"—all the equipment kicks over?" Caddy finished, realizing that the so-called "warp" had done precisely what was expected.

"As if you don't know the system restore drill by heart?" Troy scoffed. "Phone me when a real problem develops! You've got this. I am going to bed.

Caddy actually laughed out loud, her fingers automatically beginning to press the key sequences which would boot the ship's software from the hardened disc in the "storm cellar" where radiation couldn't reach.

Meanwhile, she made a silent promise to return to this place, and see her brother again. Maybe when she could bring her grandchildren, and make a holiday of it?

ABOUT THE EDITOR

Dave Creek is the author of a novel, SOME DISTANT SHORE, and the short story collections A GLIMPSE OF SPLENDOR and THE HUMAN EQUATIONS.

He's also published a series of novellas, including THE SILENT SENTINELS, A CROWD OF STARS, THE FALLEN SUN, and TRANQUILITY.

His short stories have appeared in ANALOG SCIENCE FICTION AND FACT magazine, and the anthologies FAR ORBIT APOGEE, TOUCHING THE FACE OF THE COSMOS, and DYSTOPIAN EXPRESS.

Find out more about Dave's work at www.davecreek.net, on Facebook at Fans of Dave Creek, and on Twitter, @DaveCreek

In the "real world," Dave is a retired television news producer.

Dave lives in Louisville with his wife Dana, son Andy, and two sleepy cats — Hedwig and Hemingway.